THE LIGHT
IN THE
GARDEN

MARY F. BURNS

A JOHN SINGER SARGENT /
VIOLET PAGET MYSTERY

Violet Paget, c. 1880
Born October 14, 1856, Violet Paget was Welsh-English, and like the Sargent family, hers travelled throughout Europe and Great Britain, keeping company with artists, writers, intellectuals, and many socially prominent people. She was a prolific writer, using the pen name Vernon Lee, and she and John Sargent were close friends from childhood—they met when they were ten years old, in Rome. Violet died in 1935 at her villa, Il Palmerino, near Florence.

John Singer Sargent, c. 1880 Sargent was born on January 12, 1856 to American parents living in Florence, Italy. Sargent became the most sought-after portrait painter in Europe and America from the early 1880's to his death in 1925. He produced some 900 oil paintings, mostly portraits, and 2,000 watercolors, which became his preferred medium.

THE LIGHT
IN THE
GARDEN

The Highwayman

And still of a winter's night, they say, when the wind is in the trees,
When the moon is a ghostly galleon tossed upon cloudy seas,
When the road is a ribbon of moonlight over the purple moor,
A highwayman comes riding—
    Riding—riding—
A highwayman comes riding, up to the old inn-door.

Over the cobbles he clatters and clangs in the dark inn-yard.
He taps with his whip on the shutters, but all is locked and
    barred.
He whistles a tune to the window, and who should be waiting
    there
But the landlord's black-eyed daughter,
    Bess, the landlord's daughter,
Plaiting a dark red love-knot into her long black hair.

—Alfred Noyes, 1906

PROLOGUE

The first thing that seemed odd about the village of Broadway was that nonsense about the dead bird.

John had mentioned it at the end of a short letter to me, seemingly unperturbed and yet, his note conveyed uneasiness: *"Why would someone kill the blue bird, slitting its throat and tying up its legs like that?"*

It was late summer, the year 1886; John was in Broadway and I was in London, preparing to return to Florence in a few weeks. Following our heady but tragic adventure in the Spring of '84 chasing down the Shapira Scrolls, John and I had travelled disparate ways for some time—he to face the then-unforeseen debacle of his portrait of *Madame X* and the ruin of his prospects in Paris, and I to experience—equally unforeseen—the devastating impact of my first attempt at a novel. It had been a dark two years for both of us.

My *Miss Brown*—a title that Henry James himself, to whom the book was humbly dedicated, declared was "a good one"—not only failed to ignite the favour of the ever-fickle public, but also inflicted injury and insult among my friends and acquaintances. My sad attempt at story-telling was seen to be an unkind portrayal of the London Bohemians as shallow, sensual devotées of a wayward and debauched aestheticism.

My face grows warm writing these words, even after nearly four decades. For the first time in my life, I had been subjected to the social disdain known as "being cut"—no longer invited to dinners or evening salons, the flow of cards and letters nearly dried up, and perhaps worst of all, not being greeted or acknowledged on the very sidewalks of London, or in the halls of the British Museum, by persons formerly pleased to claim my friendship.

For John, his career also teetered on the edge of extinction. He didn't actually flee Paris in the dead of night, but very nearly so. He gave up the lease on his lovely house and studio in the 17th, and had since become an established denizen of London, and even more, of Broadway. There he painted, played the piano, sang and danced and ate his way back into the confidence he had lost when Paris brutally rejected him. His most famous painting, perhaps, was created there, in Broadway, over a period of two summers and autumns.

Which brings us back to the blue bird. John hadn't actually asked me outright to come to Broadway to help, but I heard his plea in between the lines, and decided to go there for a visit—I was *persona non grata* in London (for the time being), the season was long over anyway, and the Americans in Broadway were, according to John, a most friendly, welcoming group, who moreover knew nothing about my novel and its effects. I had heard about the charming, sometimes rambunctious "artist colony"—from Edmund Gosse, that tireless gossip, and even from Henry James, who still sometimes spoke to me, and who had been known to visit Broadway and had even taken part in a country dance!

So it began, casually enough, my involvement in the sinister events that occurred in the peaceful village of Broadway, ending in more than the death of the blue bird.

ONE

FRIDAY 3 SEPTEMBER 1886

Broadway Village

"HALLOO, VI, OLD MAN! THERE YOU ARE!" John was on hand to greet me when I alighted from the coach at the venerable Horse and Hound⌿ coach house. I smiled at his enthusiastic greeting.

"Yes, indeed, my dear Twin, here I am, as you see," I said, shaking out my cloak to rid myself of the dry dust from the early autumn roads—no rain in sight as yet. Broadway had no train station, and I had taken the ancient coach (it seemed ancient to me) from the nearby village of Evesham for the final several miles of my journey from London. I glanced at the clear blue sky, the soft green hills rising behind the packed-down dirt and cobble High Street of Broadway, and drew in a deep breath of the fresh country air. It was getting on to dusk, and the edges of the sky to the west were turning a delicious pink.

"Ah!" John said, nodding approvingly. "Isn't it remarkably different air from London? Even in

Kensington," he said, with half a wink. He darted to the back of the carriage to take my bags from the coachman. "How *is* Mary?" he called to me.

"She's well," I said, thinking fondly of my dear friend. "She's very well. Another book of poems about due

out." I looked him up and down with a close eye as he strode toward me, and was satisfied with what I saw. He gestured for me to walk with him.

"And you?" I said, as we fell into step together, he carrying my two small bags and I only my reticule and a box of sweets for my hosts. "You look...better, rested maybe?"

John smiled at my concerned look. "You're as bad as Emily," he said. "My sister's letters are full of advice about country walks and hearty breakfasts." He shook his head and looked around. "I'm fine," he asserted. "Better than fine, I'm delighted to be here!"

I took him at his word, and forestalled his equivalent question about *my* well-being, as I could see it forming in his mind. "And you are painting?" I continued. "Something special, I gather, from your letters, and from what Emily tells me?"

"Yes, yes," he said somewhat impatiently. "You shall see it all—at Russell House—a marvelous place, you shall be impressed, I dare say, at all the activity—painting, acting, children tearing about in costumes and dancing and all—" He broke off as he caught the skeptical look on my face. I laughed to make light of the absolute terror his description struck in my very being. He stopped in his tracks and looked at me apologetically. "Actually, you see, there turns out to be not quite enough room at Russell House just now, so we've put you up in the village—the Lygon Arms."

"Ah, well, yes, that sounds perfectly suitable," I managed, quietly giving fervent thanks that I would not be lodging in Russell House, with all its apparent bustle and noise. We began walking again.

"You shall love Lily Millet of course, she's the most wonderful person," John rattled on as we walked. "She is the center of our little world here, along with Frank," he said. "But even more, Frank's sister Lucia, she and I are good friends, we both like Wagner, can you imagine? She is the more practical of the women—nothing would ever get done without Lucia, you'll see."

I was surprised at how absolutely *chatty* John was, and inwardly sighed at the prospect of meeting and, no doubt, being sized up by, these formidable American women—for what American woman whom I had ever met

* * *

had *not* been formidable in one way or another? Isa Boit, for instance, whom I actually rather liked, and that Mrs. Gardner from Boston, *Mrs. Jack* they called her, she was a force of nature indeed. I do not count either Emily or dear

Mrs. Sargent, John's mother, as in the least to be considered "American"—they, like John, were cosmopolitan travellers of the first water, and belonged to the best cities of Europe: Rome, Florence, Venice, Paris and London, all of which had shaped their manners, their characters, their approach to life. But these Americans in Broadway, well, we would see.

We halted at the open front door of the Lygon Arms, where a colorfully-vested and top-hatted doorman surveyed the scene with a good-natured, proprietary air. He was nearly as tall as John, with sandy hair and a tanned face.

"Good day to you, Mr. Sargent, sir," he said, tipping his hat smartly, and giving a courteous bow in my direction. "You have brought us this important lady-writer, as I understand, Miss Vernon Lee." He made it a statement rather than a question.

I nodded graciously, though somewhat surprised at his informed address. John introduced us as he handed my bags to the man, "Vi, this is Mr. Andrew Hesford. He knows everything about everything in Broadway, mind you, and if something happens at one end or other of the village, he's sure to know all about it within minutes."

"That I will, miss," the doorman said, turning and leading the way into the inn. "As my father did afore me, and his father as well."

I turned an inquiring eye toward John as we walked through the narrow passage, but he just smiled and ducked his head as we went through the inner door, a massive wooden construction of blackened wood and iron bolts. I caught glimpses of small, smoke-darkened rooms on either side of the passage, with deep, stone fireplaces, large comfortable chairs and upholstered settees, and lamps just beginning to be lighted in the early evening dusk. The welcoming aromas of roasting meat and vegetables, and a strong but not unpleasant alehouse ripeness hung in the air. My stomach lurched in its unaccustomed emptiness—it had been a long ride from London—and I found myself hoping that dinner was coming soon.

Mr. Hesford led us up the stairs to the second floor, providing a brief history of the inn—the "White Hart that was, miss, back in the day"—the day being 1377—and all the various dignitaries who bedded down over the

centuries: Charles I and Oliver Cromwell the most
illustrious. I had noted their portraits in oil facing each
other (Cromwell scowling, as I thought, at the insouciant,
patrician calm of the King's visage), as we passed through
the ground floor rooms. Various names for the inn
succeeded the centuries: the White Swan, The Swan, The
Hart and Swan—tactfully changed to meet the reigning
House of Lancashire at one time—then back to the White
Hart in 1641 until finally it became the Lygon Arms two
hundred years later.

At last we gained a door down a short hallway from
the main stairs, and with a discreet flourish, Mr. Hesford
invited me to enter the room.

The chamber was small but sufficient, with dark
wood, mullioned windows and creaking floorboards, and
an enormous wardrobe taking up a good third of the space.
Mr. Hesford peered into corners, evidently making sure all
was tidy and clean (which it was), and prepared to leave.

Feeling mischievous, I stopped him. "Mr. Hesford," I
said, taking care not to include John in my gaze. "I'm
impressed by your talent of *knowing everything about
everything* in Broadway."

"Yes, miss?" he said, looking not the least bit
affronted.

"What have you to conjecture about the incident of
the death of the blue bird?" I said, and discerned that John
started at the question.

Mr. Hesford nodded slowly. "I have thought on it," he
said after a moment. He glanced at John. "Begging your
pardon, sir, seeing as how it was your bird and all, I took it
to be a warning of some kind, and not just an ill-natured

way to get rid of a troublesome creature, again, your pardon, sir."

John half-smiled. "It *was* a troublesome creature, always pecking away at the children's legs and shrieking fit to raise the dead."

"A warning," I repeated. "For whom? And from whom? Any thoughts, Mr. Hesford?"

He gazed at me steadily. "It weren't no one from here, miss," he said. "Not a native of Broadway, that is."

"How can you tell that?" I said quickly. "And do you mean, it could have been a visitor—or even one of the American artists?"

"Yes, miss, that's what I'm saying," he admitted reluctantly, and turned to John. "You'd best watch yourself in that group, sir—as there's someone who might be up to making a bit of trouble, if you know what I mean." His tightened lips after this puzzling statement indicated he would say no more, and with a slight bow, he departed, leaving me and John staring in dismay.

TWO

SEPTEMBER 1726

Broadway Village – The Olde Swan Inn

"ELIZABETH MARY! WHERE THE DRAT IS THE GIRL? Bess? Bess!" The innkeeper bellowed up the stairs from the kitchen doorway, wiping his sweaty forehead with an old cloth. He stood gratefully in the welcoming breeze from the open back door. The heat of a long summer was loosening its grip at last, which made working over the kitchen fire slightly less intolerable, but still stoked his irascible temper.

"I'm just here, Da." His daughter's low, musical voice startled him, coming out of the gloom of the snug next to the tavern's main room. She had a mop in one hand and a bucket of sudsy water in the other, which she set down on the flagstone floor with a thump and a splash. "The snug needed cleaning after that upset last night." She half-smiled and rolled her eyes, which softened her father's mood so, he almost smiled back.

"Right, that high-nosed lady who couldn't hold her turnips," he said, shaking his head.

"Well, and the poor thing was warming a bun in the oven, weren't she?" Bess said, bending down to brush some dirt from her skirt. A lock of her wavy hair, black as night and bound in a strip of crimson ribbon, escaped the bond and fell across her forehead. She poked at it and tucked it back in again. "S'nough to make anyone lose her dinner." She looked at her father, tilting her head. The red headcloth intensified the bright darkness of her eyes, fringed with long black lashes.

"What dost thee want then, Da?" she said.*

Her father took a moment to recollect, so struck was he by the beauty of his daughter, standing in the afternoon light from the back door.

"And don't thou look the very image of thy Ma," he said softly. "God bless her for a saint in heaven."

Bess leaned in to put her hand against her father's grizzled cheek. "May she bless *us* from heaven," she said. "It's hard going without her, ain't it, Da?"

"We do the best we can," he said gruffly, trying to hide his emotion. "Get on wi'thee then, girl, I don't recall what I wanted thee for, go on then."

Bess kissed her father on his cheek, retrieved the bucket and went out to the back yard.

Her father watched her go, his heart wrung with pride and grief. Bess was just sixteen this month, and he was worried about what on earth he was supposed to do with her, with all the prospects of her being courted, and marrying, and heaven forbid! Moving away to be with some man in some other village? He wouldn't have it—he couldn't.

---

* In the chapters taking place in 1726, the characters use the older style of address: *you/ye* were used when talking to multiple persons or to a person of a higher status, to show respect. *Thou/thee* were used among familiars, intimates and to children or "inferiors".

He turned back into the kitchen with a troubled mind.

***

Bess stood in the backyard of the inn, her mop and bucket cleaned and restored to the weathered shed. The sun was lowering over the hills that rose behind their inn—the Olde Swan it was called for as long as anyone could remember. It was well-situated on the High Road at the entrance to the village on the road from London to Worcester, and was a busy, prosperous coaching inn, with large stables and a reputation for good food and clean beds. Their nearest rival was the White Hart, near the other end of the village, but there was plenty of trade for all, most years. She and her father worked hard, especially now that her mother was gone, nearly a year now, but there were others employed to help—Tim, the ostler, who slept above the stables and watched over the horses; Germaine, their recently-acquired cook, whose pies and scones were a wonder to taste; and a boy of all works, Sam, who seemed especially devoted to her, Bess, and was willing to run errands, take messages, and scurry about the village for anything she wanted.

She gazed over the low fence at the road that brought coaches and riders from London, and sighed for a sight of the only thing she wanted: the one man who had already stolen her heart. Colm Tremayne. She loved to whisper his name under her breath, like a prayer.

What she knew of him had come from himself—he was an orphan, both parents having died in Ireland of sickness when he was very young, and he'd been fetched from home by some of his mother's kin who had moved to Bristol.

He was tall and lithe, with wheat-blond hair and eyes the color of a changing sea. He spoke with a lilt and a sparkle of wit—Bess never knew when he was teasing, and had to laugh at herself when she finally caught on—he was always kind. But he was a bit of a mystery—he had a place, at times, on market days, where he sold apples and vegetables—but he hadn't told her anything about where he lived or how he made his living. He didn't live in Broadway, but one of the small hamlets further out from the village—no one else seemed to know anything about him.

The mystery of him only added to his other charms, and because he seemed interested in her above any other girls in the village, she just drank him in like heady wine, and let the questions be.

THREE
FRIDAY 3 SEPTEMBER 1886

Russell House

JOHN SAID HE WOULD WAIT IN THE TAVERN while I tucked away my things into the wardrobe and drawers, and freshened up as best I could, using the privy down the hall, and the wash basin, soap and towel on the marble-topped washstand in my chamber. I was ready in fifteen minutes, and stepped lively down the stairs, ready for a diverting adventure. Mary had made me promise to write her every day and describe all that I was to see and do, and I was already forming sentences in my head to describe my first experiences of Broadway Village.

The sun was below the trees on the high hilltop that rose to the west of the village, making it seem like a little mountain village such as I'd seen in the Swiss Alps, but the warm golden glow of Cotswold stone marked it as English a village as a village could be. John was greeted by many a person as we walked along the High Street past homes and shops, already closing for the day. We reached the green, a vaguely triangular swath of grass with two giant trees holding down one end of the park.

"That's Farnham House," John said, pointing to a solid, grey stone residence across the far side of the green. "Frank and Lily lived there first, then just this last Spring they took a lease on Russell House, which is just beyond. It's much larger." He pointed to his left up the hill, where  several high stone chimneys could be seen through the tree branches, outlined against the low sun. "And that's Abbots Grange, where some of us work," he said. "Frank has

 recently set it up as artists' studios and writing rooms for his guests to use."

"Frank Millet seems to me to be a very generous person," I said.

"He is indeed," John answered heartily.

We continued past the green and onto the road out of the village, which was flanked by orchards and fields stretching as far as one could see. In two minutes, off to our left, a handsome stone building rose up on the very edge of the village, past which the open coach highway threaded its way through green hills dotted with sheep and low-spreading trees.

Espaliered rose bushes clung to a high stone wall at the entrance, a few flowers drooping after the summer's heat. We paused at a gateway with two large square pillars on either side, and I could see, past the massive stone wall of the house, an extensive lawn rolling downhill, with flowers rioting at the foot of trimmed and shaped hedges.

"There's a lovely brook down at the bottom of the garden," John said, seeing the direction of my gaze. He sighed. "It creates the most splendid light at the end of the day—exactly when I need to be painting."

I caught at his meaning. "Dear John," I said, "I'm so very sorry that your having to fetch me has interfered with your work—is it too late to do anything now?" I laid a hand on his arm to hold him for an answer.

He shook his head and patted my hand reassuringly.

"Not a bit of it, Vi," he said. "I've only just come back myself, just this week, and frankly, haven't even looked at the painting yet." He pointed toward a large stone extension at the far end of the house. "That was a barn, a stables, too, once upon a time, when this place was an inn—a coach road inn, the Swan or the Old Swan, one of those ubiquitous country inn names—but Frank has turned it into a cracking studio for his work, and for others to use—and my painting is stored, if you can believe it, in the hayloft above one end of the barn!"

I shook my head. "As little as I know of such things, I can't imagine that's a very salubrious place to store a painting."

"It's actually very dry," John protested. "We'll have to haul it down, maybe tomorrow, and I can get started again—it's become a group project!"

Just then we heard a strong male voice calling out to John from an open window in a small square tower built just on the other side of the stone wall, some dozens of yards to our left. We looked up to see a tousle-haired man with an impish face, round glasses perched on his nose, leaning out the window of this fanciful little building.

"John, John, there you are at last! Is that Miss Vernon Lee with you?" The man laughed. "Of course it is, what am I saying? Who else were you going to fetch from the H and H?"

"Hello! Yes, Ned, this is Miss Lee indeed," John called back, grinning and clapping a hand on my shoulder quite heartily. "And I believe we may be in need of some dinner!"

Ned Abbey, for I correctly assumed it was he, Edwin Austin Abbey, who had hailed us from the window, turned away to say something to someone else in the room with him, and then disappeared altogether. John and I stood silently a moment, then with a courteous gesture, he motioned me through the front gateway. By the time we reached the courtyard and walk that led from the main house to the little square tower, a gay little party had gathered to greet us, headed by the gleeful Ned, who seemed to have absolutely flown down from the tower, followed by a woman and a little girl.

"Welcome, welcome," he cried, holding out a hand to take mine in his own, American style. He was a slightly built man, much smaller than John, but quick and lively, with a *joie de vivre* that shone out of his merry eyes, and I couldn't help but smile back as I shook his hand. "Welcome to Russell House," he said, still holding my hand as he drew me in closer. I maintained a firm grip with my other hand on the box of sweets I had brought. "Of course, it's more Frank and Lily's house than mine, but there you go!" He proceeded to tuck my arm under his and turned to present me to the others who had gathered on the broad brick walkway between the main house and the charming 'tower-house' from whose windows we had been addressed.

"I am wild to discuss crime and detection with you, Miss Lee," he said, patting my arm. "I have heard such accounts from John about all your amazing adventures, and what a sleuth you are! You will have to tell me all about everything."

While I was making suitable noises of approbation and demur, we were interrupted by a tall woman with upswept brown hair, about my own age as I determined, wearing a rumpled day dress and an apron stained with a variety of colors—paint, I thought, or were they sauces? A very young girl with luminous dark brown hair clung to her skirts.

"Dear Miss Lee," she said, taking my arm from Ned's with little ceremony and linking it to hers; Ned continued to smile broadly, not at all perturbed. "We have so longed to meet you, John's told us so much about you." She smiled with true sweetness, her blue eyes shining. "I am Lucia Millet, Frank's sister, and as you see"—she glanced down at her apron, and smoothed it with her free hand—"I am chief cook and bottlewasher here, as we say in Boston." She laughed heartily, and tugged at the child by her side. "And this is our darling Kate, one of the lights of our life."

Little Kate looked at me shyly and nodded her head. She looked to be about six or seven years old. I inclined my head in acknowledgement. "Very pleased to meet you, Miss Kate," I said. We turned to the next person in line.

I couldn't help, during this whole time, but think of the Lygon Arms doorman and his warning about the inhabitants of Russell House, and was determined to observe each of them closely, though withholding any immediate judgement. No alarums had sounded so far, but that would change when I was introduced to the third person who made up this *plein air* greeting party.

"And this is Alfred Parsons, Vi, a magnificent illustrator and a genius in the garden," John said, warmly clasping the man with an arm thrown across his shoulders. He was shorter than John (almost everyone was), and about ten years older, I judged, which would make him near forty; his short hair and trim beard were beginning to grizzle, although his rather luxuriant mustache was solidly dark brown. He bowed slightly to me (he was English, not American, you see), and as he looked me in the face, I discerned a wariness, a narrowing of the eyes that depicted to me a suspicious nature, or perhaps just a very reserved one. He presented an immediate and strong contrast to the open, chatty, fresh friendliness of the Americans.

I murmured something suitable, and was again drawn along by Lucia, who still firmly commandeered my arm.

"What shall we call you, Miss Lee?" she said. Her asking such a thing was robbed of its impertinence by her charming smile. She actually squeezed my arm a bit as she elucidated. "John always calls you 'Vi' or 'Violet', which seems ever so much nicer than 'Miss Lee'," she said, glancing at John with a laugh. "But of course, whatever you wish, we will stick to that."

"Vernon Lee is the name on my books," I said, trying to match her light tone. "In private life, I am happy with Vi or Violet, as you choose."

"Lovely!" she cried, and turned to walk into the house. She reached out to Alfred Parsons and patted his arm. "You shall have to immediately plant some violets in the garden, Alfred, to honor our new friend."

His dark eyes narrowed again. "Not the time of year for planting violets," he said, and turned away abruptly. Lucia just laughed, and told me not to mind him. "He's grumpy because John has taken over the garden patch by the brook, and Alfred can't get at it until the painting is finished."

I noted his angry stride as he left our little group to enter the house without him. Not quite the proverbial serpent in the garden, I thought, but certainly a note of discord. *I've got my eye on you, Mr. Alfred Parsons,* I thought. *We'll just see.*

● ● ●

FOUR

SEPTEMBER 1726

The Olde Swan Inn

TIM THE OSTLER STARED AT BESS from behind the half-door of the stables, trying to keep out of sight but unable to keep from watching her. She was a beauty, it was for certain, and more than that, she was kind to Tim.

The ostler was a small man, young, thin and wiry, with knobby knees and elbows, and scant brown hair that he tied back with a piece of string, leaving it long to make up for the broad, smooth front of his head where the hair had never grown. He hadn't known much kindness in his life, but he had a genius for settling horses; the landlord of the Olde Swan had seen the potential in the young man, and gladly hired him.

"Oi, Tim, wa'cher 'bout, old scruff, eh?" Tim whirled around as he recognized the voice of a sometime mate, Georgie, who more often than not was scheming his way in or out of some plan to make his fortune. They were of an age, though Tim was the elder by nearly a year; he would be twenty-one by Christmas.

"Wa'cher self," he said, stepping back into the dimness of the stables and picking up a curry brush. He

· · ·

tossed it to Georgie. "Here, make thyself useful, then, brush down Brownie, all right?"

Georgie shrugged, and hefted the brush as if considering. "Wot's in it fer me, then?" he said, but he unlatched the gate to Brownie's stall and went inside, soothing the horse with a low voice and a soft touch on her nose. He was a good deal handsomer than Tim, but it was if he didn't know his own good looks—dark brown wavy locks, big brown eyes with lashes like a girl's, and a happy-go-lucky way about him that made people think well of him—until you got to know his ways.

Tim thought about it—he knew his friend was down on his luck, doing the odd job here and there to support himself and his old mother. "I can get Bess to gi' thee a bit of stew, yes?"

Georgie nodded agreeably. "All right, thanks then."

The two young men went about their work silently for a bit; Tim was examining another horse's hooves—he'd have to call on the blacksmith, looked like.

"So what dost thou think I know?" Georgie called out.

Tim shook his head—another of Georgie's schemes coming. He merely grunted, but that was enough encouragement for his friend.

"Thou'st heard o'the Highwayman of Broadway, yes? The one that's stoppin' all them coaches on the Hill Road?"

"Course I have," Tim said scornfully. "The whole village's talked of nothing else, this half year or more."

Georgie left off his brushing and drew closer to Tim. "I'm meaning to join him." His eager brown eyes shone with hope and mischief.

"Art thou daft, then?" Tim said, letting go the horse's hoof and standing up to look his friend in the eye. "Dost thou think that's some kind of way to make a living?" He shook his head. "The King's men'll cut thee down—shoot thee, don't ye know!—just like all the other highwaymen who've come to grief. Their day is over, I tell thee, for what it ever was worth."

Georgie frowned. "Well, yes, there's that chance, the King's men and all," he said. "But he's the last of the breed, they say, and is getting rich off those merchants and squires—they don't need *all* that money, do they? Should spread it around a bit, eh?" He puffed up his chest a bit. "I think I could make a pretty terrifying highwayman, won't I? Get in for the glory while the gettin's good?"

Tim turned away from him in disgust. "Thou wouldns't terrify a rabbit," he said. "And besides," he added, turning back. "Don't know who he is, no one does, yes? How dost thou think to join up with him—stand out on the road at midnight and wait for him to pass by?" He mimicked a pleading voice. "Please, sir, can ye take me on as a 'prentice 'ighway man, I won't be no trouble, I just want a cut o'yer money."

Georgie shoved at him with a rough hand, pushing past the ostler to make for the door.

"Oi, thou didn't finish with Brownie!" Tim called after him. "Don't want that stew, then?"

"Bollocks thy stew," Georgie said, and left the stable, nearly knocking over Bess who had just come to the door.

"Hey there, watch thyself, Mr. Georgie!" she cried as he shouldered his way past her. He only walked off faster, and she stood looking at him for a moment, then turned back to Tim.

"What's gotten into him?" she said, stepping further into the stables. She carried a small basket covered with a coarse cloth, which Tim hoped was his lunch.

Tim realized she was waiting for him to answer, and he was rattled, as usual, when talking to her, so he just blurted out the truth without thinking. "Oh, him! He's daft. He says he's going to go be a highwayman, like that one everyone's talking about—silly fool."

Bess pursed her lips in a slightly disapproving smile. "Oh, I imagine as what he thinks it's a glamorous thing, riding over the hills, being daring and dangerous—and getting jewels and gold in the bargain!" She shook her head and laughed outright. "A man would have to be a fool indeed to think he would last very long at that occupation!"

"Too right," Tim agreed fervently. "And he doesn't even know who the Highwayman is, yes? As if he could just sit down with him here at the inn, and have a little chat 'bout learnin' the trade!"

Bess set down the basket on a stool near the door. "Here's thy lunch, then, Tim," she said. "Bit of stew and some bread my Da made just now." She patted him on the arm, and smiled kindly as he blushed. "Mind thou bring the basket and napkin back after thou've done, yes? I've got the washing up to do later, when I'm back from the market."

"A'course, that I will," he was able to mumble, and he watched her with all his heart and soul as she left the stable, her black hair swinging against her shoulders as she walked away with a light, firm step.

FIVE

FRIDAY 3 SEPTEMBER 1886

Russell House

CONTRARY TO JOHN'S DESCRIPTION, Russell House was quiet and peaceful. We were sitting in "Lily's Parlour" as it was called and were devouring an early tea (or a late luncheon) as we chatted.

"We have heard so much of your detecting experiences," Lucia said, her eyes bright with interest. She had seated herself next to me on a little blue satin sofa, with Kate on my other side, and Ned and John on chairs nearby.

"Oh yes," Ned chimed in. "We so hope there will be some mystery here for you to solve!"

John and I exchanged glances, and he nodded encouragement.

"Well, I must say, John's description to me of the demise of his blue bird," I said, putting down my tea cup, "is what tempted me to come to Broadway and meet you all."

"Oh, that nasty bird!" Lucia exclaimed, and Ned leaned forward eagerly to speak. "There you are," he said, "our first murder, don't you think?" He said it with considerable glee, but caught himself as Lucia shook her head and put her finger to her lips, motioning at the same time to Kate.

"*First* murder!" John repeated, not having noticed Lucia's attempt to sanitize the conversation before the child. "That's bad luck, Ned, it's tempting Fate to bring on another." I glanced at Kate to see if she was troubled by the word murder, but she seemed complacently intent on the piece of cake on her plate.

A wall clock chimed and Lucia jumped at the sound, noting the time with a start. "Lord, I must be about the dinner, Lily will be doing it all on her own," she said. She looked at me rather apologetically. "We have only one servant now, sad to say, and that one not entirely helpful, especially in the kitchen." She eyed me speculatively, and I trembled at the probable request she seemed about to make.

I was rescued by John stepping in hastily. "Oh, my dear Lucia, don't even think of asking Vi to help in the kitchen, she's preposterously unacquainted with such things, and would likely end up poisoning us all, wouldn't you, Vi?" he ended comfortably, grinning at me. "I'm rather more attuned to giving a hand, you know," he continued, "sorting the vegge and cutting things up." He stood up and cuffed Ned lightly on the shoulder. "Up, man! Your skills are needed in the scullery!" He said to Lucia, "Ned is a crack dish washer—I've seen him do it in London!" Ned sighed dramatically, stood up and bowed to Lucia.

"Then you are both drafted," Lucia said promptly, with a cheerful smile. As they left the room she nodded to Kate. "Dear, you must entertain Miss Violet while we are preparing dinner, all right?" The girl looked up at her in some dismay, I thought, but then nodded her head, and smiled shyly at me. She was a pretty little thing, with soft brown curls, very large brown eyes and a heart-shaped face; she wore a white dress with a blue pinafore over it, and in the hand that was not clutching her piece of cake, she held a drawing pad.

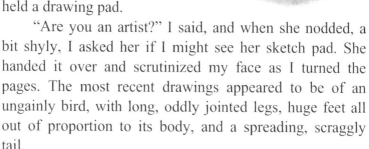

"Are you an artist?" I said, and when she nodded, a bit shyly, I asked her if I might see her sketch pad. She handed it over and scrutinized my face as I turned the pages. The most recent drawings appeared to be of an ungainly bird, with long, oddly jointed legs, huge feet all out of proportion to its body, and a spreading, scraggly tail.

"Is this Mr. Sargent's infamous blue bird?" I guessed. That seemed to open the lock to Kate's silence, and she readily responded.

"Yes, that's the blue bird," she said. "Only of course, I haven't any blue paint to make it so, and besides, he was a lot of other colors too, although mostly blue." She sighed slightly. I noted how well-spoken she was for a child her age.

"Was he a favorite pet of yours?" I asked, thinking she was missing the creature, for which I noticed she used the personal pronoun.

Kate thought this over. "Not especially," she said. "Of course, he wasn't *our* pet, he belonged to Mr. John, only he couldn't keep him in London, could he? Mr. Gosse gave the blue bird to him there, which was silly, my aunt Lucia said, as who could take care of a creature like that in an artist's studio in the city? So he left him with us to take care of."

"Ah, that seems like a wise choice," I said. We were silent for a moment.

"I have heard," I said cautiously, "that he was rather ill-tempered, at times."

"Oh yes, he was dreadful!" Kate said solemnly. "Once he got out of the garden and ran, ever so fast on those big feet, out to the village green, and when we caught up with him, dozens of people had surrounded him and were laughing and yelling at the poor thing—but he kept darting at them, pecking at their legs and screeching like a barn owl!" She looked at me earnestly. "But he also could dance," she said. "He would hold out his wings"—at this she jumped up from the sofa and spread her arms—"and then hop back and forth on one foot, then the other"—she demonstrated this prancing admirably—"all the while making a funny hooting noise, like this!" And she trilled in a high-pitched voice fit to break a crystal glass, then stopped and stood there, out of breath.

• • •

"You must surely miss this entertainment," I said.

Kate dropped back down on the sofa. "I guess so. He's only been dead and gone a few days now." She turned to me speaking gravely. "The gardener found him, down by the brook. Someone had killed him, and tied up his legs. It was very sad." She sighed again. "We buried him in the orchard, as Mummy says it would be good for the trees."

"Do you have any idea," I said carefully, "who might have killed the bird?"

She shrugged. "Any number of people, I imagine. As Aunt Lucia says, he was *not universally beloved*." She thought for a moment. "Actually, there *was* someone who really disliked the blue bird." She looked up at me. "I probably shouldn't say," she said. "It was just that the blue bird messed the garden quite a lot, and it made him angry."

Mr. Alfred Parsons, I thought. I didn't press Kate for more, and we sat companionably for some time in Lily's Parlour. Kate had become comfortable enough with me to start chattering about the denizens of Russell House, which, although coming from a child, was quite amusing and rather insightful. I suspected, however, that a good many of her opinions, stated with charming naiveté, had been imbibed from her Aunt Lucia, whose good nature apparently did not prevent her from exercising a sharp tongue now and again.

"I was the first one to pose for Mr. John," she said, sounding a little wistful. "He painted me in the garden, before anyone else, and I was very sure to stand quite still, even though it was very tiresome, and sometimes a fly or a bee would come sit on my nose, and I would have to move, but he didn't seem to mind." We were looking at a picture book as she told me this story, and I was intrigued.

"And are you posing for him now, for this garden picture I have heard about?"

"Oh! No, it's not me anymore, it's those Barnard girls, because they are older and have light hair and he thinks that's much prettier." I could see her lip trembling a bit at this admission, and my heart went out to her. How I knew the slings and arrows of a girlhood bereft of beauty! She put her head down, leaning against my arm, and murmured in a low voice. "They make fun of how I talk, because they are English and I am American."

"Well, then they are very unsophisticated, petty-minded little girls," I said firmly. "I have travelled all over Europe and England, dear little Kate, and everyone I meet has a different accent!" She glanced up at me hopefully. "It is a mark of education and liberality to accept people for who they are, for their character and their knowledge, not for how they pronounce their words. You are not to mind such things anymore."

Kate looked at me with awe. "Oh, thank you, I shall not mind them anymore indeed, Miss Violet." And she reached up and planted a kiss on my cheek, which I have to say, almost brought tears to my eyes. I'm generally not quite fond of children, but this one had stolen my heart.

"Kate! Kate my darling! Please come into the kitchen, dear," a voice called from the hallway.

Kate slipped out from under my arm, curtsied prettily, and ran off to the kitchen.

I had yet to meet her mother, the formidable Mrs. Frank Millet, but I had hopes that she would be as amiable as her sister-in-law Lucia, and that we would like each other—John had spoken so highly of both women.

I was to find, to my amusement and consternation, that this was not going to be the case.

SIX

SEPTEMBER 1726

In the High Street of Broadway Village

IT WAS MARKET DAY IN BROADWAY, and Bess set out early to the High Street, with Germaine the cook alongside her, looking out for late summer fruits and early autumn apples for the inn's larder. Her passage through the market was halted time and again as friends stopped her to chat, and especially, several young men of the village trying to claim her attention with their bashful attempts at conversation. She was polite to everyone, and pitied the young men—there was only one man she wanted to converse with, only one who could command her attention. It had been near a month since she had seen him.

An hour later, laden with a basketful of produce, Germaine bid Bess farewell and started back down the street to return to the inn, but not without a cautious hint to the young woman.

"Thou'll not want to be lingering long, I expect?" She made it sound like an ordinary question. "Thou knowest there's always more folk at t'Inn on Market Day." She glanced sideways at her employer's daughter, whose own eyes were busy scanning the remaining booths further up the street.

* * *

"Sure and I won't be long," Bess said absently, and blushed as she saw Germaine trying to hide a smile. Then they both laughed.

"Well, and be sure to give 'im my regards, when thou seest that swain o'thine, lass," said the cook, patting her arm. "But be quick about it, eh? Thy father'll be lookin' for thee."

Bess nodded, and happily turned away to search for her "swain". He was not always at Market Day, being but a small farmer, but his booth was always crowded, as his orchard fruits were well-known for quality and beauty, although he never seemed to have very much produce on offer. Occasionally, he would sell seedlings for berry bushes and flowering shrubs. His name was Colm Tremayne, and he was a great favorite with all the women.

She sped up the High Street with a light heart, hope filling her dreams, and then she saw his wagon at last, at the far end of the village, across from the White Hart Inn. There was less of a crowd than usual, and as she drew near, she could see why: most of his produce was already gone, with just a few small baskets of apples on the ground. His back was turned to her, counting out coins into a customer's hand. She watched from a little distance, her heart beating fast.

"There y'are, me darlin'," Tremayne was saying, flashing his Irish blue eyes at the woman—*that spiteful cow Mary Cummings*, Bess noted with an inward snort of contempt. *Worst flirt in the village, and nothing to show for it.* She took a few steps closer, and made as if to examine the remaining apples in the basket.

• • •

"Oh, it's you, Miss Bess," she heard Mary Cummings say, with a barely disguised sneer. "I'm surprised you have time off from all your work at the Inn." Mary Cummings was the daughter of the village clerk, and as a result of some bit of an inheritance her father had, was able to live "like a lady" as she frequently said, and do nothing more laborious than needlework, which entitled her to look down on everyone else.

Bess looked steadily at her and smiled. "Not all of us are so fortunate as to have a dead relative to help us along in life." She glanced at Tremayne, who was wisely keeping a straight face. "But I'm not ashamed of honest labor, especially at the side of such an honorable man as me Da." This was a dig she couldn't help herself from deploying—the village clerk's reputation had recently been under a little cloud due to some "misplaced" village funds.

Mary's face darkened, making her otherwise pretty face look sour and common, despite the better fabrics and ribbands she wore to enhance her appearance. She grabbed her bag of apples and laid a possessive hand on Tremayne's arm, boldly using the familiar form of address with him. "Fare thee well for now, dear Colm, but I hope to see thee at the Harvest Fair—thou must promise to dance with me, won't thee?" She tossed her head slightly, setting her yellow curls to springing about her cheeks.

Tremayne only smiled and bowed slightly, by which Bess understood that he committed to nothing, but which apparently satisfied Mary Cummings, who with a scowl cast in Bess's direction, swept away with her apples. Bess laughed aloud, and turned to Tremayne, batting her eyelashes in mock seduction.

"And won't thee be promisin' to dance with me, *dear Colm*, at the Harvest Fair?" she simpered, then caught her breath at the look in his eyes.

"Wi'thee and no one else," he said. "That I trow."

The two lovers leaned toward each other over the makeshift table of boards and boxes, as the rest of the world fell away.

"Oh, my Colm," she murmured, wishing her hands could be free with the black curls that fell across his forehead. He caught one of her hands in his and gave it a kiss on the palm, causing shivers to ride up and down her spine. But he let it go as suddenly as other customers approached the booth, and Bess turned to give her attention to a few late pears in a small basket at her feet.

When they were alone again, Bess asked him the question that had been growing in her heart for some time. Leaning forward again, she spoke in a low voice.

"Canst thee not come to the Inn, Colm, to meet my Da?" she said, her voice trembling a bit. She wasn't sure why she was so afraid to ask, but his answer confirmed to her that there was some hidden puzzle here.

"Nae, sweet, 'tis not fit, not for now," Tremayne said, looking serious. His hand swept over the mostly empty table. "I'm not in any position to present meself as courtin' thee, yes? Thy Da would toss me out on me ear, he would."

She started to protest, but he claimed her hand again, and kissed it warmly. "Soon, soon," he said. "I've some prospects as will make my fortune, and then thou shalt see, it'll all come right, lass."

Bess nodded her head, discontent that he thought such a condition necessary, as things stood between them, but then, she thought, a man has his pride, and cheered herself that he seemed to have a plan, and she was part of it.

"I must hie to the Inn," she said, slowly withdrawing her hand from his grasp. "God go with thee, my dearest," she whispered.

"And always with thee, my love," Tremayne said. Bess saw that he was watching her walk away, and he gave a little wave of his hand the last time she looked over her shoulder at him. She sighed that there was no time for them now. But she took heart, and believed in his resolve to make good on his promise, and soon.

SEVEN

FRIDAY 3 SEPTEMBER 1886

Dinner at Russell House

WE WERE TEN ALTOGETHER AT DINNER, including little Kate, somewhat to my surprise. But I recalled how Isa and Ned Boit, in Paris, encouraged their four young girls to dine with them on a regular basis, and then, they are Americans too. Fortunately, Kate was a very well-behaved young lady.

I was seated next to a very attractive and lively red-haired young woman named Kitty O'Byrne, whom I soon learned was one of Ned Abbey's regular models, from London. Two other models, both handsome, robust men, one in his twenties and the other rather older, also joined us at table. I was to discover that this was the typical procedure at Russell House—everyone and anyone came to dinner, often without an invitation.

As the newest guest (I assumed) I had the honor of being seated at Lily Millet's right hand, with her daughter Kate on her left, then the older male model next to her; Kitty the red-haired model sat on my right. I was sorry to be seated so far from Lucia, who was farther down the table, between John and Ned Abbey. The irritable Mr. Parsons sat across from them, although he appeared to be conversing affably enough. Kate smiled often at me from across the table, even though it was difficult to exchange any words.

"I understand, Miss Paget, that you are a great friend of our dear John's, from childhood," said Lily Millet, suddenly addressing me for the first time. We had nodded our heads to each other upon being introduced in the drawing room just before dinner, but had not yet spoken properly. She was a small but elegant woman, with wavy brown hair and cornflower blue eyes, though with rather a languid air about her that belied her position as active hostess of the menagerie that was Russell House. Yet, as I observed her, she seemed restless and unsettled, although perhaps unaware of it herself.

"Yes," I replied. "John and I met when we were both ten, scampering about the ruins of Rome, looking for old coins and pieces of statuary buried under the stones." My statement had caught little Kate's attention, and she leaned over her plate to talk.

"And did you find any? Any coins?" she asked.

"Oh, my yes," I said, smiling. "Loads of them! And several fingers and toes as well," I said, adding at her perturbed look, "marble or clay toes, that is, my dear, from old statues." She looked relieved.

· · ·

"Do you not think he is looking very well, happily occupied as he is, here in Broadway?" Lily asked, rather archly, I thought, as if taking the credit to herself for his improved spirits. "Miss Paget?" She said my name again as I pondered how to answer this rather impertinent question.

"Please call me Violet," I said, looking round the table and laughing a little. "There seems to be very little formality in your charming home, Lily—may I call you Lily?—and I'm sure that John is as delighted as I am to be among such friendly people." That was as close as I wanted to get to the various scandals and upsets that John and I had left in our wake, he in Paris and I in London. But my hostess was not as delicate.

"John was treated infamously in Paris," she said, taking up her glass of wine and sipping at it. "I saw that troublesome portrait of his in his studio in London—magnificent of course, but I must say I didn't think much of the lady in question." She tossed her head in dismissal of Virginie Gautreau, and looked at me coolly. "She must have used all her seductive powers to get him to paint her in the first place." She took another sip of her wine. "Do you think she succeeded?"

I have to admit I was a little shocked, and I'm not easily shocked. I answered her somewhat obliquely.

"I expect you'll have to ask John that question," I said, and was perturbed to see that this response made Lily smile a tight little smile. Then it struck me—she was jealous! Of Madame Gautreau, perhaps even of me, as impossible a thing as that might be! She was clearly very possessive of her famous guest. Another idea occurred to me, and I spoke without thinking it through.

"And where is Mr. Frank Millet?" I said. "I had hoped to meet the decorated hero of the Russo-Turkish War, especially to discuss with him how his warrior days have given way to the pursuit of Arts and Letters." I was being serious, but I couldn't help sounding a bit arch—I am no keen supporter of any kind of war.

My abrupt change of subject startled her, I could see, and she set down her glass with a slight thump. "He's in Paris," she said, and turned to speak to her daughter, who had tugged at her sleeve with some request.

I then gratefully turned to speak with Kitty the red-haired model on my right hand, as a polite guest must do, feeling a sort of queasy victory in a silly game of wits. Something about my question regarding her husband had struck a nerve, and I could see that Lily and I were going to be at odds.

"Miss O'Byrne," I said, "I understand that you have come down to Broadway from London to pose for Mr. Abbey—do tell me what character from olden times you are posing as?"

"Oh, my, do please call me Kitty," she said, and her voice was delightfully Irish, musical and lilting. She laughed, causing her red-gold curls to shake about her forehead. "I sit for both Mr. Millet and Mr. Abbey, whoever needs me. For Ned, though, right now I believe I'm someone from Shakespeare," she said. "Rosalind or Beatrice or Viola—one of those preposterous women who dress up as men or boys—as if anyone couldn't see through that disguise!" She laughed merrily.

I smiled. My own growing predilection for wearing severely tailored, "mannish" clothing gave me no little sympathy for cross-dressing, theatrical or otherwise. "You must admit," I said, feeling daring in the freer social atmosphere of Russell House, "wearing men's trousers would be infinitely more comfortable and practical than skirts."

Kitty laughed again, and looked at me more fully. "To be sure, and if I were to go out riding, trousers would suit me very well, but it would never do in a ballroom."

I nodded in agreement. "I have never learned to ride," I said. "Perhaps if I had been allowed to wear trousers, it would have been more appealing."

Our conversation was apparently of interest to the two male models who were seated across from us; the younger of the two leaned forward, grinning, his dark blue eyes alight with mischief. His thick black curls hung charmingly around his face, which had an innocent, cherubic flush. "Aye, and to see you in a pair o' *bríste* would be a *radharc álainn*, Kitty my love," and he gave a roguish wink.

She tossed her head at him and shot back. "A truly *lovely sight* would be the back o'ye walkin' away, wouldn't it, Michael?" I glanced between the two of them, then at the third, older model. "Are you all Irish?" I asked, curious. "Is modeling now an Irish pursuit?"

The three laughed and shook their heads. "I'm half and half," said the older man, whose name was David Cowan. He was broad-shouldered, but where Michael was pale, David was tanned and ruddy, with a nose slightly out of line, as if it had been broken at an early age. His brown hair was cut short, and he looked to be a sensible man. He reached for the bottle of wine on the table and poured some into his glass. "Ma is Welsh, where I get me good looks"—his companions guffawed at this boast—"but me Da gave me the Irish talent for drinking, so that's all to the good."

The younger man, who introduced himself as Michael Kelly, answered my question. "There's a few of us, actors and singers as would be, up in London, who also pose for the artists when we can." He smiled cheerily. "It's good money, and sometimes a bit o' fun on the side, like down here in Broadway." He winked again at Kitty, who shook her head and frowned at him.

"Don't you start, Michael Kelly," she warned.

"O-ho," he cried. "There's no winkin' at you, then, is it? Have you turned into a fine lady now, from wearin' all those fancy clothes Mr. Millet and Mr. Abbey have ye puttin' on day after day?"

David Cowan intervened before Kitty could answer. "Now, now, lad, we're all just earnin' our livings here, aren't we?" He gave a light poke with his elbow into Michael's side. "I've seen you in a top hat and tails, haven't I? Anyone'd think you was the finest of English gentlemen."

"Don't you ever call me that!" Michael returned, his face flushing.

"What, you don't want to be called a *gentleman*?" Kitty said, laughing. Michael narrowed his eyes at her. "It's the *English* part, thank 'ee very much, that I don't want anything to do with, as you know." He poured himself more wine and drank it down quickly.

I was about to ask a question when Lily interrupted with a question of her own, directed to all three Irish models—she had evidently overheard their exchange.

"I'm sure you hold against the English even more these days," she said, "what with the Irish Home Rule defeat this summer."

That threw a definite pall over the lively chat at our section of the table, I can tell you.

Michael Kelly gave Lily quite a black look, Kitty blanched and gripped her hands close in her lap. David Cowan poured himself another glass of wine.

I looked at Lily, puzzled by her animosity toward the models; but she was gazing particularly at Kitty, which made me wonder if Mrs. Frank Millet was perhaps jealous of the pretty model who posed for not only Ned Abbey, it would seem, but for her own husband as well.

"You Americans should understand better that the Irish want only the freedom to rule themselves independently," David Cowan said evenly. "It's nae all that long ago you fought the old King George and got your own liberty." He swallowed down the rest of his wine, and turned his face away from Lily.

"And the English need to understand us better, too," Michael Kelly muttered under his breath, giving me a dark look. I responded mildly, "Actually, I'm mostly Welsh myself, with an amalgam of Austro-Hungarian mishmash from my father." The young man looked abashed, and raised his glass to me in a cordial salute. "Let's toast to better harmony throughout the kingdom, then, shall we?" he said, raising his voice to get everyone's attention. John, Ned and Lucia turned in our direction, and willingly raised their glasses.

"To Ireland! To England! To Wales! To Scotland!" cried various voices around the table.

Lily abruptly stood up, throwing her crumpled napkin on the table, and nodded to her sister-in-law, who had glanced her way at the sudden movement.

"Lucia, if we don't clear the table now, we'll be here all night, and I believe there's sewing to be done on Ned's costumery for tomorrow," she said in a tight voice.

"And John promised to play us some selections from the *Parsifal* he just saw at Bayreuth," Lucia said as she rose, seeming to me to be trying to smooth over her sister-in-law's ill manners. "So he can entertain us as we sew."

That appeared to be the signal for everyone to spring into action. I noticed the time on the mantel clock, just gone eight, and wondered what the next few hours would bring before I could lay my head to rest.

EIGHT

LATE SEPTEMBER 1726

At the Olde Swan Inn

WHEN BESS ARRIVED HOME, her father had indeed been looking for her, as Germaine sharply informed her with a roll of her eyes and a nod toward the bar to indicate the innkeeper's whereabouts. " He's got a flea in his ear all right," the cook said. "Don' know what it's about, do I?"

Bess nodded her thanks, left the apples and other items she'd been carrying on the kitchen table, and straightened her shoulders to go meet her father. She knew his heart was kind and he was very good to her, but he could be stubborn and mulish, more since her mother died—she was the one who had kept her husband in good humour. Bess approached the tavern room quietly, scoping out the situation first, and saw that her father was not quite alone—Squire Robert Collins was sitting at a table, his large frame barely fitting the chair, and was talking to her father from where he sat, his voice loud and commanding in between sips of ale. Her father stood behind the bar, cleaning glasses and doing busy work. He looked up, sensing her arrival, and smiled fondly, although she could tell he was uneasy.

"Ah, there thou be, my Bess," he said, and she instantly detected a false heartiness in his tone.

"Hello, Da," she said, and moved to stand next to him, planting a little kiss on his cheek. She glanced at the Squire and nodded her head politely, keeping in mind her father's admonition to welcome all comers—at least initially. She didn't particularly like the Squire, though, and always kept their interactions to a minimum. "Welcome, Squire Robert," she said, making an effort. "Tis a while since we've seen ye, sir."

The man was ogling her quite openly. "That is true, little one," he said, and took a swig of his ale. "Though not so little anymore, thou've become a woman since I was here last, haven't thee?" He stroked his wiry black beard and mustache, as he looked her up and down.

Her father's face reddened a bit, hearing this, but Bess touched his arm to keep his temper down. The man's insinuations and familiar address meant nothing to her. She turned her head away and spoke in a low voice to her father.

"Was there something thou needed me for right away, Da?" she said. "Germaine said as thee were asking for me?"

"No, lass, I'm good," he said. "Just a'wondring where thou wast—on thy own in th'market."

Bess smiled and kissed him again. "I'm not a child, Da, I'm not to be looked after as if I were a wee girl still."

He sighed and nodded his head. "Aye, don't I know it," he said. "But th'art all I have, girl, and I dinnae want to lose thee—not yet. Thee'll be gone soon enow." He threw a fierce glance at the Squire, and looked down again at the mug he was cleaning. Bess saw the look and realized what was going on.

* * *

"Never him, Da," she said, her voice low and insistent. "Never."

She turned to go, but was stopped by the Squire's voice, followed by himself rising from his chair and rapidly intercepting her as she made for the door.

"Why, don't say th'art leaving so soon, my girl," he said, standing in her way. He was tall and well-made, but fleshy and too ruddy, as if the drink was more to him than food. People in the village considered him handsome, but he wasn't well-liked. "I'd been telling thy good father here as how I'd like to be better acquainted."

A glance at her father showed her he didn't like that kind of talk any more than she did, but was perhaps unwilling to discomfort the local magistrate if he could avoid it. So she swallowed her pride a bit and answered as politely as she could.

"I thank ye, sir, for the compliment, but I have many duties to attend to," she said, thinking it would be good to remind him of the difference in their status. "My father's inn doesn't run itself."

"Wait just one moment, though," the Squire said, still filling the doorway. He reached out and held her chin lightly in his hand. "Wilt thou promise me a dance at the Harvest Fair this Sunday? I'm to be there to open the games."

Bess took a step back to release herself from his clutch. "Oh, sir," she said, trying for an even tone, "I cannae think ye would want to be dancin' with one such as me."

And with that she ducked past him, thinking as she did that it was a sorry thing to be reminded twice in the same day that she was a working woman, and not a lady of leisure and class.

Not that she cared. Colm Tremayne was a farmer, and she would make a good farmer's wife, she thought as she strode away. Or, perhaps Colm would want to take over the inn, as her father was aging, and it was a good business. These thoughts made her forget the unpleasantness of the Squire's attention, and she went to work in the pantry with renewed vigor and a spirit of determination.

Her industry did not go unnoticed by Germaine, who after a few minutes came to stand at the pantry door, watching her as she sorted and shelved the stores. She was a canny woman, and had an observing eye.

"The Squire is an important man," she said. "And a widower these six months, since his wife passed, God bless her soul."

Bess sniffed in contempt. "Important is not something I long to be," she said. "Nor rich, nor idle, nor living in a big house." She looked up at the ceiling, as if contemplating the whole inn. "There's rooms enough here for me to tend to," she said with a laugh. Then she grew serious. "He cannae be serious about one such as me," she said, echoing her own words to the man. "And even if not, thou knowest my heart is set on another."

Germaine smiled at the girl, of whom she'd grown quite fond in the year or so she'd been cook at the inn. "Yes, dearie, and that glad I am thou hast such a one to dream of." She contemplated the young woman for a moment longer. "Wilt thou be bringing him to meet thy father soon?"

Bess hesitated, then nodded. She was sure it would happen soon; she would try again to get Colm to show himself to her father—he needn't fear he wasn't good enough, or rich enough. He was enough in himself, for her part—he must know that.

NINE

FRIDAY 3 SEPTEMBER 1886

After Dinner at Russell House

BY NINE O'CLOCK ALL WAS SETTLED and relatively calm at Russell House. Kate and her infant brother Laurence, of whom I had not yet had a glimpse, were abed in the nursery. Lucia, Lily and Kitty were all seated at a large table brightly lighted by tall work candles and two oil lamps in the drawing room, sewing and stitching and discussing the costumes they were creating. Mr. Parsons had disappeared, and Ned Abbey hovered over the seamstresses, commenting and advising as to tassels and trims. David and Michael, the models, had sat down to a game of cards at a little table near the fireplace, and seemed content to focus on their game.

John was seated at the piano at the other end of the room, and was playing Wagner from memory; the still-controversial composer, dead some three years now, was gaining a greater reputation than ever with his final opera

* * *

Parsifal; the story of the Holy Grail had been staged to great acclaim at Bayreuth in August, and John had come back filled with admiration.

I sat somewhere in the middle of all this activity, and set myself to observing the inhabitants of Russell House; my lack of seamstress skills having been duly noted, I was free to play the *flaneur*, albeit stationary. Lily Millet seemed calmer, but quite self-absorbed and withdrawn. I could see that Lucia bent toward her frequently, whispering, and occasionally Lily responded with a small smile. Kitty chatted and laughed with Ned Abbey in particular, but I noticed that she looked restless, and often glanced out the window, as if expecting someone to appear.

I felt a nagging sense of impatience—after all, what was I doing here, scrutinizing all these presumably respectable people, and all for the sake of a stupid dead bird! I began to find the blue bird as irksome as everyone said it was, and sympathized with Mr. Alfred Parsons, who probably *did* slit its throat because it messed in his precious garden once too often.

I was seated nearest to the two Irishmen playing their card game, and as I turned my attention to them, Michael caught my eye and smiled as David Cowan slapped his hand of cards on the table and stood up. "Miss Lee," said the younger model, "would you take up a hand or two in David's place? He's a sore loser, he is." David smiled broadly at that, disproving the young man's taunt, and bowed to me as he pulled out the chair for me to sit upon.

Thus encouraged, I thought *why not?* and stepped over to sit at the little table.

• • •

"I'm not at all a card player," I said to Michael, who was shuffling the cards at an alarming rate. "I don't believe I know any game whatsoever."

He paused and looked thoughtfully at me. "Shall I tell your fortune then, Miss Lee?" he said.

"You are a man of many talents, Mr. Kelly," I said, quite amused by the idea. "But can you tell fortunes with ordinary playing cards?"

He placed the deck, faces down, on the table, and spread them easily in a fan. "Oh, the original of the Tarot cards, don't you know, they were just plain playing cards, so, yes, a fortune is easily teased out from a deck."

He motioned with one hand to the fan of cards. "Pick three, now, if you please, from anywhere, and then lay them face up on the table, in the order you chose them. But first," he continued, "think in your mind some question, or thought, or worry, that you would want an answer for."

Still amused, but beginning to  feel a bit uneasy—I had never had my fortune told before—I studied the array of cards, thinking at the same time: *I want to know what's going on here in Broadway*; then put my hand out to pick one, then another, then the third.

I did as Michael told me, and lay them face down.

He surveyed them intently for a few moments, then leaned forward, in a whisper only I could hear, he told me what they meant. "The Jack of Spades," he said, "in the Tarot he is the Knight of Swords. He's a fighting man, one who defends the honor of his land with his sword, when needs must—he is gallant, and young, and high-spirited, and he does what he must do to bring about justice and the right for his people. He is not alone, though, he has brothers at his side." I watched, fascinated, as Michael's face seemed lighted by his own words—I could swear he was describing himself—but how was this an answer to *my* question? *Wait and see*—it was as if a ghostly voice had whispered in my ear. *Wait and see.*

Michael continued. "The Queen of Hearts next," he said, smiling a little, then a troubled look passed over his

brow. "This Queen is both here and not here," he said, sounding puzzled. "She is of another time, but is making herself felt now, here. Her heart is sore to breaking, and her love calls out through Time to be heard."

Very poetic, I'm sure, I thought to myself, cynic that I am. What was this tending toward? *Wait and see....*

"And then we have the Jolly Joker," Michael said, picking up the card and looking at it closely. "In the Tarot, he is The Fool—the young searcher who wanders here and there, seeking Truth, seeking Wisdom, desiring to know all the ways of humankind so that he can help bring about a better world." He put the card down and looked intently at me. "The Fool is the wisest one, because he asks questions, and listens to the answers." He pointed to the Queen and the Knight. "The Fool must find these two—they hold the key."

I felt entranced in the moment, as if a magic web had spun itself around the two of us so we were a world apart. I wanted to speak, and ask him to tell me more of the meaning of the cards, but before I could gather my wits, we were interrupted by a sharp cry from Lily.

Little Kate Millet had appeared in the doorway of the drawing room, her feet bare under her long white nightdress, holding some sort of stuffed toy animal in her arms. Lily, facing the door, saw the look of trouble on her daughter's face, and jumped up to go to her.

"My darling, whatever is the matter? Did something awaken you?" she said, kneeling down to draw the child into her arms. The rest of us watched, concerned as the girl nodded. We couldn't hear what she said, but her mother obligingly repeated it.

"Someone in the garden?" Lily smoothed Kate's soft brown curls. "It's probably just Mr. Alfred, don't you know? He often is in the garden late, dear." But Kate shook her head, and raising her face to her mother's, spoke more clearly. "It was like a faery light, mama, it floated here and there, and then all along the ground, very fast, and I saw it come right up to the house, to the window, there." And she pointed to a far window of the drawing room.

I couldn't help but look at Kitty, who had seemed to be expecting some visitor, and I saw that her face had gone all rosy with blushing, and her hands were clutched nervously in her lap.

John stood up from the piano and came over to talk to Kate. "I'll just pop out into the garden and see what I can see, shall I, Kate? Will that put your mind at ease?" Kate nodded earnestly, and John patted her on the head.

"I shall accompany you, John," I said, rising quickly from my seat. "I should like a turn in the garden anyway," I added, somewhat lamely, "I'm sure it's quite warm still, al-though it is dark."

"Come along then, Vi," John said, although he shot a curious look my way. I looked down at Michael Kelly, who still seemed to be a world away, inside his own mind, and laid a gentle hand on his arm. "Thank you," I said. "I don't know all that your reading portends, but somehow, intuitively, it seems to make sense to me."

He looked up at me and smiled. "The Welsh, like the Irish, have the second sight," he said. "You'll find the answers, I'm sure of it." We shook hands very cordially, and I turned to leave the room with John.

"Take the kitchen lantern," Lucia called out as we left, and John guided us toward the kitchen, where we would exit to the back of the house and to the garden from there.

A frisson of excitement thrilled through me, although I'm sure I couldn't say exactly why. *Something* was going on, I could feel it, but I didn't know what it might be. *The Knight of Swords and the Queen of Hearts, all right,* I thought. *I'll find you out.* I almost laughed aloud. *And I am The Fool, no doubt of that!*

I breathed deeply of the cooling night air when we stepped out of the kitchen a few minutes later. I felt as if

I'd been holding my breath all evening; I hadn't realized the tension had been building so much until I was able to release it in a big sigh of relief, once outdoors.

"Are you all right, Vi?" John asked, pausing a moment before we stepped through the garden gate. He was holding the kitchen lantern above us, but its uneven and flickering light did little to dispel the shadows lurking among the bushes and trees. In the sudden silence, I heard the gurgle and swoosh of water from the brook at the far end of the garden, where it made its way through the orchards and fields.

"Yes, yes, I'm fine, John," I said, not wanting to concern my friend. "Probably a little too much company all at once," I added.

"You're hardly a recluse, old man," he said, smiling, then pushed open the gate.

"Shutter the lantern," I said softly, and as he did so, the garden fell into greater darkness; then gradually, as our eyes adjusted to the outdoors, everything grew more distinct. It was a clear night, and the moon was rising to a midpoint in the sky, its cool light draining the color from the flowers and plants.

"No sign of any faery light," John murmured.

"Any sign of Mr. Alfred Parsons?" I murmured back, and John stifled a laugh.

We walked cautiously along the flagstone path, keeping to one side of the garden, farthest from the house, and we stopped as we came upon a rough stone wall, with equally rough steps leading down into the ground.

"What is this?" I said, shivering a little. "It looks like the entrance to a warlock's cave."

"Ice house," John said. But as he raised the lantern to illuminate the steps, we heard a muffled groan coming from below. The light revealed the crumpled form of a man at the bottom of the steps.

"Good Lord!" John cried, and started down the steps. He thrust the lantern at me, and I held it high, staying a few steps above him.

"It's Alfred, he's hurt!" John said. "But conscious, thank God." He looked up at me, his face white. "Call the others, Vi! Tell Lucia to get the doctor!"

I carefully set the lantern on a step where it could afford some light for John, and raced back to the house. Gasping, I threw open the door to the drawing room, but seeing that little Kate was still there, sitting with her mother, I immediately composed myself and addressed the group with insouciant calm. "So sorry to burst in, but could we have Lucia for a few moments? Won't take long."

Puzzled, Lucia nonetheless put down her sewing and came to the door. I hustled her away toward the kitchen.

"John and I have found Mr. Parsons in the garden, perhaps he stumbled down the steps, the ice house, he appears to be hurt," I managed to say as we walked.

Lucia flew from me at this, running out the back door and into the garden, towards the lantern light on the ice house steps.

I stood silently for a moment, catching my breath. Faery light, indeed! Something very sinister was afoot here in the garden of Russell House, and I meant to find it out.

* * *

TEN

29 September 1726

*The Feast of St. Michael and
The Harvest Fair*

ALL BROADWAY AND THE SURROUNDING HAMLETS in the countryside turned out for the Michelmas Harvest Fair, held on the wide swath of green on the High Street. The Olde Swan was doing a brisk business, with folk from other villages having come to spend a few nights, and some on horseback wanting to stable their mounts there for the day. Tim and Sam were kept busy from early in the morning, with extra help from Georgie, but Bess made sure there would be time for them to get away and enjoy some of the Fair's activities from time to time.

She and Germaine kept the kitchen running, although there was more call on her father's ales in the tavern than the need for food—the booths at the Fair drew most of their visitors out to sample the wares offered—roast ducklings, fruit and savory pies to be eaten out of hand, and enough sweets in twisted paper packets to satisfy even the greediest child. But Bess and the cook had put together plenty of hearty stew and fresh bread and preserves to keep any tavern customers from starving in the meantime.

"The two of ye should be off soon, or ye'll miss all the fun."

Bess looked up from the stove, where she was stirring up some chicken stew, and saw her father standing in the doorway. She smiled and shook her head.

"Can't be leaving all the work here to thee, Da," she said. "I don't mind staying."

"Nonsense," her father said, coming over to the stove to give her a kiss on her flushed cheek. "Young people should be out for having a good time, and there's that dance to be starting soon, eh? Thou'll have plenty of partners, I warrant."

"Aye, that she will," Germaine piped up, wiping her hands on a cloth. "I'll be there along with her, just to have some older head to keep an eye out."

"Go along with ye both, then," the innkeeper said. "I've got old Tully in the bar to gi' me a hand when I need something, and I can fetch a bowl of stew and some bread, should anyone want anything." He turned to go back to the tavern. "Besides, near everyone is gone down to the Fair, and I'm thinking I might just lock up after a bit and have a look myself, yes?"

"Oh thou should, Da, thou should do that!" Bess cried. Instantly she had thought if Tremayne actually was going to show up at the Fair, that it might be an opportunity to introduce them to each other, in less formal circumstances than an awkward home visit. She ran over and took his hands in hers. "We could dance a jig or two, then, yes? Like we used to do when I was little!" Her shining black eyes were filled with glee, and her father had to gulp back the sorrow he felt at her request—he didn't know if he could face dancing with anyone but his wife, even his daughter. But he put on a brave face, and answered her

* * *

gruffly as he left the kitchen. "Maybe so, lass, maybe so, we'll see."

* * *

As the early autumn twilight set in, gentling the heat of the day, the village took on a golden, magical glow—deepened by the Cotswold stone so famous for its sunny color—and it gave every man, woman and child a sheen of glamour. The rougher sports and competitions were over for the day, the last wagonload of corn sheaves had been paraded about the village, and the husks had been distributed for the children and women to make corn dolls, which would find their place on fireplace mantels, blessing the house for the winter until they would be given back to the earth on Ploughing Monday, early in the Spring.

People were slowly making their way to the green, where a rough platform of boards had been set up for dancing. Local musicians were tuning their fiddles, and a couple of flutes could be heard trilling in the background.

First to come, however, was the Harvest Masque.

As Bess and Germaine approached the green, they could see a couple of jesters in motley motioning to the crowd to be seated on the grass, if they would, which the children all complied with readily; others preferred to stand behind them, and the two women from the Olde Swan slipped into the crowd and found places to sit on the warm grass, just behind the last row of children.

One of the jesters, whose mask and costume disguised whether it was a man or a woman, started to beat time slowly on a hand drum, walking with measured steps around the perimeter of the boards, and calling out "Hey!" every once in a while, which made the children start and cry out "Hey!" in reply.

Finally, the drum was beat three times, sonorously, calling for quiet, and the whole crowd settled down. Even the birds were quiet. The sun was an hour from setting, so there was plenty of light still to see the masquers as they assembled on the makeshift stage.

"I hear they are a group of hardened players from Canterbury," Germaine whispered to Bess. "We should be in for a good show."

The players stood in a line, and one man, dressed very elaborately in a large hat with long feathers, a bejeweled cape over a striped doublet and pants and knee-high boots, stepped forward as a trumpet announced the beginning of the play. The audience applauded and shouted greetings. He bowed to the sides and the front, then held up a hand for silence. He began to speak, pointing to the various actors behind him as he introduced them.

"Gentles, perchance you wonder at this show;
But wonder on, till truth make all things plain.
This man is Pyramus, if you would know;
This beauteous lady Thisby is certain.
This man, with lime and rough-cast, doth present
Wall, that vile Wall which did these lovers sunder;
And through Wall's chink, poor souls, they are content
To whisper. At the which let no man wonder.
This man, with lanthorn, dog, and bush of thorn,
Presenteth Moonshine; for, if you will know,
By moonshine did these lovers think no scorn
To meet at Ninus' tomb, there, there to woo."

The well-known and beloved tale of the ancient lovers Pyramus and Thisby was thus begun, and the audience watched with rapt attention.

Bess held her hand to her throat, feeling the pulse throbbing there as she felt deep in her heart that the tragic lovers' story was too close to her own—she and Colm, separated but longing to be close, uncertain where and when they could meet. She took a deep breath and shook herself, mentally. *Da is not an ogre, nor will he forbid me seeing Colm. We are not warring families with a grudge. We won't make a pact to meet in a graveyard and mistakenly think the other is dead.* She shivered to think of it. Suddenly she didn't want to stay for the end of the masque—even though the actors were comical, and played their parts broadly, with a simpering, eyelash-fluttering Thisby (played by a man for certain) and a blustering, rather old-looking Pyramus—nonetheless, it had an unhappy ending.

She whispered to Germaine that she needed to go for a bit, but would be back. In truth, although they had been in the village but a short time, she had not caught sight of Tremayne, and hoped perhaps to see him among the crowd gathering around the stage.

Bess made her way through the standing crowd, excusing herself in a low voice. After much pushing and a little shoving, she was finally at the outer edge of the audience, and felt able to breathe better. She made her way to one of the shops that had a stone bench outside the door, and sat down gratefully. It had been a long day, and she was looking forward to dancing—if Colm could but find her here.

• • •

But it wasn't Colm Tremayne who came upon her on the stone bench—it was Squire Robert—and without ceremony, he sat himself down beside her and began to talk.

"What think ye, good miss, of the Harvest Fair this year?" Squire Robert was in a good mood, enhanced by several tankards of ale no doubt, and Bess noticed that he seemed to be trying hard to be polite and gentlemanly toward her. Perhaps it was the effect of being out in public, where he had a reputation to maintain, she thought. Upon observing him more keenly, however, she could see that he was clear-headed, and had not been drinking, or not much.

"I do believe, sir, that there are a great many more folk here than last year," Bess said calmly. "Which is good for the village, of course."

The Squire glanced back toward the stage, where some comic nonsense had caused the audience to roar with laughter. "Are ye not interested in the masque?" he asked, looking at her intently. His dark good looks were enhanced by better manners, she thought.

"I do enjoy a good play, sir," she said. "This one, I think, is too sad for me today."

"Ah, yes," he agreed. "Pyramus and Thisby, doomed lovers." He looked pained for a moment, and Bess wondered if he was actually missing his dead wife—for what did she know, other than the gossip of the village, whether the couple were happy in their marriage or not? The thought softened her heart a little towards him, so she was unprepared with a better answer when he leant forward and spoke.

• • •

"May I have the honor of your hand for a dance this evening, then, mistress Bess of the Olde Swan?" His eyes were gentle as he said this, and his politeness, she felt, deserved a fair answer.

"Oh, well, I—" Bess stumbled for a response, then said firmly, "Yes, I thank ye, sir, I will dance with ye tonight."

His eyes gleamed with a happy look, and as if to ward off a change of mind on Bess's part, he rose, bowed to her, and made his way back through the crowd to watch the end of the masque.

Oh dear, thought Bess. *Why did I do that? But it's only one dance, and after all, even if Tremayne is here, I cannot dance every dance with him anyway.*

At that she, too, rose from the stone bench and walked off into the village to see if she could find the man she loved.

ELEVEN

FRIDAY 3 SEPTEMBER 1886

The Night Ends at Russell House

SEATED IN THE KITCHEN, MR. PARSONS submitted to being examined by Lucia, who shortly declared that the cut on his forehead was not deep and would not require stitching. This led the victim to insist, therefore, that no doctor be called.

John, after seeing his fellow artist settled in the kitchen with Lucia, had gone to the drawing room to assure little Kate that it was only Mr. Parsons after all, out in the garden, and that she could go back to sleep in full security. But he returned to the kitchen with Lily only steps behind him.

"Oh! Alfred, what has happened?" she cried out when she saw her sister-in-law carefully bandaging his head.

"Now, Lily, don't make a fuss," he said to her, reaching out to take her hand. "Just tripped down those ice house steps in the dark, didn't I?" He patted her hand and winced a trifle as Lucia pressed the bandage into place firmly.

"Were you not carrying a light to see by?" Lily pressed him.

"Nay," he shook his head. "The moon gave enough light for what I wanted to see, I had no lantern."

* * *

I found this exceedingly curious, given Kate's story of the 'faery light.'

"Did you see any other lights around the garden?" I asked. He looked at me, puzzled by my question. I hastened to explain. "You see, Mr. Parsons, the reason John and I were in the garden—and luckily happened to find you—was that Kate was awakened by flickering lights dancing about in the garden."

Everyone seemed to hold their breath for a moment. I added, "And if it wasn't you, and you saw nothing, then what—or who—could it have been?"

John stepped forward, looking concerned, and addressed his friend. "Are you sure you tripped, Alfred?" he said. "Was it possible you were...pushed?"

Alfred tightened his lips at this question, and his eyes narrowed. I thought at first he would curtly deny it, but it appeared as if he were thinking about the possibility.

"I may have been," he said at last, causing both Lily and Lucia to gasp slightly. He raised a hand to feel the back of one shoulder. "Now that you say it, I seem to recall a shove, just as I got near the top of those steps." He looked sheepish. "I thought I'd just trod on a loose rock or something."

"But who would do such a thing?" Lucia exclaimed.

"Someone who was afraid of being seen," I said quietly. Everyone turned to look at me then.

"We were all in the drawing room," Lily started to say, sounding defensive, then stopped suddenly.

I nodded. "Not quite all—didn't Mr. David Cowan leave the room a while ago?"

"But why on earth would he shove Alfred down the steps?" Lucia cried.

I shook my head. "I'm not saying it was him."

"Or creep about the garden with a flickering light?" Lucia continued. "They have no need of secrecy here, they come and go as the rest of us do."

I shrugged and shook my head. "I'm sure I don't know about all that as well as the rest of you must do."

"You don't," Lily said sternly. "It must have been a dream illusion, my daughter has them often." But she looked troubled. "She said she saw the ghost the other night."

"Ghost!" Both John and I repeated the word in unison. "There's a ghost at Russell House?" I added.

Just then Ned Abbey appeared at the kitchen door, and having heard the last exchange, chuckled heartily.

"Yes, yes, we have a ghost, like all good old English houses," he said, but then cut off short at the sight of Alfred and his bandaged head. Upon hearing the story told over, Ned responded with great indignation.

"We must search the garden," he declared.

"Now?" Lucia interposed. "In the dark? What could you hope to do, other than fall down the steps yourself?"

"Nonetheless," Ned insisted. He turned to John. "Will you join me?"

"Of course, Ned," John said reassuringly. "I'm ready to look wherever you want."

"And I too," I spoke up. I had an idea about this garden adventure.

"And I," Lily said, her lips a tight line.

Alfred Parsons made to rise from his chair but was held there by Lucia's firm hand. "No, Alfred, no more garden wanderings for you tonight, you should get yourself to bed. You're leaving in the morning, remember?"

This was news to me, but I forebore to ask questions at the moment; I would be able to query John at leisure, when he walked me back to the hotel—which I hoped would be soon.

Arming ourselves with lanterns, four of us went back into the garden—John, myself, Ned and Lily. We must have made a strange sight indeed, four spots of light meandering through the bushes and trees. Not being familiar with the layout, I decided to stick closer to the building and let the others fan out across the lawn. Besides, I wanted to particularly check the area by the drawing room windows, where Kitty had kept glancing out.

As I neared the window, I saw what everyone familiar with light and darkness knows well—I could see every detail of persons and furniture inside the drawing room, and knew that they could see nothing outside beyond the reflecting glass of the windows; all would be blackness to someone inside the room. Surely Kitty must know this, so why had she been attempting to look out the window?

I raised the lantern to illuminate a tall, sturdy azalea bush that grew against the wall, and as I did so, Kitty appeared at the window above me, as if called by my thoughts of her. She brought her face close to the window, shading her eyes with her hands, so that she would be able to see to the outside. The lantern lighted up my face, and I saw her give a start as she noticed me, and her eyes widened as she glanced toward a little wooden bird house that hung from a strong branch of the azalea. She looked away quickly, and walked back into the room, but it was enough for me.

I poked a finger into the bird house and felt a curled up piece of paper. I carefully withdrew it, uncurled it, and eager to see it, held the lantern over it. The message was brief.

féar—meán oíche.

I knew enough of languages to comprehend that the words were Celtic—Irish, in fact. A smattering of Welsh remained in my childhood subconscious, and the last two words came to me soon—*midnight*. So, an assignation! Kitty had a secret lover, I presumed. But was it one of the gentlemen of Russell House? One of the Irish models? Or someone else entirely? And what did *féar* mean?

I contemplated whether to take the note with me, and perhaps present it to Kitty in the drawing room, but a moment's consideration suggested that the better course of action might be to just return the note to its hiding place, and leave it for Kitty to find.

And perhaps, at midnight, for me to follow her to the meeting place and discover who it was who had probably shoved poor Mr. Parsons down those stairs, whilst he was leaving the note.

I heard John calling my name from no far distance, so I hastily rolled the paper up and slipped it back into the birdhouse, and turned to take a few steps to meet him.

"Anything?" he asked, coming up to me and glancing up at the lighted window.

I shook my head, not wanting to speak of the hidden note where someone might overhear; I would tell John later. "You?" I queried.

"Nothing," he said. He peered into my face. "You look rather tired, Vi, I haven't been very thoughtful, have I? You must be longing to get to your rest!" He tucked my arm under his and began to walk back toward the house. "Shall I walk you to the hotel now?" He smiled. "I imagine you've just about had your fill of Russell House shenanigans for one night!"

I laughed and nodded my head, and allowed him to lead me back into the house where I could make my *adieux* and collect my reticule. Lily and Ned had already gone back inside, their searches having been as fruitless as John's, and when we entered the drawing room, Alfred Parsons was just taking his leave of the ladies. Michael Kelly was nowhere to been seen, nor had David Cowan returned. Kitty seemed to avoid looking at me, although I caught her glancing at me all the while I was there. I approached her to say good-night in order to get her to look me in the face, but she managed a pleasant farewell with no sign of any nervousness or disorder.

Well, we would see what the night would bring.

TWELVE

29 SEPTEMBER 1726

The Harvest Dance

THE PLAYERS TOOK THEIR WELL-DESERVED BOWS to the cheers and applause of their audience, and then followed a piper who led them off the stage and around to their dressing tent farther along the green. A couple of men from the village proceeded to light lanterns, which were hung from poles planted around the stage, transforming it into a platform suited to dancing. The flutists had returned, along with the fiddle players and a guitarist; they set up in a corner of the dance floor and began to practice a lively tune.

Bess joined the throng of young people who gathered cheerfully on the dance floor, forming a ring of girls in the middle and boys around the outside. The drummer hit his drum three times, and the two circles began to revolve, the girls to their left and the boys to their right. The drum beat faster and faster and the circles kept to the pace; then the pounding beat suddenly ceased, and partners for the first dance were aligned wherever they were when the drumming stopped. There was much laughing and gaiety among the young people, and Bess was satisfied when she saw that her first partner was a nice-looking young man named Bill whom she'd known since they were children together. She knew he was already affianced to another childhood friend, so this first dance would be just fun and nothing else.

Although the dancing required paying some attention, Bess couldn't help but glance about past the dance floor to see if Colm Tremayne had yet made an appearance. Her search through the village, after she parted from Squire Robert, had turned up no sign of him, and vendors of whom she casually inquired said they had not seen him set up his booth that day. Disappointed, she had wandered back to the green, and upon rejoining Germaine in the crowd, had been persuaded by her to join the young folks for the opening of the dance.

After the first dance, the floor was open to all and sundry, and lines were formed to dance quadrilles or squares, according to the music being played. Bess found herself besieged by the young men of the village, and was at no loss for a partner for several dances. Finally she begged off for lack of breath, and went to find Germaine who was standing with her father off to one side. The evening had set in and the lanterns around the dance floor only accentuated the shadows.

"Here, my dear child, have a sip of this ale," the innkeeper said, holding up a tankard for his daughter, who drank gratefully. "Th'art having a fine time of it, eh?"

"I'm that out of breath, Da," Bess said. "I'm thinking I may be getting too old for such exercise!"

"Pah! Nonsense!" cried Germaine. "Ne'er too old to dance, I say—it makes thee young again!"

"Then the two of ye should give it a try," Bess said impulsively. She took the tankard from her father's hand,

THE LIGHT IN THE GARDEN

and placing Germaine's hand in his, gave them a little push toward the dance floor. Richard was about to beg off but he saw the hopeful look in Germaine's eyes, and agreed gruffly to "try a step or two." Bess watched happily as the couple gained the dance floor and joined the line of dancers, her father stepping as lightly as any youth could do, and Germaine smiling and laughing through the turns and twists.

A gentle tap on her shoulder brought her round to gaze on the face she had longed to see: Tremayne had come at last.

"My lady Bess," he whispered to her, drawing close. "Wilt thou not dance wi'me, love?" She was about to answer joyfully when a larger figure loomed above them—Squire Robert.

"I believe this dance is mine," he said, swaggering a bit. Bess could see that he had been drinking since she saw him last, and the demon ale had altered him for the worse.

Tremayne stood his ground coolly. "I think ye're mistaken, sir," he said politely. "I've just asked the lady meself."

"Irish swine," the Squire sneered, and roughly seized Bess's arm. "She's better off with me than a poor farmer."

"I believe that's for me to decide, Squire," Bess spoke up in a firm voice, and shook his hand off her arm. "Ye'd best come back when your head is not so full of ale." She turned to Tremayne and linked her arm in his.

But Squire Robert wouldn't give way. He drew back an arm, ready to punch his rival, but Tremayne swiftly side-stepped the blow, pulling Bess with him. The Squire stumbled forward, losing his footing. He barreled into another very large man, jostling his arm and causing his ale to spill, which enraged the man, who then turned to land a blow on the Squire's head. This resulted in a number of men and boys tumbling and swinging arms and legs, many gleefully joining in the fray for the fun of it.

Tremayne hustled Bess away from the free-for-all and they made their way to the dance floor, where they joined the other couples in a round dance. Half-way through, Bess found herself and Tremayne linking hands with her father and Germaine, who winked at her. Richard threw a narrow glance at Tremayne and at Bess, but there was no time for talk as the dance swept them onward.

The musicians took a little time out for refreshments after that dance, and the dancers drifted down toward the ale and food stands. Night was all around them, in the shadows past the green, and light clouds covered the half moon, which showed herself with a gleam now and then. Couples sneaked off under the trees and behind nearby buildings for a little private time, and Bess boldly decided to take the opportunity to introduce Tremayne to her father.

"Da," she said, drawing near, her lover's arm in hers, "I want thee to meet this man I was dancing with." The lovelight that shone in her eyes was not missed by either her father or Germaine, who stood next to him. Richard pulled himself up to his full height, but was still a head shorter than the tall young man his daughter presented.

"An' who might this be, daughter?" he said.

"My name is Colm Tremayne, sir," the young man said, and glancing at Bess, he continued. "I've a small farm over to Moreton-in-Marsh, good freehold land. And

I'd like your permission to court your daughter, sir." Bess opened her eyes wide when she heard this—she could scarcely breathe for happiness.

Richard stared at him for a long moment. "Irish, are ye?" He half-smiled. "No need to be *sirr* in me," he said. "I'm just an innkeeper and no more."

He looked at Bess, and his heart gave in. "Is it thy wish to be courted by this man, daughter?" he asked, feeling sad and happy at the same time.

"Oh, Da, it is, it is truly," she said.

He nodded briskly. "Then go along wi'ye," he said. "The music is starting up again, and young folk have but few opportunities to dance in this life."

Bess kissed his cheek quickly, and fled away with Tremayne back to the dance. Germaine stood quietly at Richard's side, and put a tentative hand on his arm. "Sure," she said, "and we older folk might have one more go at it, dost thou not think?"

He looked at the merry brown eyes that gazed up at him, and felt a warmth begin to grow around his heart. He laughed aloud, and taking her arm, led her back to the dance.

But both couples, intent on their own happiness, missed the dark eyes that followed them with ill will—a disheveled and even more drunken Squire Robert, disengaged from the brawl he'd inadvertently started. Clinging to his arm, with her white scrap of a handkerchief patting ineffectively at a cut on the Squire's lip, was Mary Cummings, whose narrowed eyes revealed the animosity she, too, felt toward the oblivious couple who had slighted both of them.

THIRTEEN

FRIDAY 3 SEPTEMBER 1886

Around Midnight

"I SHALL KEEP WATCH, THEN, VI, NOT YOU!" John was vehement in his insistence that I not attempt to follow Kitty to her assignation point. I had mistakenly supposed he would be as keen as I was to discover her secret, which, although he *was* interested, it was not enough to override his concern for my safety.

"You are not familiar with the village, first of all," he said, beginning to enumerate his objections. We were halfway to the Lygon Arms, it was nearing eleven o'clock, and the village, in darkness, was as silent as a cemetery. The light from the lantern John held flashed and wavered as he punctuated his remarks with flourishes of his arms. "Second, it's black as pitch, the moon's almost down, and you have no lantern," he continued. "And third, how do you think you'll get in and out of the Lygon Arms at such a time of night?" I acknowledged this with a reluctant shrug, and he harrumphed his satisfaction. "Even you, Vi, unconventional as you are, would consider that to be scandalous as well as reckless behavior."

He stopped me some twenty paces short of the Lygon Arms, whose main door, though closed, was illuminated by two robust lights on either side, and I could see cheerful fires inside the front rooms, where a few wakeful patrons seemed to be comfortably sipping at cordials and wine.

"Will you promise me not to attempt it, Vi?" John said, watching my face closely. I sighed.

"Yes, I promise," I said.

He smiled at last, and put a friendly hand on my shoulder. "And to reward your obedience," he chuckled, "I'll promise to stay awake myself, and watch the house, and if anyone creeps about, I'll see what I can do to keep an eye out for any midnight meetings."

He wasn't actually promising to *follow* Kitty, but I suppose it was the most that I could expect.

The door to the Lygon Arms opened, and the genial doorman stepped out to greet us and welcome me in.

"Miss Vernon Lee," he said, bowing slightly. "We thought perhaps you had found shelter elsewhere for the night."

"Not at all, Mr. Hesford," I said, smiling. "The evening activities at Russell House are so entertaining, I could scarcely tear myself away!"

I turned to John and reached up to give him a kiss on the cheek, and bade him good night. He pressed my hand and strode off back down the High Street to Russell House again. A sudden anxiety struck me, and I turned to Mr. Hesford, still standing there holding the door open.

"There aren't any robbers or highwaymen around these days, are there, Mr. Hesford?" I immediately felt silly asking such a question.

He was serious in his answer. "One can never be too careful, late in the night, Miss Lee," he said. "But no, there hasn't been a highwayman for almost two hundred years now in this county—not since the Highwayman of the Hill Road, as they called him, and I'd like to see the robber that would dare try his trade in our village." His voice took on a stern, judicial tone, which I found very reassuring.

As he stepped to one side to allow me to enter, I thought of another question I might ask him.

"Mr. Hesford," I said, "are there many Irish people living in Broadway, or visiting in the area?"

He hesitated, then answered briefly. "There's a small party of Irish over to the Horse and Hounds, now, last two days—with the famous athlete Thomas St. George McCarthy, d'ye know of him?" When I shook my head, he only added, "Well, he's that good of a rugby player, and has gone and founded a society of some sort, an athletic association, to bring the Irish up to speed wi' the rest of us."

"Ah," I said, "I know nothing of sports, Irish or otherwise. Is there to be some kind of exhibition or something?"

Mr. Hesford smiled slightly at my ignorance.

"I believe they're just passing through on the way to London, but I have heard tell that Mr. McCarthy *might* be persuaded to play a few rounds, for charity, don't you know," he said. He thought for a moment. "Other than them, there *have* been more visitors from Ireland than usual, last few months," he added. "That trouble in Belfast, you know, set a lot of the young men fleeing the city." He paused. "Seems they take ship for Cardiff, and make their way across here, off to London. They don't cause any trouble, and they don't stay long."

"What is the general feeling here, in Broadway, about the Irish Home Rule question?" I asked, remembering the brief exchange between Lily and the Irish models at dinner. I was keen on the issue myself, and had been sorely disappointed when the Commons trounced Gladstone's valorous attempt to procure justice and independence for the Irish, just two months ago. I waited for the doorman's answer while he turned and secured the great inn door.

"As much for it as against it, Miss Lee," he said evenly. "It's not as if we're much affected here, in this small village, by the greater goings-on of the nation." At this, he bowed and went to stand at his post further inside the inn.

I approached the desk, where I was handed my key, and made my way thoughtfully up the stair to my ancient room, where I felt sure my dreams would be filled with queens and knights and jesters all chasing each other in a maze.

The Next Morning – 4 September 1886

Perhaps due to all the day's variety of excitements, I am ashamed to admit I slept well and soundly, and woke to a bright, cheerful sun casting warm rays into my chamber. My first thought was, of course, to wonder if anything had happened at midnight that John may have witnessed. I felt astonished that the very thought had not kept me awake all night, and so I rushed out of bed, made a hasty toilette, and descended the stairway with less than my usual dignity in order to get to Russell House as soon as I could.

* * *

It was a lovely warm day, and sculpted white clouds hung in the deep blue sky like bunting at a celebration. Walking quickly through the dry, dusty street, with villagers having been out and about some two or three hours already, I arrived at Russell House in less than ten minutes, and was there met by a house completely in uproar.

I had walked through the open gate at the side of the house, where I had entered the day before, and saw before me several people standing about, talking and lamenting, seemingly all grouped in front of something they were intently observing on the ground before them. There was Lily Millet and Lucia and Kate; John, of course, and Ned Abbey, along with a woman I took to be the housemaid. No sign of Kitty or Alfred Parsons—perhaps he had already departed on his travels. David Cowan, the older male model, was there also, but not Michael Kelly.

I approached, all but unseen, and stopped at the edge of the group to see what they were scrutinizing. John was looking down at a very large, rectangular canvas, on which I could discern the figures of two girls, and a great many flowers and lanterns strung about a garden scene—this must be the much talked about painting that John had been working on for so long.

Lucia Millet, next to whom I came to stand, suddenly noticed me and instantly drew my arm under hers, and spoke in a low voice. "My dear Violet, it's so good that you are here, John is quite distraught!"

"Whatever has happened?" I said.

"John went up to the hayloft to retrieve his painting, for you know, the Barnards are due to arrive today, and then he can begin painting again," she said.

I must have looked puzzled, because she explained further. "The Barnard girls, Polly and Dolly, they are the models for this painting, you see."

"Ah, of course," I said, remembering what little Kate Millet had told me, about those two girls making fun of her American accent. "Go on, please."

"Well, John brought the painting down, and set it here on the bricks to take a look at it, and lo and behold! Someone has ripped three great holes in it! See there," and she moved with me a little to the side, and pointed to a part of the canvas, on the lower right. There were indeed at least three holes torn quite through, with the ragged edges of the canvas sticking out.

"Oh, what a shame," I cried, and looked up to see John grimacing and shaking his head. He heard my voice, and smiled grimly.

"Well," he said, as if after some consideration, "there's nothing for it but to cut that part off, and see what *that* will look like."

Ned Abbey spoke up in an encouraging voice. "You can make it a square painting, John, you see," he said. "And that's not so bad, you know, it's a different look—like your *Daughters*, if I remember correctly, eh? Those four girls in the large room? That made quite a splash."

"It certainly looks like it was done deliberately," Lily Millet said, bending down to take a closer look. "But who on earth would do such a thing? And why?"

I had stepped closer to the painting to examine it better.

"This was the painting that was stored in the hayloft, yes?" I said. John nodded. "Those holes look to me to be made by a pitchfork."

Everyone leaned in to look again.

"By Jove, I believe you're right!" cried Ned. "I suppose that means it was just an unfortunate accident, don't you think? I mean, there's still hay up there, and maybe..." His voice trailed off, speculating.

David Cowan came up to stand beside me, taking in the destruction. I had a sudden thought, and leaned up to whisper to him. I was taking a chance, but I felt it was worth the risk.

"What is the Irish word for *hay*, Mr. Cowan?" I asked.

He raised his eyebrows at my curious question, but answered promptly enough. "*Féar*," he said. He didn't seem perturbed by the question, or curious, either, as to why I had asked.

Hay. Midnight.

Now I really needed to speak to John to learn if he had seen anything in the night that would help unravel this new mystery.

FOURTEEN

29 SEPTEMBER 1726

After The Harvest Dance

TREMAYNE LEFT THE DANCE EARLY ON—he had animals at the farm to tend to, he said—but he and Bess had stolen a few moment's quiet talk as he walked his horse down the road from the village. The night's cooling air fell in waves around them, and Bess shivered after having become heated with dancing. Tremayne pulled a black cloak from his saddlebag and wrapped it around her, pulling her close to him. Bess breathed in the scent of him— woodsmoke and cinnamon, a whiff of a hard-ridden horse, and the warmth of leather boots and vest—and she nestled into his embrace.

"Colm Tremayne," she whispered, pulling away slightly. "Canst thou come to visit me, up to the inn?" She gasped as he kissed her, taking her breath, but spoke again when she could. "Now that thou'ast met my Da, it would be good for the two of ye to know more of each other."

"Soon, my love," he said, soothing her, stroking her face with his hand. "There's much I must do to be worthy of thee, and build a life for us. Thy father seems a good man, and I want him to be proud of me." His horse nickered softly, and he patted the animal on its long face, tracing the white star on its forehead with his fingers. He turned back to Bess. "Thou'rt the only woman for me, dear Bess," he said. "I feel I have found family at last, and with thee, we can have our own home, our own bairns." He kissed her cheek, and seemed to choke back tears. "But nae just yet, love, soon, soon."

Bess sighed. She knew in her heart he was a good man, but there was something about him—was he really just a farmer?—but she feared to ask, if she was honest with herself. It was a wayward feeling she had, perhaps what her mother would have termed her "Irish eye", but his long absences, his pride, even his fearlessness in standing up to the Squire—something didn't fit with the image of a simple farmer who tilled the land.

The clatter of a wagon and voices coming round the bend alerted them to an intrusion, and before Bess could do more than touch his cheek, Tremayne had swiftly mounted his black horse and disappeared into the shadows, and she was alone. She shook herself, and began walking again, steadying herself to greet the farmer and his son with their wagon who soon came into sight, with a smile and a wave that belied her fast-beating heart.

Bess found her way back to her father and Germaine, whom she had seen dancing at least one more time. Tim the ostler and Sam she had seen once or twice, at games of dice or just talking with friends, but she didn't see them now. Upon hearing the village crier call nine of the clock, Richard was dismayed at the hour.

"Our customers and lodgers will be wanting us at the inn," he said, greatly disconcerted. The two women immediately declared they would go with him—they'd had enough of dancing and the fair.

"No one worth dancin' with here now, is there?" Germaine said slyly as she and Bess hastened down the High Road back to the Olde Swan. But all was well at the Inn, with Tim and Sam back at their duties, and Richard's old friend Tully holding down the tavern, which was now beginning to fill up. Bess and Germaine repaired to the kitchen, and the rest of the evening was spent in work and merriment.

* * *

It was some time after midnight when an uproar in the courtyard wakened all within—a mad rush of hooves, then a pounding on the door, with a harsh voice calling for the innkeeper. Bess flung aside her blankets, drew her robe around her and opened the shutters at the window to see lighted lanterns swinging from a coach, and four restive horses filling the courtyard in front of the stables. She heard her father shouting that he would open the door in a moment, and she rushed down the stairs.

"Glory be to God and His saints," her father cried as he opened the door to the travellers. The coachman, known to them for many years, had sprung down from his seat, and was holding up an older man as he nearly fell out of the carriage, well-dressed by the cut of his coat and hat, who was struggling to walk. A white strip of linen was wrapped around his upper left arm, and was alarmingly turning red. Following him was a woman and a young lad, presumably his family—the woman was white as a sheet, and her son was supporting her forward with some difficulty. They were dressed well, quality folk, as Bess could see from the fine embroidery on the lady's coat, and the well-made shoes they all wore.

Bess took charge of the lady and her son and escorted them into the tavern to sit, while her father and the coachman settled the gentleman into a comfortable chair just inside the door. Germaine, unkempt but alert, had already stoked the fire and was putting a kettle on to boil for tea. Bess nodded to her and could see she understood what was wanted.

"I'm Bess," she said to the lady. "Sit ye down, ma'am, and all will be well."

"A wee dram might go a good way to restorin' our spirits, Richard," the coachman muttered to the innkeeper, who looked up at him sharply.

"What happened, then, Tom?" the innkeeper said.

"We've been robbed, 'aven't we, by that blasted 'ighwayman o' the 'ill road."

The innkeeper quickly produced some whisky and a round of small glasses, pouring for all, including the wife and son, who sat shaking by the window.

"There, there, missus," he said as he handed her the glass.

"Thank you," the lady said softly, and taking a deep breath, seemed to pull herself together. "I am Mrs. Wells," she said. "And this is our son, Jonathan." The boy nodded politely, looking anxiously at his mother as he did so. "I fear my husband may be badly wounded, is there a doctor near?"

"There's none in the village, ma'am," Bess said, turning away to tend to the gentleman. "But I am used to caring for such things."

"Ye'll be all right, then," the innkeeper said to Mrs. Wells, "and yer man as well, it's no more than a bother, his arm, my Bess'll see it right." He turned as he heard his daughter call to him.

"More light, Da?"

Bess carefully unwound the linen cloth from the man's arm, and folded back the ragged edges of his coat and the shirt beneath to reveal an ugly cut, some three inches long, but not over-deep. Her father held a lantern to shine more light for her to see by; Germaine appeared at her side with a bowl of warm water, clean linen strips, and a fine needle and thread.

"It needs stitching," Bess said, and glanced at the man, who was older than he had first looked; his scant beard was grey, and his face lined. He lay back with his eyes closed, as if all his strength were spent. She nodded to her father to get the man to drink some spirits, which he did while she tore away his shirt and coat further from the wound. She glanced up at Germaine, and nodded toward the man's arm. The cook put her hands on either side of the wound and held the arm down firmly.

"This'll burn a bit," Bess said, and dribbled a bit of whisky onto the wound. The man started but Germaine held his arm still. Bess swiftly threaded the needle, wiped away the now slowly seeping blood, and stitched up the wound, so quickly the man had time for only one gasp of pain, then blessedly fainted while she finished the stitching.

"Edward!" His wife rose from her chair and stumbled forward, but the innkeeper forestalled her from intervening. "There now, missus, he's fine, just a stitch or

two, he'll come round in a minute, ye'll see." The woman
looked about to faint herself, so the innkeeper led her back
to her chair, and gave her another tot of whisky with some
water. The son looked excited and overwrought, and
started talking rapidly as he began to be assured that his
father was going to be all right.

"You should have seen him, sir!" he cried. "He was a
giant of a man, tall, with a great scar across his cheek, and
a black cloak whirling all around him!"

"Ye're daft, ye are," interrupted Tom the coachmen,
holding out his glass for another whisky. "'e din't 'ave no
scar, and I saw 'is face plain in the lamp."

The boy was not deterred from his flights of fancy.
"His horse was fourteen hands high at least, and all black,
too, like his cloak, with a white star on its forehead." He
leaped up from his chair and started slashing the air with
an imaginary sword. "There! And there!" he cried. "And
my father, he was so brave! He told the highwayman that
he was 'outside the law' and he had no right to harry
honest people on their journey."

"And what did the Highwayman say to that?" the
innkeeper asked. He looked up at the coachman, who
shook his head.

"He laughed," the boy said. "He said he had always
been outside the law, and the law was a fraud, and then he
whipped his sword at my father's arm, and..." At this, the
boy shivered, and suddenly was just a child looking for his
mother, who drew him into her arms to soothe him.

"Did he take anything from you, then?" Bess asked,
looking at Mrs. Wells. She had finished her task, and
bound the wound with clean linen—her 'patient' was

resting quietly—and she had walked over to join the group at the window.

The woman nodded. "My reticule," she said, and laughed without humor. "There was but a few pence in it, so I hope the little things he took will serve him well—some smelling salts, and an old brooch that was my mother's, and a small book of Proverbs." She shook her head, then seemed thoughtful. "I thought he would have searched my husband's person for some money then, but something stopped him." She looked fondly at her son, who was starting to fall asleep, lying with his head in her lap. "I believe he saw my Jonny here, saw that he was trembling, and decided to leave us alone at that point." She looked severe. "After he wounded my husband, the blackguard!"

"And he escaped without injury to himself?" Bess said. She held her hand to her throat as she asked the question, almost holding her breath. Her father gave her a strange look.

The coachman snorted. "If I'm not afooled," he said with quiet pride, "I myself gave 'im a blow to 'is leg as 'e leaped upon 'is 'orse—I 'eard 'im grunt as 'e mounted." He patted a heavy club that was slung through a loop on his belt. "Ol' Trow 'ere allus comes in 'andy in a fight."

"Well," the innkeeper said, putting the cork back in the bottle of whisky, "what you folks need is a good night's sleep, and lucky ye are that the inn has a room above just ready for the three of you." He looked at the coachman. "And you, Tom, will ye be going on, or will you rest the night above the stables—nice and clean it is, and the horses below to keep an eye on them."

The coachman shook his head, reg~
push on this very night to Oxford," he sai
bite o' something good wi' me, if you ca..
looked hopefully at Germaine, who smiled at him ..
invited him back to the kitchen.

Bess saw that both Tim Ostler and their boy of all works, Sam, were standing in the doorway, and she gave them orders to bring in the travellers' luggage, and told them that the coach would be on its way soon, so Tim should see to the horses. As they went back out to the courtyard, she stood in the doorway herself, looking up at the half crescent of moon high in the sky, and trying to push away the serpent-streak of fear that pierced her heart.

She had wondered before, but now she couldn't hide the question from herself—the black horse with the white star on its forehead seemed to give ominous evidence— was Tremayne the Highwayman of the Hill Road?

FIFTEEN

SATURDAY 4 SEPTEMBER 1886

Russell House

"I LIKE THE WAY IT LOOKS," NED ABBEY SAID firmly, squinting his eyes at the now square canvas that lay on the paving stones in the courtyard at Russell House. "I like it square, I really do," he continued. "It gives the two figures more prominence, makes it more than just a garden painting."

"I do like the asymmetry of it," John admitted. "It's

rather more full on the upper right, with that nice dark empty space in the lower left corner to balance it out." After a few more nods and comments from the group, John proclaimed himself satisfied, and proceeded to carefully roll up the canvas and store it somewhere other than the hayloft.

I walked after John to see if I could engage him in conversation about last evening, and we were at a distance from the others, heading toward the Tower house, when a little stir at the gate caught everyone's attention, and we all turned at Lucia's cry of greeting.

"Why, it's Mr. Henry James! Lord, I had forgotten, in all the excitement, that you were to arrive this morning!" She hastened to the gate, along with Ned Abbey, who took the writer's small valise from his grip, and ushered him in.

"Did you walk all the way alone from the Horse and Hound?" Ned asked in dismay. "How stupid we have been to forget you, my dear Mr. James! It's just that we've had an unusually chaotic morning here," he continued, but Lucia interrupted him.

"Yes, infernally thoughtless of us, and for you to have to walk all that way," she said, although I somehow had the sense that she didn't think such a walk would hurt Mr. James one bit. "Please do come into the house, my dear Mr. James, and have some tea, and rest yourself. We'll tell you all about everything when we're inside." And she positively hustled the man inside, leaving the rest of us, dispersed as we were, to go about our ways for the time being.

As for myself, I was glad of a bit of reprieve in meeting with Mr. Henry James so unexpectedly. He had never really responded to my inquiries about whether he liked or had even read my novel *Miss Brown*, but I had heard, through some cruel gossips, that he did not think highly of it, to say the least. I think he disapproved of how my book had made such a stir in town, with people thinking all the wrong sorts of things about my characters, and trying to put names to them of real people, in order to discover secret vices and propensities of the famous people they presumably depicted. I knew him to be a very private person, and a very reserved type of man, who intensely disliked the wrong kind of public attention—that is, aimed at the "personality" of a writer or artist, rather than the importance of the person's writing or painting—although I also knew that he relished gossip while pretending to hold it in disdain.

I think I was afraid to see him face to face, and that troubled me on several counts, not the least of which was showing me how cowardly I was.

"Vi? Are you there, old man?"

I came out of my sorry reverie at the sound of John's voice. "Oh!" I said. "Sorry, just, um, thinking." I roused myself and smiled. "Will Mr. James be staying at Russell House?"

John half-smiled. "Yes, probably much to his dismay. Lucia insisted on it, she's quite taken with him, you know, but I fancy he'd rather be somewhere where it is a bit quieter. He needs a good deal of quiet, does Mr. James."

My eyes brightened at this. "Do you think it could be proposed to him," I said, "that he and I exchange places? Wouldn't he prefer the Lygon Arms to Russell House?"

"Well, yes I think so," John said. "But do you really want to be in the middle of all this? It gets quite active, especially when the Barnards show up."

I grimaced slightly, but nodded. "I think it will be better for our, well, investigation I must call it, if I am on the spot here." I smiled at him. "I'm hoping I might catch a glimpse of the famous Russell House ghost as well!"

John laughed. "Good luck there," he said, then thought a moment. "I shall approach Lucia about this change of places, I hope she'll consider it."

I thanked him heartily, then switched to the subject most on my mind as we continued toward the Tower house, where John thought to stow his canvas now. I told him that I had further deciphered the meaning of the note I had seen the night before: *hay—midnight*, and proceeded to ask, "Did you see our young lady last night, John? Or anyone else for that matter?" I said, keeping my voice low.

To my disappointment, he shook his head. "I was awake til long past midnight, and all was quiet," he said. "But I fell asleep at some point, I'm afraid, so may have missed something." He opened the door to the Tower and we stepped inside.

I nodded slowly. "It had occurred to me that all the fuss of finding Mr. Parsons in the garden may have put the ardent lovers off for the night, and there was no meeting."

"But the pitchfork holes in the painting!" John protested. "Doesn't that seem to point to someone having been in the hayloft?"

"Yes, of course," I said, "but not necessarily last night. When was the last time you saw the canvas?"

"True," John admitted. "I hadn't yet gone to look at it since I came back, late last week, so the holes could have been made at any time since last winter."

"And yet," I mused, "the rips in the canvas do look recent." We stopped then and unrolled the section of the canvas that John had just cut off, spreading it on a nearby table. We examined the canvas piece minutely and became convinced that the rips were of recent origin.

"We shall have to ask the others if any of them were in the hayloft—and using the pitchfork—recently," I said.

"Alfred is the one mostly up in the hayloft," John said, looking uneasy. "I mean, he often goes to get hay to cover seedlings and such, or to make mulch, I gather."

"Where is Mr. Parsons?" I asked. "Did not his head injury keep him from his planned journey today?"

John shook his head. "No, as a matter of fact, I saw him walking down toward the stables just after first breakfast this morning, valise in hand, and carrying fishing poles. I expect he feels fine enough to keep to his plans."

I was chagrined to think that a chief suspect—but also victim—in our ongoing investigation of the death of the blue bird was now beyond our reach.

"When is he expected back?" I said, watching John roll up the canvas again and look for a good place to stow it.

"Three or four days, I believe," he said. He looked at me as he straightened up from placing the canvas in a low cabinet. "Surely you don't suspect him, Vi, he's quite a lovely person, despite all his gruffness."

"Oh, you know me," I said airily. "I suspect everyone. Guilty until proven innocent, that's my motto."

He grinned, and we walked back to the door. "Well, at least you don't have to suspect Henry James," he said. "The poor man has just arrived."

"Ah, but he may have confederates close at hand," I joked. We walked out into the bright sunshine, and I glanced toward the garden walk that led down to the brook.

"I think I'll take a little stroll for a few moments, John, before joining you all in the house," I said, and started to turn down the path, when a piercing, bloodcurdling scream tore through the quiet air.

"That came from down by the brook," John said, and we both started to run. Before we had gone halfway, Kitty appeared, gasping and stumbling up from the brook path.

Upon seeing us, she collapsed in a sad little bundle on the gravel, and when we reached her, she spoke but a few words.

"He's dead, he's dead," she moaned.

Then she fainted.

SIXTEEN

30 SEPTEMBER 1726

At the Olde Swan

IN THE MORNING, OVER A HEARTY BREAKFAST, more of the story of the Highwayman was told. Bess strained to hear as she went back and forth between the kitchen and the tavern, bringing hot dishes of ham and eggs, kippers, sliced bread and butter in the crock. Mr. Wells, the gentleman who had been wounded, seeming much recovered, was speaking to the innkeeper who stood at the bar, wiping tankards and glasses.

"My lad's not far wrong," the man said, between bites of egg and fried fish. "He was a giant of a man, but tall only, not broad." His wife murmured something to him, which he answered with an agreeing nod.

"Aye, he wore a large cocked hat, with a black feather," he said. "That would have made him seem all the taller." He waved a hand at his throat. "Bunch of lacy stuff for a collar, and high-topped boots, like a Cavalier." He snorted in contempt.

"What did he sound like?" Bess asked, trying to keep her voice even and indifferent. When the man look puzzled, she added, "I mean, by way of accent or speech—could ye put him in any near county, or afar?"

"Interesting you should ask that, young miss," the man said. "It struck me that he was putting on a cultured English way of speaking, didn't you think so too, my dear?" He addressed his wife, who shrugged and nodded. Mr. Wells laughed. "But it couldn't quite disguise his real speech, which was Irish, without a doubt." He went back to eating his breakfast.

"Irish you say?" said the innkeeper, with a quick glance at his daughter, who had all but dropped a plate on the floor. "We get but few Irish round these parts, more Welsh, you see, and Cornish."

"The Irish have always been troublemakers, damnable Papists," the gentleman said, wiping his mouth with the napkin. He shrugged as his wife nudged him. "I will say so, my dear," he said to her. "You know what trouble my own brother has had with all that lot down near Oxford."

"Your brother?" the innkeeper asked, curious.

"Aye, he's a magistrate there," the gentleman said proudly. "And he'll hear of this crime against us, he will, soon as we've arrived, I guarantee you that."

"Well," the innkeeper said, smiling, "I'm glad of it, sir, that you have such connections, and mayhap this will bring down the rascal and free us from his misadventures." He glanced uneasily at Bess, but he couldn't quite tell what was bothering him—perhaps just the sight of her face, all pale and woebegone. There was something here he didn't understand, and didn't like.

The small party of travellers went back up to their room to pack for the rest of their journey, and Bess offered to go to the stables to let Tim know to get the inn's coach and horses ready soon—he was to drive them to Oxford

* * *

103

and return the same day, though it would be late. Bess mused on this circumstance as she walked outside, taking deep breaths of the cool morning air—this gentleman must be tolerably rich to spend that kind of money for his convenience. But his remarks about the Irish set her heart hard against any trouble that had befallen him. She felt a desperate need to be alone, and snatched at these few moments to help her get her head and heart straight.

She had hoped that what she thought last night was but a feverish dream, but the additional evidence of the Highwayman being Irish put it beyond imagining. Tremayne was Irish—it was one of the things that had attracted her to him, as she was half-Irish herself, from her mother's side. And, although her mother had kept to her Catholic faith in secrecy, they had all attended proper Church of England services at the ancient St. Eadburgha's church in the old village down the Snow's Hill road. Indeed, her mother often said that St. Eadburgha's, which had been Roman Catholic before "that devil Henry" stole it, was nearly as Catholic as she could imagine, what with the incense and the prayers and the priest's lacy vestments.

She arrived at the stables to see Tim already leading the horses out to hitch them up to the coach. She managed a smile when he looked over at her, so clearly wanting her approval.

"Thou hast gotten ahead of my telling thee, Tim," she said. "What need is there for me to come ask thee to do the work thou already know so well?"

Tim blushed to the roots of his hair at this unexpected compliment, and he muttered something that sounded like thanks. Bess stepped further into the stables, and idly took up a curry brush that had been set on the floor.

"They've been telling us about the Highwayman, the gentlefolk at the inn just now, over their breakfast," she said, trying to sound nonchalant. "Did Tom the coachman have anything more to say about it last night, when he came for his horses?"

Tim shrugged as he buckled the first horse into its traces, patting it gently and giving it a bit of feed from his palm to keep it still. "Not much, just like that the man was tallish, wore fancy high-top boots, that sort of thing."

"Tom said that he hit the man with his club, didn't he," she said cautiously. She found she was torn between condemning her lover as a criminal and worried that he was injured.

The ostler laughed. "Yes, and didn't he make it into a bigger story every time he told it over? I'd expect the poor Highwayman to never be walkin' again, to hear old Tom tell the tale."

Bess shivered in spite of herself and bit her lip to keep from saying more. She laid the curry brush on a shelf and turned to go.

"Well, those folks'll be ready to go any time now," she said. She paused and put a gentle hand on his arm. "Mind thou go careful, now, especially coming back in the dark night." She glanced up at the sky. "And there's no more'n a half-moon to guide. Dost think thou should take Sam along too?"

Tim, touched by her concern, shook his head and looked away. "Nay, and what help is that boy if trouble happens? And I've got naught any highwayman might want of me. I'll be fine, Miss Bess, don't thee worry 'bout me." As she started to leave, he called after her, "And I've gotten that Georgie mate o'mine to come by the rest of the day to take care of whatever is needing done in the stables til I get back—I spoke to thy Da about it already."

Bess smiled at him. "Sure, and thou thinkest of everything, yes Tim? Thou art like a good brother to me, and a son to Da, which he never had."

Tim just stood with a harness in his hand, looking after the love of his life as she walked back to the inn.

SEVENTEEN

SATURDAY 4 SEPTEMBER 1886

Russell House

A STIFF DOSE OF SMELLING SALTS brought Kitty back to her senses, and as I stashed the vial again in my reticule, I thanked my mother's staid propriety that kept that handy substance always within reach. I helped John raise the girl from the ground and, supported mainly by him, as he was nearly twice her size, we slowly brought her back to the house. She was perilously close to fainting again, and was utterly unable to speak.

Her scream had roused the inmates of Russell House, and chief among the first to reach us in the garden was the indomitable Lucia. She sized up the situation and instructed John and me to bring the young woman to a sofa in a small sitting room next to the kitchen. Lily whisked Kate away to another part of the house, chattering to her about something they might do, and distracting her from the situation.

Directly he had laid Kitty upon the sofa, John turned to Ned Abbey and David Cowan, who had also run to join us, and gestured for them to follow him instantly back down to the brook. I caught John's arm as he passed by me, and was able to whisper a reminder to look carefully at the body and its surroundings before they moved it. He nodded, patted my arm, and left.

My initial ministrations done, I gave way to the greater skills of Lucia and the housemaid for Kitty, and stepped to the window to watch the three men hurrying away into the garden. I was wild with curiosity to know who the poor dead person was, and I longed to run after them but held myself in check for the time being. It was then I noticed Henry James, who was hovering discreetly at the door to the sitting room, looking as if he wished to be of service but, much like myself, wasn't quite sure what form that would take. I took pity on his feelings, and walking over to him, suggested we retire to Lily's parlour for the moment while the ladies revived Kitty, who had recovered a spot of color in her cheeks, though her eyes had not yet opened.

"I agree completely, Miss Lee," he said gravely. "I am of no more use than a lamppost in such situations." We began to walk down the hall, and he continued talking in his soft, calm voice, his grey eyes glancing over at me (he wasn't that much taller than I) as he spoke. "I cannot say I am *surprised* to see you here at Russell House, Miss Lee," he said. "Half of Chelsea and Kensington make their way to this Mecca of literature and art." He smiled faintly. "But I am *glad* to see you here, and hope we may pass some time in conversation, so that I may sharpen my poor wit against your prodigious one."

I was relieved at his tone, although it was impossible to imagine that Henry James would not treat me with the utmost politeness, however much he might find my novel distasteful or *outré*.

* * *

"Our friend John," he continued, "has occasionally entertained me with accounts of your joint endeavours at solving mysteries." He paused on the threshold of Lily's parlour to allow me to enter before him. "I would venture to assume that you are on the brink of one at this very moment."

We entered the parlour; we were its only inhabitants. I seated myself in an upright chair next to the little yellow sofa, from where I could see out the back window and into the garden. Mr. James sat, after a moment, on the sofa, catching up a plump cushion to place it behind his back, wincing slightly. I recalled that he had always seemed to be cautious in his movements, as if he were an elderly man, although I happened to know he was just forty-three this year. Still, that was thirteen years older than John and

"Russell House *would* seem to be suddenly at the center of some sinister goings-on," I said, smoothing my skirt and glancing out the window—there was no sign of John and the other two men who had run down to the brook.

"Perhaps the local constable should be called," Mr. James said mildly.

I frowned. "In my experience, Mr. James," I said, "local constables are rather more in the way of solving a crime than just about anyone I can imagine."

"How very unconventional of you, Miss Lee," he said, although he didn't seem particularly disturbed about it. He looked around the room uneasily, however. "I must say," he said, his voice low, "it's possible *I* might be more in the

• • •

way here, than any kind of help or comfort, and perhaps ought to take myself off again. What is your opinion?"

Here was my opportunity! "That is very thoughtful of you, Mr. James," I said promptly. "And, as it occurs to me that I might possibly be of *more* use here than elsewhere, under the circumstances, I wonder if you would consent to establish yourself in my quarters at the Lygon Arms, and I could take your place here, at Russell House? I have already mentioned it to John," I pursued, "and he was quite of my opinion that you would find the hotel more comfortable, and especially now, with everything in such disarray."

His still youthful face, even with the trim brown beard and clipped mustache, clearly showed his relief, although instantly covered up by a look of sanguine unconcern. "If it would oblige you and the Millets," he said. "I would be happy to change accommodations." He looked around the room again. "Do you think it would be acceptable for me to return to the Lygon Arms now, and make the arrangements?"

"Assuredly," I said. "Let me just write a note to an excellent man, Mr. Andrew Hesford, at the hotel, and he will take care of all the details." I rose and went to a desk on the far side of the parlour, found paper and pen and ink, and wrote a quick letter to the doorman, asking him to have my things packed up and delivered to Russell House forthwith, and to prepare the room that had been mine for Mr. Henry James, the eminent American author and critic.

We discovered Mr. James's valise in the hall, where it had been unceremoniously deposited, and he set off with no little alacrity, my note in his vest pocket, to establish himself at the Lygon Arms in all the quiet and comfort it could afford.

I saw him depart, then immediately went to the kitchen, where Kitty was coming back to herself, half-lying on the sofa but attempting to drink some tea, with Lucia hovering over her solicitously.

"Oh, Violet!" she cried, stepping over to me. "Such a thing to happen!"

"Who is it?" I asked her, keeping my voice low. "Did Kitty recognize the, ah, the person?"

Lucia nodded solemnly, and whispered, "Michael Kelly." She swallowed hard, and looked at Kitty, who had put down her teacup and closed her eyes.

"Michael Kelly!" I repeated softly, but not low enough to escape Kitty's hearing. She moaned and turned her head aside, her hand to her lips. We both went to her quickly.

"Kitty," I said, taking her hand gently. "You've had a terrible shock," I said. "Believe me, I know what it is like to find someone..." I stumbled a bit, not knowing how to put the obvious. "I too, have experienced such a devastation."

She opened her eyes at this, and gazed at me intently.

"Too horrible," she murmured, and started to cry. "Poor Michael!"

I knew it was wrong, but I felt I had to press for some answers. "Was it Michael with you in the hayloft last night?" I said softly.

The effect of my words was astonishing—Kitty sat bolt upright and then seemed to shrink back into the sofa pillows. "What...who...what do you know?" She was stunned, but kept trying to speak. "Have you the Sight? No, no, not Michael, no one, no one, I was all alone. He...he..."

Then she fainted dead away again.

EIGHTEEN

30 SEPTEMBER 1726

On the Road to Oxford

THE ROAD TO OXFORD WAS WELL-MAINTAINED, and there had been no rain for some weeks; it was dusty, but it was dry, and Tim reckoned he could make fair time the day he drove the Wells family from Broadway, perhaps five or six miles an hour.

"Six hours there, and the same back again," he told his mate Georgie, who had remarkably showed up just as Tim was placing the family's luggage in the carriage. Richard the innkeeper had bought the carriage at a good price from the old Lord Peter at the Manor, one of the many carriages the landed family had owned. But Lord Peter was the last of the last, and had taken to selling off the odd piece of property now and again, to support his various genteel habits. Tim kept the carriage in superb condition, and the velvet lining inside was barely worn, so infrequently was it used.

"Well, ye'll have fast going," Georgie said. "The roads be dry and hard. Will ye stop at Moreton-in-Marsh?"

"Maybe so," Tim said. "And why?"

Georgie shrugged. "Folks say it's where the Highwayman lives—disguised, he is, like any ordinary farmer or shopkeeper." He smiled cheerily. "Ye might take a look about for him!"

Tim shook his head in disgust. "Thou'rt as daft as a drunken cat," he said. "Now mind thee take care of things here til I'm back—stay as late as thou can, yes? I reckon I'll be back some time after midnight."

The carriage pulled out of the inn yard as the clock struck nine. Bess fingered the coin Mrs. Wells had slipped to her as they bade farewell. "Thank you, my dear, for your attention to my dear husband," the lady had said. "You are quite a capable lass. His wound seems fair to healing very well already." Mr. Wells' parting words were less than comforting for Bess to hear, for he swore again that he would relate their encounter with the Highwayman to his brother the magistrate, and get the King's men on the road to deal with him.

The Highwayman was on Tim's mind as well, as he drove the well-fed team up the High Road and out the other end of the village. But he consoled himself by thinking he had no money or personal effects worth stealing, and he assumed highwaymen in general weren't foolish enough to steal a whole carriage—for how could they ever sell it on?

Folks stopped to watch as the carriage went by, a rare enough sight that it captured the attention of the village, and Tim nodded and waved, feeling proud, as people hailed him from doorways.

"Ye're looking a proper coachman, ye are, Tim boy!" called the butcher's wife, smiling approvingly.

• • •

"Fit for a lord, that carriage is!" This from the doorman at the White Hart.

"Watch out for the Highwayman, won't ye!" called a stableman as they passed the Horse and Hounds, just at the other end of the village.

They made very good time, stopping once to allow the horses to rest and feed at Chipping Norton and then again a very brief stop at Woodstock. There had been little conversation between the coachman and his passengers, although the lad Jonathan had taken a great interest in the horses when they were stopped, and Tim found him an intelligent boy and very polite. It was at Woodstock, their last post before coming into Oxford, that Mr. Wells grew more chatty as he walked around the inn yard while his wife made use of the inn's facilities.

"Now, then, young man," the gentleman addressed Tim all at once. "As I said to your innkeeper, I shall be acting on my word about this Highwayman, and my brother will, I know, be keen to get the King's men on his tail as soon as will be. So I want to charge you," he went on, pausing in his earnestness to look Tim in the eye. "If you see or hear aught of this villain, if he strike again, mayhap, or show himself, you may send word to me here in Oxford, at Lavender House, Stewart Street. Do you know your letters, boy?"

Tim nodded. Bess had been teaching him the past few years, and he was able to write a passable sentence, and read a bit, if it was simple enough. "Lavender House, Stewart Street, Oxford," he repeated dutifully.

"Good, good," Mr. Wells said. "I understand he works the Hill Road a good deal—perhaps he is lazy and won't go far afield! We shall catch him, I swear. And there will be a good reward posted for anyone who aids us in his capture."

Soon after that, they entered Oxford as the day was cooling and the college bells were ringing out for evening prayers. Mr. Wells directed Tim to Stewart Street, and he pulled up the carriage at the front of a grand stone house, with several large windows on the ground floor, and smaller ones above on two more stories, a very grand house indeed.

As the family alighted, Mr. Wells pressed several coins into Tim's hand—he had already paid the innkeeper for the coach before they left—and thanked him for his assistance.

"Take the carriage around the back, through the mews," Mr. Wells said. "My stableman will see to your horses, and you are welcome to bed down the night there if you wish."

"I thank 'ee, sir, but I told Mr. Richard I would be back home tonight," Tim said.

"And you do not fear such a long trip all on your own?" asked Mrs. Wells, who had stopped a moment to oversee their servants who had come out to bring in the luggage.

"No, ma'am, thank 'ee kindly, I've no cause to fear," said Tim.

"Well, be sure to stop by the kitchen door in the back and get yourself something to take with you on your journey home," said the kindly Mrs. Wells.

So, after bidding them farewell, and taking the carriage and horses around the back for rest and food for them and for himself, Tim was back on the road to Broadway before the sun had set. He didn't mind travelling on his own, and was content to move along in the mild autumn night. The moon was only at the half, but waxing, and the sky was clear and full of stars. He thought about what Mr. Wells had said about the reward for capturing the Highwayman—what if he were to catch the brigand, and reap the reward?

Possibilities opened before him such as he had never thought of before. He could use the money to purchase a partnership in the Olde Swan, and marry Bess! He was practically a son to old Richard, Bess had said so herself—but far from a brother to her, is what he meant to be.

Such musings and happy plans helped the hours speed away as he travelled without mishap, stopping briefly at the same coaching inns as before, and found himself more than eager to be going home.

● ● ●

NINETEEN

SATURDAY 4 SEPTEMBER 1886

Russell House

THEY HAD LAID POOR MICHAEL KELLY GENTLY on a large table in one of the outbuildings, a large storage shed, formerly part of the stables. Lucia had dispatched the housemaid to the village to call in the doctor, who arrived in haste shortly after John, Ned and David had brought the body to the shed.

I had left Lucia to tend the mostly unconscious Kitty, and hurried to the shed to find out what I could. I entered by a set of large double doors, one of which was partly open, and managed to slip in and to the side without being seen by anyone but John, who, when he noticed me, grimly shook his head, glancing down at the body on the table. I put my finger to my lips to indicate I wanted to remain undetected, and he nodded slightly in understanding.

The other men had their backs to me, and thus obscured the body from my sight, but I could clearly see the doctor as he turned and moved the arms and legs and head of the dead man, muttering to himself as he did so. I felt a sudden sharp pang as I thought of the young Irishman, so mischievous and lively at dinner the night before—and so imbued with a kind of magic, it seemed,

* * *

when he was telling my fortune. I had to shake myself to stay in the present, and not fall into pondering the Queen and the Knight, and whom they might represent.

The doctor spoke up then, addressing himself mainly to Ned and John. He sounded calm, but as if he repressed some excitement underlying his even tones—perhaps he had not seen many dead bodies. I could see the side of his face—he sported a short beard, dark brown, and his hair was rather long. A youngish man, I thought.

"Other than this severe contusion on the side of his head, I see nothing like a knife wound or the like," he said. "Rigor has begun to pass off, probably due to the warming day. Where did you find the body?"

John spoke up as Ned remained silent. "He was on the edge of the brook, with his feet in the water." I could see Michael's feet, and noticed his leather shoes were dark with soaking, as were the bottoms of his trousers. "He was facing downwards, with his hands above his head."

The doctor pulled at his beard, thinking. He leaned forward and gently unfastened the man's shirt, pulling it open to inspect the body further. I couldn't see what he saw, but I saw him nodding his head as if in affirmation of his thoughts.

"Bruising here, and here," he said, pointing. "It looks as if he had been crossing the brook—it's at a relatively low point now, is it not?—and perhaps lost his footing or tripped, came down on the rocks, bruising his chest, then hitting his head, then managed to get to the shore before he succumbed." He bent to examine the head wound again. "It's quite a deep gash," he said. "I expect there was a concussion, and inflammation in the brain, and it took him in the night."

So, not murder. I felt somewhat relieved and, shamefully, a little disappointed.

Just then the door swung open next to me and I had to quickly step back to avoid being thumped—but it hid me from view as the intruder barreled into the room.

The village constable.

As I had said to Mr. James, my estimation of policemen in general was not high, and as for village constables (as opposed to City policemen), I had been able to reduce them to two types: the one big, burly, bewhiskered and blundering; the other, more typical, small and rodent-like, sharp-eyed and suspicious. Broadway's constable was of the latter type.

"Ah, Mr. Poole," the doctor said, upon turning round and seeing the man. "It would appear you have been called out to Russell House in vain."

Mr. Poole, raising his chin to increase his height (so it seemed to me), touched his stiff-brimmed hat by way of greeting, and tucked a thumb under the wide white belt that girded his thin frame. "With all respect, Doctor White, and to the gentlemen here, I'll be the judge of that." He walked slowly to the foot of the table and surveyed the body. The door, which had been left open, and was apparently hung unevenly, began to close on its own, exposing my presence—and it was not missed by the vigilant Mr. Poole.

"Eh? Who's this?" he said, causing the doctor, Ned and David, all on one side of the table, to turn and regard me. "A female!" cried the constable. "What's a female doin' here?" I saw John roll his eyes.

It was an awkward moment. I admit I was at a bit of a loss, for once, but was about to stammer out some explanation when Ned Abbey, of all people, came to my rescue.

"Miss Lee is here at my express wish," he said in a decisive tone, but with a slight twinkle in his eye as he looked at me. "She is a practitioner of the new science of detecting, and as she happens to be a guest in our house at this moment, we luckily have her expertise to assist us in this most tragic incident."

"Detectin', is it?" Mr. Poole said, his twisty eyebrows scrunched in deep suspicion. He looked as if he might have a good deal to say on the subject of female detectives.

"Regardless," the young doctor cut in, looking rather amused, "this poor fellow has had an accident, fell while crossing the brook, hit his head, and came up a goner on the bank, and there's an end to it." He turned back to the table and began to button poor Michael's shirt up again. "There's no crime, and therefore, no need for you, Mr. Poole, that is, in your official capacity as a policeman."

Mr. Poole gazed at him, mildly affronted, but looking as if he were used to sparring with the doctor. "Might I have a look at the body meself, Doctor White?" he said politely.

The doctor stepped back and waved a hand at the table, inviting the constable forward.

I watched, curious, as Mr. Poole conducted a careful and minute scrutiny from head to toe, not touching anything, until at last, he gently slipped a hand into the pocket of the young man's trousers, and drew forth a slip of damp paper.

Everyone leaned in, and I moved to the table, unnoticed while everyone's attention was fixed on this interesting discovery.

Mr. Poole carefully unfolded the paper, and we could all see there was writing on it.

sruthán mheán oíche

"Looks like that Gaelic writin' the Irish are tryin' to use again," the constable said, with a twist to his mouth that clearly revealed his low estimate of such an enterprise. I was surprised at his knowledge of the Gaelic revival; I was only peripherally aware of it myself.

I involuntarily glanced up at David Cowan, who, standing next to the constable, had seen the writing and from the look on his face, clearly had understood the meaning of the words. He spoke the Gaelic aloud, and I caught at the second word. I spoke up without thinking.

"*Midnight* again," I said, my voice cutting into the fraught silence. "And although I don't know Gaelic, I'd bet my bonnet that the other word means *brook*." Mr. Cowan grunted a brief *aye*.

Mr. Poole was quick to catch at my words. "You said *again*, miss?" He peered into all our faces, one after the other. "Has there been someone else 'had an accident'?"

I inwardly cursed myself for my impetuous remark. No one knew about the first Irish note but John and me— and perhaps Kitty.

"Mr. Alfred Parsons," Ned said smoothly. "He is also a guest here. He fell down some steps last night, in the garden, and hit his head. But he's fine, it was only a slight cut." John and I exchanged very brief glances at this statement of Ned's—why was he disguising the truth?

Mr. Poole gazed keenly at me. "And what is the significance of 'midnight', if I may ask, miss?"

I thought it best to play into the constable's prejudice against women. "Oh, just my wayward mind, constable, thinking that as Mr. Parsons had fallen down at around ten o'clock, last night, which is *close* to midnight, and this note had that word in it, it seemed like an unspeakable coincidence to me, you see."

He sniffed, looked superior, but seemed content to accept my ridiculous explanation.

"Nonetheless," the constable continued, folding the note up again and putting it in his wallet, much to my dismay. "It would appear someone requested his presence at the *brook*—" he looked suspiciously at me, then David Cowan, and resumed—"and it might be of great interest to discover who that party is." He looked around at us all but no one seemed inclined to suggest any names. I had had only a very quick glimpse of this second note, so felt I needed to examine it more thoroughly to see if the handwriting matched the first note, which although I had only seen it by the light from the parlour window, my photographic memory still held a crisp image of it.

"But if it is just a sad, sad accident," I decided to state the obvious, for clarity's sake, "then it really doesn't matter who wanted to meet him at the brook—one presumes that is was likely a friend, and that poor Mr. Kelly's accident occurred *after* the meeting, if there even was one, or his companion would surely have raised the alarm upon him falling on the rocks."

"One can presume all one wants, miss," the constable said smugly. "What we want is *evidence*, you see," he added, smirking. "Evidence is a key element of detectin', as I understand it, or do you have different methods in *your* way of detectin'?" He suddenly seemed greatly perturbed, and interrupted himself. "Did you say *Kelly*?" He looked down at the body again, and shook his head, a slight smirk glimmering at his lips. "So this lad was Irish, too?"

David Cowan spoke up. "Aye, he was," he said, cautiously but with some defiance. "And what if he was?" It made me think how terrible it is to have to live one's life in fear of discrimination and suspicion—not unlike being a woman in this day and age, only one doesn't usually get arrested for being female. Not yet.

Mr. Poole pursed his lips, then shrugged. "It's all their own business, ain't it, and they can go kill one another all they like, says I, but we don't need 'em bringin' it over to our door," he said, and he began to turn away. I noted his face looked flushed to a dark redness.

But Cowan persisted. "Is there news of more unrest in Belfast, then?" he said. "Are you saying it's spilling over to here?"

The constable eyed him speculatively, then shook his head again. "Only rumors," he said. "Nothin' as is troublin' us here in Broadway. And if it did, we'd show 'em quick enough how we deal with such kind of rebels." He looked as if he could say more but chose not to. Or perhaps he was just being arrogant.

* * *

I decided to take a chance, I was that fixed upon seeing the note. "That note, constable," I ventured, holding out my hand (I have often seen that presuming someone will do what one wants often makes them do it). "Might we here take a look at it, to see if any one of us can recognize the hand?"

"I can't imagine any one of us could tell," Ned started to say, but upon seeing my questioning look at him, he amended his objection. "But of course, if you wish, Violet."

With a frown, Mr. Poole retrieved the note from his wallet, and handed it, not to me, but to Ned, who motioned me to come closer to study the writing. John leaned in to look at it, too. I called up the image of the writing on the birdhouse note in my memory, the curves of the letters, especially the words that meant *midnight*. I was not at all convinced that both notes were written by the same hand, which troubled me greatly. Ned looked at me, but, nonplussed, I shook my head; John did the same, and we handed the note back to the constable. "It is not a hand we recognize," Ned told him.

Mr. Poole straightened up, gave a half salute to the doctor, and left the shed, but only after giving me a veiled glare of contempt, and remarking that he would be back if he had more questions. Dr. White prepared to leave as well, only noting to Ned that he would inform the village undertaker that there was a body to be collected and prepared for burial. "In this weather," he added, "best to be taken care of soon."

I looked at Ned Abbey, whose face was flushed, his hands nervous. It occurred to me to wonder if he had, after all, recognized the handwriting. I might want to have a good long conversation with this amiable artist.

* * *

TWENTY

1 OCTOBER 1726

At the Olde Swan Inn

THE MOON HAD JUST SET, it was the deepest part of night, and Bess heard the bell from St. Eadburgha's, off in the fields, toll three times. A scattering of small pebbles hit her window—a sign she knew—and she rose quickly and went to unlatch the casement.

Down in the courtyard, in the shadows, she could just discern the black horse, the white star on its forehead gleaming from the lantern kept lighted in the yard for Tim's return from Oxford. That the lantern was still lighted told her that Tim had not yet come back, which worried her a little, but all her attention was quickly drawn to the tall, cloaked shape that moved to stand beneath her window.

"Tremayne!" she whispered, and her voice reached him easily in the still night.

"Bess my lovely," he said. "Wilt thou come down?"

She hesitated, but then nodded. Closing the casement, she donned her robe and slipped on her shoes, then made her way down the back staircase, which was away from where her father slept, and Germaine. A moment later she was in the arms of her Highwayman, and glad for it.

"Art thou hurt, then?" she gasped, drawing him out of the lantern's light and into the shadow, where his horse stood quietly. "That gentleman traveller, he was wounded, and Tom said he cudgelled thee..." Words burst from her lips without her knowing exactly what she was saying.

"Shush, shush, now, what art thou sayin'?" Tremayne whispered into her hair. "I've nought to complain of, I'm fit as a fiddle." He pulled back then, and looked her in the face, searching for her thoughts.

"Thou knowest, then?" he said softly. "Canst thou bear it, Bess?"

It melted her heart that he would think of her and how she would think and feel about this secret of his.

"But, it's so dangerous!" she whispered back. "What I can't bear is the thought of thee hurt, or killed—the King's men—they'll hunt thee down!" Her heart beat fast.

Tremayne smiled and shook his head. "They'll never catch me," he said, and it didn't sound like a mere boast. "And besides, dearest, I don't intend to make this my living much longer—I've saved what I've earned, see— and soon I'll have enough to offer my hand like an honest man." He gazed at her and touched her face. "Canst thou wait just a little longer, love? Wilt thou marry me when I ask then?"

"Yes, oh yes," she said, reaching up to kiss him soundly. "And do not worry," she added. "I will tell no one, not even my father." He kissed her again, then moved to mount his horse, all in a quick motion, silent and swift.

• • •

"Watch for me," he said. "The day after the full moon, in about a fortnight, I'll ride up to the door in the broad daylight and claim thy hand, love."

Bess kissed her hand to him, and watched him ride out the gateway. She turned back to the inn, and slipping round the side, went back up the stairs to her room. All was silent around her. She gave a final thought to wonder why Tim the ostler was so late in coming home, but then fell asleep with a little sigh, into her dreams.

But she was mistaken. Tim had already come home, and had been seeing to the horses for the night, but had not yet come round to put out the lantern at the door. He had stepped into the courtyard just as the Highwayman tossed the pebbles to Bess's window—and he hid in the shadows, watching and hearing all that had passed between the two lovers. His heart was black with rage and sorrow, and he crept back to his stable room like a whipped dog.

• • •

TWENTY-ONE

SATURDAY 4 SEPTEMBER 1886

Russell House

WITH THE DOCTOR AND THE CONSTABLE both departed, the four of us remaining with Michael Kelly's body were left to determine what to do next. David Cowan was the first to break the silence.

"Kitty will know the whereabouts of his kin," he said, his voice rough with sorrow. "She knew Michael's family, back in Belfast, where her folks lived before moving to London, some years since." He laid a tentative hand on the young man's cold forehead, and I saw him trace the sign of the cross.

Ned took a deep, steadying breath. "I shall of course," he said, "see to transporting the body to wherever the family wants it, or else pay for the burial here in Broadway, should that be desirable." I thought this exceedingly generous of him, and admired him all the more for it.

"I should go back in to Kitty," I said, thinking she was probably more revived, and might be heartened by hearing that the doctor affirmed that Michael's death was purely accidental, sad as that was, and not the result of foul play. I was curious, however, as to one thing, and turned to David Cowan before I left the room.

"Mr. Cowan," I said, "do you have any notion as to why Michael would have been down at the brook in the middle of the night?" He did not look at me, his gaze still fixed on his dead friend, and then shook his head. "Nae, miss," he said. "A warm late summer night, wasn't it? Young men have plenty of reasons to be abroad on such a night, I'm thinking." He turned away abruptly and strode out the door, with the rest of us—me, Ned and John—following slowly, after securing the door against any accidental entry.

We found Lucia and the housemaid still in the small sitting room near the kitchen, tending to Kitty, who was indeed revived, sitting up, and drinking some tea. All three women looked up as we entered.

"What did Dr. White have to say?" Lucia spoke first.

"A tragic accident," Ned answered. "He found no evidence of anything that suggested otherwise." He shrugged slightly, and walked over to the sofa where Kitty was. He sat beside her and took her hand in his tenderly. "Dear girl," he said, "it appears that Michael was out on some lark of his own, perhaps, and unhappily slipped on the rocks in the brook, hitting his head fatally, and died upon the bank. I'm so sorry, my dear," he said, and kissed her hand, and then her forehead.

The red-haired model bore this news rather better than I expected, perhaps because the worst was already known. She nodded her thanks to Ned.

"David said you might know where Michael's family is, so we can send the sad news and see what they want done," Ned continued. Kitty hesitated, seemed uncertain about something, then nodded. "I know where to write to them in Belfast," she said softly. "I will do it right away." And she rose, stood swaying unsteadily for a moment, then squared her shoulders and made her way to the door. As she passed by me, I felt her shrink a bit and look away, as if she didn't want me to accost her with questions.

Lucia turned to Ned. "What is to be done with poor Michael's body?" she asked, and he told her the doctor was going to alert the undertaker to come collect it. With a firm nod of her head, Lucia rose, gestured to the housemaid to return to her duties, and walked over to John.

"We have had word that the Barnards have arrived, and are at their usual lodgings nearby," she said. "I have it in mind that, sad and sorry as all this is, we should try, for the sake of the children as well as our own spirits, to carry on as normally as possible, yes?" She laid a hand on his arm and smiled up at him. "Despite everything, I know you must be eager to paint, are you not?"

John smiled back, and put his hand on top of hers. "You know me well, dear Lucia," he said. "I quite agree that we should try to keep all our spirits up." He looked at Ned, who sat, brooding, on the sofa. "Don't you think so as well, Ned?"

"Eh? What?" Ned awoke from his reverie. "Yes, yes, carry on, as you all say here, it will be for the best."

Lucia looked over at me. "I saw you leave earlier, Violet," she said, "escorting Mr. James out of this sad scene. Where have you left him?"

This was awkward, but there was nothing for it. "As it turns out," I said, trying for a decidedly reasonable tone, "Mr. James felt he would be in the way here, just at this time, so he and I came to an agreement that he would take my room at the Lygon Arms, and I would come to stay here, at Russell House, in his place." At the slight frown that formed on Lucia's face, I hastened to add, embroidering the truth only slightly, "I hope that is agreeable to you, Lucia. I fear Mr. James might have taken himself directly back to London if we hadn't hit upon the scheme of exchanging rooms."

"Of course," she said, recovering her equanimity, and her manners, quickly. "The room is all prepared anyway, so we'll get you established there as soon as you collect your things from the inn."

"I think they are arriving as we speak," I said, pointing out the window to the courtyard, where a lad in Lygon Arms livery was standing, my valise in his hand, looking about as if to determine upon which door he should knock. I hastened outside, to escape Lucia as much as to claim my belongings.

"Here, lad," I called.

"I'm to deliver this to Miss Vernon Lee personally in person," the boy said, not relinquishing his burden without proof, seemingly, "or Mr. 'esford will 'ave me 'ead on a pike."

"Very good," I said, smiling. "I am Miss Vernon Lee, and you may tell Mr. Hesford that his charge has been duly accomplished." He peered at me closely, then, apparently satisfied I was who I said, he set the valise at my feet, and drew from his pocket a small white envelope.

"Mr. 'esford said as I was to give ye this, miss," he said, handing over the envelope.

* * *

I had no coins on my person, so I told the boy to wait just a moment while I went back in the house.

"John?" I called in a low voice through the sitting room door, and it was opened in a moment by the very person I was seeking.

"Have you a penny or two I could borrow?" I said, and as he handed it over, I clarified, "the boy from the Lygon Arms has just brought my valise. Thank you, I shall pay you back shortly."

"No need, Vi," John said, smiling. "I'm always in your debt for various things, anyway. You can take this on account."

I turned back outside, smiling myself, and gave the boy his coins and saw him run off happily. I still had Mr. Hesford's missive in my hand, and curious about what the doorman might want to convey to me, I opened it as I stood there alone in the courtyard. What he had written, though brief, astonished me.

There were two young men by the brook last night. A.H.

***

The undertaker arrived to remove Michael's body from the premises while I was standing in the courtyard, transfixed by the message from the Lygon Arms doorman, so I hastily stuffed the note in a pocket and alerted Lucia to the next sad duty to be performed. Within minutes, I saw from the parlour windows the little procession leave the grounds: a two-wheeled cart which bore a plain pine coffin in which the remains of the Irish youth were carried off. David Cowan, the older model, accompanied it solemnly.

I stood quietly as the sad procession left through the gate, which David closed behind him, and realized I was not satisfied with the doctor's pronouncement of accidental death. I went back into the house, carrying my valise and looking for John, but the sitting room was empty. I heard voices in the parlour further down the hall, and a moment's listening told me that Ned and Kitty, at least, were in there, probably writing the letter to Michael Kelly's family.

I then entreated the housemaid to show me where my bedchamber was, and she obligingly led me upstairs, to a perfectly lovely room with casement windows facing the front, framing a view across the wall to the orchards and fields, as well as of the coach road that led into the village. I found it a little odd that the woman did not enter the room, but stood at the doorway while I went in, her eyes wide and darting here and there. She curtsied hastily and disappeared back down the stairs when I thanked her and told her she could go.

I disposed my few items of clothing and such around the room, and after sitting a few moments in renewed contemplation of the doorman's note, I was about to return downstairs, when it occurred to me I might have a look round at the rooms on this floor—a little nudge from my conscience observed it would be wrong to look for Kitty's room and search it, but I paid it no mind.

I seemed to be all alone on this upper floor, so stepped quietly to one door and another, and on the third try, at the far end of the hall, I hit upon a bed chamber that I could easily see belonged to Kitty—a bright green shawl, beautifully worked with flowers of many colors, lay across the bed; I had seen her wearing it the previous night.

Closing the door quietly, I quickly surveyed the room. Where was one likely to stow a note that must be kept secret? I opened the drawers, one after another, of a chest that stood by a window—nothing. Then I spied her reticule, on the floor near the window, and snatched it up. Just then I heard voices and steps rising up the stairway. I pulled open the little bag, felt around inside and eureka! My fingers grasped a little slip of paper curled up like the one I had found in the birdhouse the night before. There was no time to peruse it now; there was nothing for it but to take it with me, and hope it would not be missed until I had an opportunity to return it.

Stepping softly to the door, I opened it a crack—no one was to be seen, but I heard voices coming nearer. I slipped out quickly, and seeing across the hall a worn door that indicated to me it was the servants' stairway, I opened it quickly and was gratified to see I was correct. I closed the door quietly behind me, and waited with baited breath. I heard Lucia's voice and Lily's, companionably chatting as they gained the hall—and sighed with relief as they proceeded to the next floor above us, probably the nursery. I waited until I could no longer hear them, then cautiously opened the door. Seeing no one, I slipped out again and back to my own room.

I breathed more easily as, safe inside my chamber, I leaned against the closed door, and looked at the slip of paper in my hand. To my great surprise, it was *not* the note from the birdhouse, but another one entirely—and this note was in English, not Gaelic, so it was impossible for me to ascertain if they were by the same hand.

Please come to the exhibition match—I shall play all the better for seeing your bright eyes upon me. Love, McC

TWENTY-TWO
3 OCTOBER 1726

At the Olde Swan Inn

THE FRIVOLITIES OF HARVEST DAY soon gave way to daily labours at the Olde Swan—for the women, it was cooking up preserves from the autumn fruits, salting beef and pork to hang in the larder, and making tallow candles to store up against the coming darkness of winter. Bess and Germaine were busy from morning to night, and the men had no less free time with all the chores and preparations for winter—sealing cracks in the inn's walls, repairing chairs and tables worn and split from the summer's heat outdoors, and always seeing to the horses and their welfare.

Bess was counting the days until she might see Tremayne again—she hoped that he would fulfill his promise and present himself at their door, ready to ask for her hand in marriage. He'd said he would return in a fortnight from Michelmas, so that would be around the feast of Edward the Confessor, mid-October. He had told her he had to lay low for a while, and would not be coming into the village—but if she needed him, she could leave a note at St. Eadburgha's—the first tombstone to the right-hand of the main door had a loose stone at the base—one Cwynedd Bowhill was buried there.

Her heart was full as she scrubbed and cleaned and worked in the Inn, not allowing herself to think what it would be like for her father, if she were to marry and leave him behind. She shoved away the thought with a desperate *but I'll be nearby, won't I?* to quiet her sense of abandoning him. She went to bed tired out, and dreamed of moonlight and roads winding through the hills.

The wind had shifted during the night, and the third morning after the Harvest Fair showed frost settled on the village, and a sky so clear and blue it hurt to look up. Bess gazed with longing out the front door of the inn and, making up her mind, called out to Germaine in the kitchen.

"I'll just be taking myself to the village," she said. "We need more rough muslin for the preserve jars, don't we?" Germaine appeared at the door, wiping her hands on a cloth, and nodded.

"Sure and we're needin' more o'that stout string, too, canst thou get some?" She looked at Bess, a question strong on her face. "Thou'rt restless, lass, what's takin' thee so?"

Bess just shook her head and smiled. There was so much to say she couldn't possibly begin, and besides, she had promised Tremayne she wouldn't betray him—she was afraid if she started talking about him, she wouldn't be able to stop herself, especially with someone as sympathetic as Germaine.

"I'll be back before anyone knows I'm gone," she said, and taking up the market basket, she quickly left the inn.

As she left the courtyard, she couldn't keep from peering up the road that went to London—it was empty of all travellers just now, and she could see the dry, hard track wind its way across the browning hills. When would her love come riding down the road to her?

She turned toward the village, and hummed a little old tune as she walked, swinging her basket and rejoicing in the crisp air. The frost had turned the trees from green to crimson, rust, yellow and brown, and soon the north wind would blow them all to the ground, and dreary winter would set in.

But not dreary for me! she thought, and pictured herself and Colm, snug in his farmhouse, man and wife.

A few minutes later she was passing by the green, where no trace of the Harvest Fair was to be seen, just some sheep grazing and a young shepherd gnawing at a bannock as he poked straying members of the herd with his crook from time to time, his dog sitting alert at his side.

She turned in to the apothecary's shop, which the proprietor, Mr. Samuel, had ingeniously stocked with an array of useful dry goods—cloth for aprons, cloaks and shirts; glass bottles and jars; sewing needles in paper packets, with china thimbles; paper and string of all kinds, even some nails and small tools. It was everyone's favorite store—and so there was a bit of a crowd this morning as always.

Bess waited patiently as customers came forward and Mr. Samuel found the things they wanted; and then she noticed that Mary Cummings was also in the shop, and was before her in the line. She turned slightly away, not really wanting to be drawn into any kind of exchange with the woman, but all heads were turned in that direction when Mary began to enumerate her requirements to Mr. Samuel in a loud voice, so that everyone might hear.

"Squire Robert is feeling a little poorly, you see," she said, leaning over the counter as if to whisper this news confidentially. "And I am charged with bringing him some remedies and such like—he said you, Mr. Samuel, would know the kind of thing that is needed for his condition." She stood up straight again and glanced around at the crowd in the shop, all eagerly listening. Bess kept her eyes cast down, avoiding contact, but she was listening too. Mary Cummings...and Squire Robert? How had this come about?

"He trusts only me to take care of him in his time of need," Mary was saying, with a grand, careless air. "Dear man, he is so worthy, and depends upon me so much, I swear, sometimes I don't know which way to look in his company."

Bess saw Mary's lips form a satisfied smile, as she pretended to a modesty she didn't possess. Mr. Samuel bowed slightly, said he would prepare the solutions immediately, and would the lady please wait a few moments?

The other ladies in the shop began to whisper among themselves, whilst Mary idled at the counter, picking up one thing after another, to await the apothecary's treatments. Bess wondered what they could be, and amused herself with thinking they were remedies for a bad head and stomach after too much drink, or possibly some bruising from having been roughed up at the Harvest Fair. But what had Mary to do with the Squire, that she was fetching and carrying for him, and attending to him in this manner?

The apothecary returned quickly with a small box, tied with string, and handed it to the waiting Mary.

"I shall put it to the Squire's account, Miss Cummings," he said. "His housekeeper understands how to mix the powders with milk and tea. Please do not hesitate to send for me, should his condition require my personal attention." Mr. Samuel was the closest thing to a doctor the village had, and was used to treating the ordinary complaints of the villagers.

"Oh!" said Mary, taking the box, her nose in the air. "Oh, I am all he needs in regard to *personal attention*," she said, with great emphasis on the last two words. She turned to sweep out of the shop, and came to an abrupt halt when she nearly bumped into Bess.

"Ah, I did not see thee there, Miss Bess," she said, giving Bess's clothes the once-over, with a cluck of disdain. "Buying muslin for a new apron, are we? Well, we wouldn't want that lovely day dress stained with persimmon jam, now would we?" She laughed, a high, strained sound, and looked around at the women in the shop. "Papa lets me order all the jam I need from London—no need for aprons and hot kitchens in our home."

Bess was so angry she almost slapped the insolent woman, but her better self told her to calm down and ignore the insults. She took a breath and was about to reply, when one of the other women in the shop, an older lady of means who was quite one of the principal women in the village, spoke out in a steely tone.

"Why, thou nasty piece of baggage!" she said, causing all the other women to look at her in surprise, and then satisfaction. "Our Bess here is a good, hard-working, respectable woman, and thou'rt no better than a common slag to say such things and think thyself so high and mighty, just because thou eat boughten preserves from a shop in London!" She rustled her silk shawl about her, and delivered her closing line. "Thou ought to be ashamed of thyself, useless, frivolous thing that thou art!"

Mary flushed bright red with shock and anger, her mouth open but unable to speak. Turning to Bess again, she muttered so only Bess could hear: "Thou mayest think thou'rt respectable, but thy lover is not. The Squire will see to him!" She then fled the shop in great haste, but not soon enough to avoid hearing the laughter and chatter that broke the tension as she ran out the door.

"Mrs. Damson," Bess said, turning to the lady who had defended her. "I do thank ye with all my heart, ma'am, but her words are as flies in the yard to me. They cannae hurt me."

The good lady patted Bess's arm and smiled. "Nonetheless, she needed taking down a peg or two," she said. "And I'm happy to be the one to do it. When you get to my age, dear, you have the luxury of saying just what you think!" She winked at Bess, and soon left with her maid to continue her shopping in the village.

Bess made her purchases swiftly, and was free to walk back to the Inn, and think with wonder about the possible connection between Mary Cummings and Squire Robert. Well, anything that turned the Squire's attention away from herself was a good thing, although how the Squire could be attracted to Mary—or for how long—was quite the puzzle.

But what really worried her was that bizarre statement Mary had hissed at her—what on earth could she mean, about Tremayne not being "respectable" such that the Squire would be dealing with him? Surely they could have no notion of him being the Highwayman! She hurried home, trouble creasing her brow.

TWENTY-THREE
SATURDAY 4 SEPTEMBER 1886

Russell House

THE SOUND OF VOICES RAISED IN JOYFUL GREETING reached my chamber as I sat musing over Mr. Hesford's note—the Barnards had arrived. Everyone in Russell House gathered from the far corners of garden and house to greet their friends. I had earlier heard both Lily and Lucia return from the upstairs nursery, and after a moment, I had swiftly run to Kitty's room and replaced the note in her reticule. Now I hastened down from my room upon hearing the clamour, and encountered Ned, leaving Kitty behind in the parlour, and the two of us reached it in due time to join the welcoming party—Lily and Kate already there, and Lucia and John who appeared together coming from the direction of the Tower house.

The Barnards had three children, a handsome young lad of fourteen or so, Geoffrey, who made a very fine appearance, although he said little. The girls, Polly and Dolly, were indeed bright and pretty, but I harbored an ill feeling toward them on little Kate's behalf, and soon satisfied myself they seemed rather smug and self-centered.

. . .

I saw Kate lingering on the edges of the group, so I sidled over to her and bent down to whisper in her ear whilst the others were busy chatting.

"Remember what I told you, dear Kate," I said. "They are not superior to you in any way, and you have a regal bearing about you, which they do not. We must be queenly and beneficent towards those who have not our intelligence and keen insight."

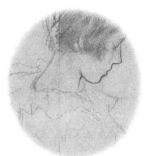

Her response was to take my hand in hers and hold it tightly, and stand up a little straighter. Just then the two Barnard girls ran over to where we were standing, and paid their addresses to Kate. One of them kissed her on both cheeks, and spoke very politely. I have no idea whether it was Polly or Dolly, they were so alike, fair-haired and slim little creatures; I never really ever discerned the difference between the two, although one *was* a bit taller and older than the other.

"Dear little Kate, it is so good to see you looking so well," said Polly (or Dolly). She glanced inquisitively at me. "Won't you introduce us to your friend?"

Kate did the honors very creditably, and both Barnard girls dropped quick curtsies as I nodded my head, regally, I presumed.

"We understand you are a famous writer, Miss Lee," said Dolly (or Polly). She beamed up at me, shyly. "I do so want to write stories myself, perhaps we might discuss writing and books some time, while you are visiting."

Softened by their good manners, and better treatment of Kate, I assented graciously. "Of course, I shall be delighted to discuss literature and the art of writing with you, perhaps over tea one day soon."

There was a whirlwind of activity as the sound of the luncheon bell gonged throughout the house—although I didn't know at the time that's what it was, I soon learned—and Lucia began shepherding everyone into the dining room where a much welcome feast was being delivered to the sideboard and the table. I was amazed to see by my little timepiece that it was a little after one o'clock. The informality of the proceedings at Russell House left me without introduction to Mr. and Mrs. Barnard, but I assumed it would happen eventually.

My attention was drawn once more to the front gate, where a small, sedate figure had appeared—Henry James had returned just in time for luncheon. Lucia smiled her welcome and immediately ran to him, took his arm in hers and led him into the house, calling out to the Barnards, who had gone on ahead, that "Henry" was here.

Kate held fast to my hand as we ambled after the others, and when we entered the dining room, she insisted on my sitting next to her; and, as Ned Abbey sat to my left, I was glad of her choice, as I had wanted to become more acquainted with him, and now had the opportunity to converse at leisure, as we were situated at one end of the table, and no one near enough to overhear our conversation.

But he surprised me by anticipating my first question. Looking around at the others, busily filling their plates, he practically whispered to me as he poured some wine in our glasses.

"I am not satisfied with Dr. White's findings, Violet," he said. "I think there's more going on here than meets the eye." He took a sip of his wine. "You see, Violet, I have been infected with the detecting bug, thanks to you and John." He smiled slightly as he said this to me, but his aspect was grim as he told me his suspicions. "I cannot believe that so lithe and able a young man as Michael Kelly could so easily slip on some rocks and fall so heavily as to incur a fatal blow to his head." He leaned back a little, toying with his wine glass. "And if he had tripped up while actually in the brook," he continued, "wouldn't he have just fallen there and drowned?"

I wasn't sure how to answer him at first, then merely said what I was thinking. "I wish I had been able to examine the area where you found his body," I said. "There was something strange to me at the time, when one of you mentioned that he was lying on the bank, with his arms stretched over his head."

"Exactly so!" Ned exclaimed, though keeping his voice low. "I thought the very same, as it really did not look to me as if he had been grasping at the bank in order to pull himself up—his hands, for instance, were not at all muddy or dirty with blades of grass, as if he had been pulling at the grasses or bushes."

● ● ●

I tilted my head to look at him thoughtfully. "Why did you not say this before? When the doctor was examining him? Or to the constable?" I reserved to myself my own estimation of constables, as I wanted to hear what Ned had to say.

He looked, if possible, even grimmer, and shook his head. "Dr. White is a very young man, but not keen," he said. "And the constable is notoriously anti-Irish, as you may have discerned, and would be more likely to dismiss my concerns than not."

I pondered all for a few moments, and realized that the two of us were the only ones at table who had not retrieved any food from the sideboard. Ned seemed to see this at the same time, so we both rose and walked over to collect some food, however much I felt we neither of us had an appetite for anything.

Plates full, and no one seeming to be paying any attention to us (except for little Kate, at whom I smiled warmly as she anxiously watched me until I returned to my seat), we continued talking in low voices.

"Did you notice anything else at the scene?" I asked, wondering if it were too late to go down to the brook myself to take a look. "Evidence of another person, perhaps?"

Ned shook his head. "It was dark, of course," he said, "and I suppose now, after all and sundry have been walking about down there, that it may be impossible to discern any one footprint from another."

I remembered Ned's prevarication about the assault on Alfred Parsons. "Why did you dissemble about Alfred being shoved?" I asked boldly. As I thought it would, my

Constable
M.

sudden change of subject caught him off guard. His round face grew pink, and he brushed back a lock of his rich brown hair from his brow.

"Oh!" he said, picking up his fork and shoving some potatoes around his plate. "I, well, you see, I thought ... actually, I thought it might just complicate things, and as Alfred isn't here to speak about it, and he was really quite all right, I simply didn't want Constable Poole thinking we were all imagining things." He smiled ruefully. "Last summer, we played a hide and seek game—adults and children both!—and it somehow spilled out onto the green from Farnham house, where we lived until this Spring—and we all ran screeching and jumping across the village, and the villagers, poor people, just rolled their eyes and said 'It's them Americans again' and went on their way." He took a sip of wine and shook his head. "The whole village thinks we're all crazy here as it is—this isn't going to help."

I nodded, mostly satisfied with his answer. I quite liked that word *crazy*—it seemed to fit this unusual group of people. Ned was looking at me intently.

"What do you think we ought to do, Violet?" he said simply. I was getting quite used to the American familiarity of using first names, and I felt pleased, silly me, at his deferential attitude. But I couldn't help fearing that his show of faith would be disappointed.

"I would like, despite all you say, Ned, to go down to the brook and see the place for myself," I said.

"I shall be happy to accompany you," he said, and made as if to rise immediately. I put my hand on his arm to hold him in place, and whispered, "Will not everyone

* * *

wonder what we are doing, leaving luncheon so precipitously?"

Ned looked down the length of the table at the chattering, laughing group, thoroughly engaged in conversation and eating. "Frankly, I don't think they'll even notice," he said. He leaned over to whisper in my ear. "I'll go first, then you join me in two minutes, at the back door." I nodded my approval, and turned to speak to Kate as Ned rose and drifted away.

"Dear girl," I said, "I've barely had a chance to chat with you, but I find I must absent myself for a short time."

She looked up at me, her eyes bright with interest. "Cannot I go with you and Mr. Ned, Miss Violet?" she said, folding up her napkin. She was clearly an astute listener.

"Oh, no, dear, this is something done best by grownups," I said. "I shall be back in a trice, and then perhaps after luncheon you would be so good as to show me more of your drawings? I've become a great admirer, you see, of all the artists at Russell House."

Kate looked at me solemnly, as if she weren't quite sure she could believe me, but I kissed the soft curls on the top of her head, and rising, made my way to the kitchen and the back door, where Ned was waiting for me. I felt a quickened sense of interest in the situation—and I also very much wanted to query Ned about whether he recognized the handwriting in the note found in Michael's pocket.

TWENTY-FOUR

4 OCTOBER 1726

At the Olde Swan Inn

"TIM! OY, TIM ME LAD, where're ye hidin'?" Georgie's voice echoed in the stable, quiet but for the occasional snorts and soft whinnying of the horses, restless in their stalls. It was nearing noon, when Tim was often taking a lunch break, sitting in front of the stables and resting. The ostler's mate poked his head here and there, then finally knocked politely at the closed door that led to Tim's small quarters in a corner of the barn.

"Are ye sleepin' then, Tim?" he called softly, and was startled when the door was jerked open suddenly, revealing a serious-faced Tim, but fully dressed and not at all looking sleepy.

"Cannae a man have a moment to hisself?" Tim groused, but Georgie took it good-naturedly, and stepped back as Tim indicated they should go into the barn. He had a small flat parcel in one hand, wrapped in brown paper.

"Wacher got there, Tim?" Georgie asked. "Love letter is it?"

"Never thou mind, mate," Tim said. He held the parcel close to his chest, and motioned that he was going out into the courtyard, where at that moment the county mail coach lumbered up to the inn. Tim held up his hand, showing the letter to the coachman, and handed it up to him as he slowed to a stop.

"That's all for ye today, then?" the coachman asked, taking the letter and frowning at it. "Where's that lovely lass who is alwas 'ere to favor me wi' a smile, then?"

"Ye mean Miss Bess, d'ye?" Georgie piped up.

The coachman shook his head. "Nae, not the wee lass, t'other, who alwas 'as a fresh bannock wi' a slice o'cheese or sommat for me, eh?"

"And here I am, ye greedy old thing," called Germaine from the doorway of the inn. She had a pouch of letters and parcels that various customers had consigned over to the innkeeper to post for them when the mail came next. She smiled at the coachman, though, and handed him a large apple scone wrapped in a cloth. "That'll have to do ye for today, too busy to be bakin' on behalf of a no good scoundrel like yerself," she said, chuckling as she did so.

The coachman tucked the scone away in one of his large pockets, stowed the bag of mail in a larger bag behind him, and realized he still had Tim's letter in his hand.

"Oxford?" he said, looking at Tim curiously.

"Never ye mind," Tim said roughly.

The coachman shrugged and put it with the rest of the mail. It was none of his business, after all. He clucked to the horses, slapped the reins lightly on their backs, and was off.

Georgie was importuning Germaine to part with another scone, as he was *near starvin' to death*, he told her. But Germaine just motioned him into the kitchen with a nod of her head; she had heard the destination of Tim's letter, and wondered at it, an uneasy feeling creeping into her heart. She'd have to keep an eye on that one—something was up.

Tim turned back to the stables, his heart thumping like a trapped bird. He tried to soothe his wayward feelings by thinking about the reward that would surely be his, in a fortnight or so. And it must be that he was doing Bess a favor, keeping her from further entanglement with a scoundrel and a criminal! He ignored Georgie's calling out to him as he walked away, or rather, he didn't really hear his friend, so caught up he was in his own unfortunate dreams.

* * *

On Stewart Street in Oxford the next morning, the mail was delivered as usual, and the housemaid brought it in to Edward Wells's study on a silver tray, curtsying as she left it on a corner of his large desk.

Mr. Wells, his wife and son were all fairly recovered from the scare they'd had on the Hill Road a few weeks back; certainly his arm was well healed, thanks to Bess's ministrations and care. His son still told the tale to his schoolmates, embellishing it with every telling, and his wife had settled down after about a week, and no longer talked about it.

But the indignity and mortification of the midnight assault still had a bitter taste in Edward Wells's mouth. He had, as he had sworn to do, brought the matter to his brother, the local magistrate, and his brother's indignation equalled his own. They were still talking about how best they might approach the authorities to get the response they desired—to have a cohort of King's men apprehend the rogue and have him summarily hanged in the public square.

His eyes lightened, therefore, when he saw the brown paper in his stack of mail, with the careful, childish writing showing it had come from *Tim Ostler, Olde Swan Inn, Broadway.* He'd had a feeling that young man would come through with information sooner or later.

He slit open the folded paper with a silver knife, and read with increasing interest and excitement. The contents made up for the lack of style and inconsistent spelling.

To Mister Wells, sir, I have such to tell you that will get justiss done. The hiwayman will come to the Olde Swan on the day after the full moon to see the innkeepers dotter. He can be taken then with ease. Do not forget the reward, good sir, and this help from yer humbel frend, Tim Ostler

Edward Wells read the note a second time, and folding it up again, tapped it against his desk with a growing sense of satisfaction. Excellent! He would go to his brother at once, and now they could easily persuade the local regiment's captain to lay a trap for this scoundrel.

TWENTY-FIVE

SATURDAY 4 SEPTEMBER 1886

Russell House

NED ABBEY AND I WALKED BRISKLY across the back garden, down the sloping lawn toward the brook. The sun was bright but the occasional cloud floated by to shield us from its intensity. There was a tennis court at a flat space

where the lawn ended, with gravel paths on either side of the court leading off into a riot of flowering bushes and fruit trees, heavy with the coming autumn harvest of apples and pears.

"Is this where John sets up to paint the Barnard girls?" I asked as we passed a little clearing among the trees, still at some height above the brook, which I could see flashing in the sunlight through a shifting curtain of leaves.

"Yes, yes indeed, this is the spot," Ned said. "We are in high hopes of setting up this afternoon at—" he consulted the sky and the position of the sun, and then his watch—"around half-past four—that's when John says the light is just perfect."

"So precise!" I said, though not really surprised. Artists are sticklers when it comes to light and shadow, and John was especially keen on getting the right effect.

A few more steps past the clearing, and Ned led the way down a rocky path to the very edge of the brook. It was at a low point and there were large, flat rocks, like a path across the water to the other side, one or two just barely below the surface, with others clearly above the water line.

"Those look to me like rather solid stepping stones," I said, pointing to the flat rocks that led to the far bank. I moved closer to the edge of the brook. "They don't look mossy or slippery, do you think?"

Ned came up beside me. "No, most of them are fairly clean, especially this time of year, with the water so low." We surveyed the brook a few moments. "Shall I attempt to cross and test them?" he asked. I nodded, and watched with held breath as he set off to ford the brook. A few minutes was all that was needed, as Ned reached the other side, turned and came back, all without mishap, and barely even wetting his shoes.

"I didn't feel a single rock shift beneath me," he said.

He then touched my elbow to turn me to a section of the bank that rose at a slight angle. The long grasses on it were smashed down into the dirt.

"This is where we found him," Ned said, grief rough in his voice.

There was a flat ledge of sorts above the incline of the bank where Michael's body had lain, and I carefully walked back up the path and over to that spot, where I leaned down and examined it closely.

"Did you or John or Mr. Cowan stand here, on this ledge?" I asked. Ned thought a moment and shook his head.

"No," he said decisively. "We were all down here, alongside the body, and at his feet. I don't believe any of us were up there at all." He looked up at me. "What do you see?"

"The grasses here are all crushed down," I said, trying to keep the excitement from my voice. "There are deep divots in the mud here, as if someone had dug in his heels."

"As if dragging Michael up the bank?" Ned jumped to this next thought quickly. He came round the path to stand beside me and observe what I pointed to him to see.

"That would explain why Michael's hands didn't show any signs of grasping onto the hillside, or grasses, or dirt," I said. "Someone pulled him up out of the water."

"And he wasn't completely wet, Violet," Ned said in an anguished tone. "Only his feet and ankles, from being in the water as he lay on the bank, so it's clear he didn't *fall* in the brook, or his clothes would have been all wet. Why didn't we see that before?"

We turned to each other, grim-faced, but I still speculated. "What we're seeing here *could* be proof of murder," I said. "But if someone was with him, perhaps Michael did fall after all, and the other person pulled him up out of the brook, but then ... perhaps, panicked and ran away?" It was deeply puzzling.

"But why panic?" Ned protested. "If it was just an accident, why not call for help? And who could just leave him there, for dead?"

I hesitated, but decided to keep back the information I had received from Mr. Hesford, about there being "two young men" at the brook last night—I wanted to talk to Mr. Hesford first, and find out what his sources were, before I sounded the alarm any further.

"Shall we call the constable back?" Ned asked uncertainly. I shook my head vigorously.

"He will be of no use if, as you say, he's prejudiced against the Irish as well as against yourselves, here at Russell House," I said. "He won't care." I put a hand on Ned's arm, reassuringly. "John and I, and you, Ned, need to investigate this more thoroughly, and when we have incontrovertible evidence, we can turn it over to the authorities."

He nodded his head, although he looked troubled.

"We will only speak of this to John," I said, and waited for him to agree.

"All right," he said at last.

* * *

We started to walk back to the house, and I took the opportunity of our relative solitude when we reached the tennis court to say what was on my mind.

"Ned, please tell me the truth," I said, stopping and looking straight in his pleasant face. "Did you recognize the handwriting—even though in Gaelic—on the note in Michael Kelly's pocket?"

Ned turned very red, his eyes wide, and looked away. He swallowed audibly, and took hold of the branch of an azalea bush nearby, twisting the leaves until they snapped off.

A sudden spark of intuition, and sympathy, gave me the answer.

"*You* wrote that note to Michael," I said very softly.

Ned nodded; I could see he was fearful of my judging him, but I had no notion of doing so. I pondered what to say next. "And *did* you meet, last night at the brook?" I finally said, deciding to just stick to the facts.

He shook his head vehemently, and turned to look at me, anguish and grief in his whole frame. "No! I...I wanted to, but I didn't...couldn't. If only I had, perhaps..."

He left his sentence unfinished, but of course I knew what he was thinking. I put my hand on his arm, not looking at him. "You are not responsible for Michael's death, Ned," I said quietly. "Please do not take on that grief, you have sorrow enough." He pressed my hand with his, and we spoke no more, but made our way back to the house. I walked slowly, to give Ned time to compose himself.

I felt convinced that he was telling me the truth. That explained one of the three notes that were now vexing my brain to make sense of. But the other two—both of them for Kitty, one in Gaelic, one in English.

Who were they from, and were they connected to the death of Michael Kelly?

TWENTY-SIX

5 OCTOBER 1726

At Oakehurst, Home of Squire Robert

MARY CUMMINGS HAD QUICKLY DETERMINED that the Squire was much easier to deal with, from her point of view, when he'd been drinking. His increasingly rare moments of sobriety made him withdraw from her, or worse, question her presence in his study, or dining room, or drawing room, wherever they happened to be when he

"woke up." But when he was drunk, he paid her such lavish and lascivious attention that it wasn't long before she began to plan how to secure her future—as the Squire's new wife.

She was making a second visit to Oakehurst, the Squire's estate, with more of the apothecary's treatment for his "condition," as Robert had not been improving much. She stood at the kitchen door talking to the housekeeper, Mrs. Reynolds, an older woman who seemed to have taken a fancy to her. The housekeeper was a spare woman, with greying hair tightly bound in a bun at the back of her neck, and her dress was severely cut, quite black, with the only ornament being a small cameo at her throat. It was hard to tell, as the profile on it was very small, whether it was of a man or a woman. The housekeeper was resting after luncheon before resuming her duties, and took a moment to chat with Mary.

"The Squire's in sore need of a woman taking care of him," said Mrs. Reynolds, sighing a little. "I do what I can, of course, but it's not the same thing, is it?"

"I'm sure you've done everything in your power, Mrs. Reynolds, and a great help to him you are indeed," Mary said. She was canny enough to know that being on the housekeeper's good side was worth her weight in gold.

"Here's what Mr. Samuel gave me for Squire Robert," she said, handing the box to Mrs. Reynolds. "I'm sure you know much better than I how to mix it or set it up for him, so it's done properly?"

Mrs. Reynolds acquiesced with a gratified smile, and invited Mary in for a cup of tea and a chat while she made up the potion for her master.

Which is exactly what Mary wanted her to do.

* * *

"Who is that? Who's there?" The Squire's gravelly voice came from somewhere in a pile of bedclothes heaped upon the canopied, four-posted bed in his chamber. October had brought with it the beginnings of the north wind, calling for greater warmth at night as well as the late afternoons, and a fire was burning brightly in the grate across from his bed. The door opening, and the housemaid arriving with a tea tray, accompanied by Mary a step or two behind, had awakened him from his uneasy slumbering.

"It's jest me, Susan, yer honor," said the maid, speaking softly. "Mrs. Reynolds says as how the 'pothecary has put a potion together for you, and ye're to drink it, and there is tea here for ye as well, sir." The girl set the tray on a small table near the window, not far from the bed, and proceeded to open the curtains, letting in some late western sunlight.

"Good God, child, don't open those!" Robert cried, partially throwing back some of the covers and attempting to sit up. "My head hurts something awful." He buried his face in his hands and rubbed his eyes. This was no mere hangover, he was thinking—he felt there was something more, something wrong happening to him this time. Or maybe he was just getting old.

"Here, then, dear Squire, try this," Mary spoke in the most soothing voice she could muster, and drew near, holding out a warm, lavender-scented cloth. Robert looked up slowly, then looked away, closing his eyes and lying down again.

"Oh, it's you again, is it?" he said. Nonetheless, he let her come closer, and only sighed when she carefully laid the warm cloth on his forehead and over his eyes.

"Thank you," he said after a moment, although it was grudging. "That feels good."

Mary held her tongue. She was beginning to learn how to manage this changeable man. She moved quietly to the table and took up the cup with the apothecary's remedy in it, along with a cup of warm water to swallow afterwards.

"Here you are, here's what will make it all better," she said. She hadn't yet called him by his Christian name, but she could sense it would happen soon.

"Aye," he said, and lifted himself into a sitting position again. He took the potion, drank it, made a face, then accepted the cup of warm water and drank that. Whatever was in it—and he wasn't at all sure he knew—it began its work almost immediately, and he felt a new warmth flow through his body. Now he would be himself again, soon.

"Do you think you could eat something?" Mary asked. "Mrs. Reynolds has sent up all your favorite things— poached egg and toast, peach marmalade, that nice strong China tea you like?" Her soft, wheedling tone suited his weariness and temper, and he nodded, feeling a bit like a sick child—and somehow, not minding it. Mary, watching him like a hawk, turned as if to leave the room.

"Will you not sit by while I eat?" he asked suddenly. "I've been abed too long, and know nothing of what's going on in the house or the village," he added. "Perhaps you have a bit of cheery gossip to wake up my poor head?"

Mary's smile, if he could have seen it, was triumphant, but she composed herself as she turned around and seated herself at a chair near—but not too near—his bed. Susan was still in the room, and after placing the bed tray across the Squire's lap, curtsied to both of them and left the chamber, closing the door as she did so.

● ● ●

172

Robert found he had an appetite after all, and began eating the eggs and toast with renewed appreciation.

"So, then, Mary," he said. "Tell me what's new in the village."

Mary relayed such news as she had, and added some well-timed information about the state of his own house, which she had garnered during her talk with Mrs. Reynolds, about a lame carriage horse, and a visit from a neighbouring magistrate, who had left his card and a brief message about wanting to speak to him regarding some local land rights he was dealing with.

"Well," Robert said, drinking the last of his tea. "You've got quite the administrative head, don't you? I'm very impressed." He leaned back on his pillows, feeling better than he had in a long time. He looked with a new interest at the pretty blonde woman who was tending to him. "And what do you think this magistrate's message— rather cryptic—was all about? Can you enlighten me?" He'd said it jokingly, but Mary was prepared to take him seriously. This was the chance she had been hoping for, and although she felt it might be risking a change for the worse in Robert's mood, it was too opportune to pass by.

"Well," she said, smoothing a non-existent wrinkly in her skirt, "and I say this because it is what some villagers have been saying, it seems possible he means that Irish scoundrel Colm Tremayne, whose property, it is rumored, is not at all what he has been saying it is—that the farm is not his freehold, and he has been claiming rights that are not his—fooling us all with his charming ways and orchard fruits he is selling as a fraud!" Her voice rose slightly with mild indignation as she spoke, and she

• • •

observed the Squire closely as he listened. His looks darkened, and his lips thinned. She knew that everything she was saying was a lie—no one was talking about it or anything like it—but she comforted herself by saying it *could or could not* be true—who was she to say?

She hastened to add, "I don't know the truth of it, and I daresay, it might all be nothing."

"But that sort of rumor doesn't get started from nothing," said Robert. He started to throw back the covers, then suddenly seemed to realize that he and Mary were alone in his bedchamber. She perceived his consternation straightaway, and immediately rose, taking the breakfast tray from his bed. She swept away to the door, calling back over her shoulder, "I'll just take this all away, Robert. Mrs. Reynolds will be so pleased to see that you had an appetite for all the good things she had sent up for you." She paused for a moment, then said, "Perhaps I may call again to see how you are doing?" She looked (she hoped) very fetching in her good blue gown that matched her eyes and made her golden curls shine.

Robert nodded curtly, then said, "Actually, I'd prefer it if you could stay a bit, and I'll come down to you, in the small drawing room, when I'm presentable." He said it more as a command than a request, but Mary rejoiced to hear the words.

"Of course, Robert, if that is what you wish," she said, and quietly left the room before he could speak again.

TWENTY-SEVEN
SATURDAY 4 SEPTEMBER 1886

Russell House

CONTRARY TO NED'S CAVALIER SURMISE, we *were* missed at the luncheon table, and upon our arrival back at the house, were accosted with much outcry and curiosity.

Lily Millet was the most direct, audaciously so. "Well," she said coolly, "I never expected this particular pairing-off, the two of you, of all people."

I was a bit taken aback, but Ned, perhaps used to Lily's ways, answered cheerily, if not much to the point. "Oh, my, yes, Violet here was insistent on being shown where our resident ghost often turns up, don't you know? She's that interested in writing up some ghost stories, she says."

This statement was greeted with exclamations of surprise and interest—and I tried very hard not to look completely surprised myself.

"Oh, that would be too delicious," cried Lucia, "I love a good ghost story, don't you, Henry?"

This appeal to Henry James, spoken with some gaiety, produced only a solemn look on the writer's face, following which he touched his napkin to his lips, and appeared to be about to respond. However, that process took entirely too long (apparently) for Lily, who jumped in again with an expression of disapproval. "Let us not talk of such things at the luncheon table," she said. "Not at all suitable before the children."

The Barnard girls and their parents protested mightily and noisily that ghost stories were their favorite fireside entertainment, and amidst all the resulting chatter, whatever Mr. James was going to say was lost under their more strident voices.

I had seated myself again next to little Kate, who now looked up at me and said in all seriousness, "I have seen the Russell House ghost, Miss Violet."

"Have you indeed?" I said, looking closely at the little girl's intent face. "I would like very much to hear about it." I glanced at her mother at the other end of the table. "But perhaps we should wait for a more appropriate time to discuss it, is that acceptable?"

She nodded, and turned back to finishing her pudding.

We had arrived at the very end of luncheon, and the women were busy helping the housemaid remove plates and setting the table back to rights. They all seemed to know so very competently what they were doing that I hesitated to insert myself into the process, imagining I would only be in the way. Just then John called my name and motioned for me to join him and the other gentlemen at the head of the table.

"Vi, I want to introduce you to Mr. Frederick Barnard," he said, moving an empty chair forward to the table for me to sit upon. I nodded at the man, noting his full mustache with upturned tips and his head covered in a riot of unruly dark curls, and said sincerely, "I am absolutely delighted to meet the artist who has given visual

life to the wonderful characters of
Charles Dickens! I am quite an
admirer of your illustrations, sir."

"Thank you, thank you," he
said, beaming pleasantly. He
caught at the arm of a lovely
woman who was just passing
behind him, collecting dishes
from the sideboard. "Here,
Alice, come meet Miss Vernon
Lee." Alice Faraday Barnard was a
subject worthy of the best of John's
art—in fact, he was working on a portrait of her, as I was
to find out later—with thick auburn hair, flawless
pearlescent skin and a long, swan-like neck.
She looked regal, but was as frank and
friendly as could be.

"Miss Lee! I have been entranced
by your works, and I must say, your
Miss Brown as well, I've just been
reading it! I do hope we will have an
opportunity to discuss it at some
length, as I have many questions."
Her smile was warm and brilliant,
and I was immediately taken by her.

"As you like, Mrs. Barnard," I
said. "You may be one of the few
persons who wish to discuss that book, but
I am happy to oblige you."

"Oh, please call me Alice, and," she said airily, "I've
heard all that nonsense from those thin-skinned people,

heavens, are they bereft of common-sense, to be so ticklish about such things?" And with that she freed herself from her husband's fond grasp and continued on her way to the kitchen.

While I was talking with the Barnards, Ned had obliged John to stand up so he could talk with him with some privacy; I was sure I knew what he had to say, especially as after a few moments, John touched my shoulder to get my attention, and addressed Mr. Barnard.

"Fred, I find I must take Violet away for a bit, I hope you don't mind," he said, with the ease and familiarity of long acquaintance.

"Not at all, not at all," said Mr. Barnard (he had an odd way of saying many things twice). "I've been commanded by my wife to see to the girls taking their naps before the painting begins today, so must be off now." He looked around the table happily. "Must be off!"

"Very good!" John said. "They will be fresh and ready to pose!" He consulted his watch. "Say four o'clock? It may take a bit to get started with this lot."

With a friendly nod, Mr. Barnard then departed, along with Polly and Dolly, who, contrary to their mother's directions, were clinging to their father and begging to be taken into the village for ice cream. Their brother Geoffrey, with a half bow to the company, strolled silently behind them.

I began to rise from my seat when I noticed that Henry James was still seated at the table not far from me— observing everything and everyone in his usual quiet way; those grey eyes of his missed nothing.

* * *

"Mr. James," I said, sitting back down for a moment, and leaning toward him. "Did you find the room to your liking, at the Lygon Arms?"

He gave a half-smile and nodded. "Most comfortable, Miss Lee, thank you. Your Mr. Hesford was excessively attentive, and very kind."

"Oh, he's not my Mr. Hesford," I disclaimed, "but I am glad to hear you were well-treated."

Mr. James looked at me a moment. "You have made a conquest there, Miss Lee, whether you will or no. I believe the good man would consult the devil if you asked him to."

With that, he rose slowly, bowed, and ambled out of the room. I felt no little astonishment at his statement, and wondered what the doorman had said or done to give such an impression. But that reminded me of my desire to speak with Mr. Hesford about his note, and I turned back to John and Ned to see what was next to be done. Ned was saying something about Kitty.

"... should check to see that she's holding up, and whether her letter to Michael's family is done and ready to be posted." He shook his head. "So many sad details."

"If you speak with her, Ned," I said, though glancing at John, "perhaps you could try to find out more about why she was looking for a person—and perhaps a message— last night, while we were all gathered in the parlour."

Ned, rightfully so, was puzzled, so I hastened to explain. "The scrap of paper found in Michael's pocket wasn't the only one with Gaelic writing on it, although in a different hand," I said. I wanted to make it clear to him that I believed the note to Kitty was from someone other

* * *

than himself, and the relieved look on his face told me he understood I would keep silent about his note to Michael. I continued. "When we went to look in the garden last night, I found a slip of paper inside the birdhouse on the tree near the window." I paused. "It said, translated, *Hay. Midnight.*"

Ned's eyes widened, and he clutched at John's arm. "The hayloft! John, do you think that has something to do with the pitchfork holes in your painting?"

John shrugged. "There's no telling exactly when that happened, but we have determined that it was fairly recent. It *could* have been last night."

"Shall we go up and take a look in the hayloft now?" I said. "Perhaps there may be *something...?*"

The two men nodded, and John led the way to the former barn, now converted to a comfortable artist's studio. It was connected to the main house by a short passageway, with windows that looked out to the gardens. In the studio, the old stone floor had been covered with warm wooden boards, and a fireplace was newly building in the center wall of the long room.

As I entered the studio, I was seized with a sudden feeling, as of fear and dread. A whirl of voices filled my head, rough sounds as of soldiers shouting orders, horses neighing and hooves pounding. I stood aghast for a moment, one hand on the wall to support myself, and surrounded by noise, then it slowly faded away. Coming back to my senses, I realized that neither John nor Ned had noticed any-thing amiss, either in me or in the atmosphere—they were busy mounting the sturdy ladder that led to the hayloft. I was back in the present moment and though a little dazed, shook off the hallucination as a lack of proper nourishment, as I had barely touched my luncheon. I promised myself I would eat well at tea this afternoon.

I declined to mount the ladder, being encumbered by my skirts, but trusted John and Ned to search thoroughly; Ned had already proved to be an able detective, down at the brook, and I knew John's keen eyes missed little.

In the event, there was nothing unusual to be found. Disappointed, we gathered on the ground floor again and considered what to do.

"There is something I must ask Mr. Hesford at the Lygon Arms," I said, and when both men pressed me for more, I shook my head. "I will tell you all once I've spoken with him. Ned, you are going to see to Kitty?"

He nodded, and we started to walk back through the door and hallway that led to the house.

"What will you do, John?" I asked.

"I have promised Henry that I will escort him over to Abbots Grange, where we can get him settled in his favorite room—he generally writes for a few hours in the mornings, and he would like to prepare himself for tomorrow." John glanced out the window; Mr. James was walking sedately around the near garden. "There he is now, awaiting me." He consulted his watch. "It is now nearing half past two o'clock, shall we meet back here in forty-five minutes or an hour, and hear what we have found?" He grimaced, then smiled more cheerfully. "After that, I believe the plan is to set up the garden painting and start all that up again."

* * *

We agreed it was a good plan, and I turned to the stairway to get my reticule from my room before setting off for the Lygon Arms.

Where I was going to get the shock of my life.

TWENTY-EIGHT

7 OCTOBER 1726

At the Olde Swan Inn

RICHARD WAS STARTLED BY THE SOUND of a hard-driven horse pounding the cobblestones of the inn's courtyard. It was mid-afternoon and the tavern was nearly empty, awaiting the evening drinkers, mostly locals from the village now, with winter coming on and fewer travellers on the London Road. He stepped from the bar to the front windows and saw it was Squire Robert, just alighting from his high-fed horse. Tim was holding on to the reins, soothing the nervous animal to a calm. Richard heard the Squire's harsh command to "Tend to the beast—I won't be long" and prepared himself for something unpleasant—he could feel the dread growing in his bones.

The Squire filled the doorway as he paused before entering the tavern; his big frame loomed like a dark shadow, and his eyes were fierce above the black beard. With an innkeeper's practiced eye, Richard could see that the Squire was in his cups, even at this time of day, and all the more belligerent for it. The innkeeper turned from the window and was once again behind the bar; he felt it a needed barrier at the moment.

Robert scanned the room, nodded in seeming satisfaction at its emptiness, and strode forward to the bar.

Richard, though inwardly cautious, was his own man, and used to dealing with rough sorts—which is what the Squire ultimately appeared to him to be.

"Squire," he said, nodding his head in a half-salute. "Ridin' hard ye are," he continued easily, glancing at the shivering horse in the courtyard, being tended by Tim. "What is it now I can do for ye?"

Robert laughed, a short bark of a sound. "It's more what I can do for you, innkeeper," he said. He took off his riding gloves and tossed them on a nearby table. His glance took in the bottles and kegs lined up behind the bar. "But I wouldn't say no to a dram of that Irish whisky," he said, taking a seat at the table, but with his eyes trained on Richard. "And come to that, pour one for yourself, it's on me," he added, with a sour smile. "You may be needing it."

Richard complied with his requests, noting that the drink addled the Squire's head enough that he was addressing Richard as an equal. He poured out two neat whiskies in small glasses; he carried them to the table and at a gesture from the Squire, he sat down with him.

"To the stinkin' Irish," Robert said, raising his glass. He drank it down, burped and said, "At least the thieving devils make a good whisky."

Richard paused, his arm half-raised, then he lowered the glass. "I'll not drink to such an insult," he said. "My Mary, God bless her soul, was Irish." He challenged the Squire with fierce eyes.

Robert wasn't so drunk that he needed to fight, so after a moment's pause, he merely shrugged, reached over and took up the innkeeper's glass himself, downing it in a gulp.

"You may be more inclined to drink to the insult after you've heard what I have come to tell you," the Squire said.

Richard stood up and stepped away. "Then say what ye have to say and get on with it."

"It's about that no good Irish farmer who's taken up with your Bess," the Squire said, looking square at the innkeeper. "Turns out he's not the man she thinks he is."

Richard felt a stab of fear, but stood his ground. "And what might he be then? Don't dance around, man." In his fear and growing anger, he was in danger of forgetting the respect due to the Squire, but it seemed Robert didn't notice.

"I've made inquiries in the next county," Robert said. "And this morning I went there myself, to *his farm*." He paused, but Richard waited for him to speak again.

"Sure, and there's a farm all right, but not such a one as he says he owns free and clear," he said.

"But Tremayne regularly comes to market, with produce to sell," Richard protested.

Robert smiled smugly. "He's just a hired hand on that farm," he said. He leaned forward across the table, looking up at Richard. "I talked to the owner myself—he says he sends Tremayne to market as himself is too old for it anymore." He sat back, satisfied that the bolt had struck fair, given the look on the innkeeper's face. "And the old man tells me how he hasn't seen Tremayne for near a week now—and there's a little matter of some missing money." That this was *almost* true was enough for the

Squire; he saw no need to add that the "old man" had told him he looked upon Tremayne as an only son, and heir to the farm and all its holdings at the old man's death.

Richard was tongue-tied, thinking of the implications for his beloved daughter, and just stood staring at the other man. Finally he found words to say. "And what is it ye're saying to me? What does this mean to my Bess?"

The Squire laughed again. "Just that Tremayne's a fraud, and a trickster! And knowing we'd be on to him sooner or later, he's gone off, hasn't he? All that pretty talking, no doubt, to your poor Bess, just playing with her heart, and now he's taken himself off, and left her without a word of fare thee well."

As the innkeeper continued standing in a dumbfounded way, the Squire rose to depart.

"But I wouldn't put it past the scoundrel," Robert said, "to try his luck with your Bess still, bring her round to his side, so as to marry her and do you right out of this inn and all that belongs to you." He picked up his gloves from the table and turned to go. "If she were a daughter of mine, I'd keep her under lock and key for a time, to be sure."

At the door, he turned once again to deliver a final statement. "If Tremayne steps foot in Broadway, I'll see to it personally that he's arrested and arraigned for fraud and thievery." He paused fractionally. "And anyone else that might be inclined to help him or warn him off in any way."

He left quickly then, feeling a slight sting of his conscience that intimated he was doing Bess a great wrong. But the drink buzzing his grievance in him—and

Mary Cumming's persuasive voice—had a stronger presence in his head, and quieted his uneasy feelings.

TWENTY-NINE

SATURDAY 4 SEPTEMBER 1886

The Lygon Arms and Broadway High Street

I FELT THE NEED FOR A BRISK WALK up the High Street, so decided to venture past the Lygon Arms, and go as far as the Horse and Hounds, a quarter-mile or so further. I told myself my mission was probably foolish, but I couldn't get out of my head what Mr. Hesford had told me about the "Irish party" that was lodged at the old coaching inn, and thought that perhaps a glimpse of the travellers might reveal *something* to me that could be useful.

Call it intuition, if you will, or some nascent glimmering of connection behind a seeming coincidence. I had learned to trust my inner voice, and this was too serious a case to ignore it now.

Mr. Hesford was not at the door of the Lygon Arms, so I slipped by without being tempted to draw him into conversation immediately, and continued on my way up the High Street. The mid-afternoon sun was warm, but the clouds were increasing and helped to cool the air. The morning market crowds had dispersed, and a quiet somnolence pervaded the village, as if everyone were taking a post-prandial nap. I almost felt like one myself! As I neared the Horse and Hounds, I saw the Royal Mail coach coming to a halt before its doors. The arrival of the mail caused quite a stir—the innkeeper himself came to the door, as well as several people who, from the looks of them, were staying at the inn.

Suddenly I saw someone in the little crowd whom I recognized—good God, it was Michael Kelly!

The same curling black hair and slender figure, the same height and youthfulness, only rather better dressed than when I had seen him last. He called out to the coachman, and I clearly heard his Irish accent. But this voice was deeper, more commanding, than I remembered from dinner last night.

Just then he turned toward me—we were some twelve feet or so apart—and looking straight at me, he gave a polite nod, and continued looking past me as if in search of someone else. I could see then that I had been mistaken— this man was not Michael Kelly; his eyes were a warm brown, where Michael's had been sky blue. But the similarity was striking. The coachman hailed the young man, calling out a name he read from a package—Thomas St. George McCarthy.

I remembered the name immediately. Mr. Hesford had told me that the Irish party consisted of the famous rugby player McCarthy and his crew—and also I instantly saw before my eyes the hand-written note to Kitty, referencing the exhibition match and signed *McC.*

My mind ran rapidly over the possibilities: McCarthy and Michael Kelly looked almost like twins; Mr. Hesford's note said *there were two young men at the brook last night*. Could this be a case of mistaken identity? Had McCarthy come to leave a note for Kitty, and for some reason had gone down to the brook where Michael met his fate? And if so, was McCarthy the real target or was Michael? And why?

Or was McCarthy the killer?

I turned away abruptly and sped back to the Lygon Arms. This time Mr. Hesford was stationed at the front door, calmly surveying his village, and I accosted him with a gasping sort of entreaty.

"Oh, Mr. Hesford," I said. "I must speak with you, please, it is urgent business." I'm afraid I alarmed the good man, who immediately drew me to a small table and chairs that stood on the flagstone in front of the inn, some way from the door.

"Miss Lee, I fear you have fatigued yourself, please be seated," he said, and I sat down, out of breath. "Shall I get you a glass of water?" He stood patiently while I composed myself.

"No, no I thank you," I said at last. I looked up at him, frowning. "Do you have a moment, Mr. Hesford," I said, "to explain that extraordinary note you sent to me this morning along with my valise?"

He stepped a little closer, and bent from his tall height to speak to me in a low voice.

"I must be quick, but my facts are few. We have a young person, here, who runs errands and such—in fact, the boy who brought your valise to Russell House. After I heard of the unfortunate event discovered there this morning"—and here again I marvelled at the scope of Mr. Hesford's information—"I noticed our Sam looking queer, so I asked him a few questions. The long and short of it, Miss Lee," said the stately doorman, "is that Sam was out

• • •
191

larking about the orchards in the night, and happened to see two men at the brook below Russell House. By fading moonlight, he only saw they were of a height and shape together, both with curling hair."

Mr. Hesford fell silent as I pondered this information.

"Sam didn't say if he had heard them talking, or saw anything unusual?" I stood up now, having recovered my breath, and to allow Mr. Hesford to straighten up from leaning over me.

He shook his head. "I asked him in several ways, but he said although he knew they were speaking, it was not anything he understood, and their voices were low. But it seemed it was a friendly conversation, at least, there did not seem to be any kind of altercation or harsh words between the two. He did say," Mr. Hesford added after a moment, "that he saw one man walk away, leaving the other standing by the brook. Then he ran off himself, so as not to be discovered."

I gazed out onto the High Street, in the direction of the Horse and Hounds, my mind working rapidly.

"Thank you, Mr. Hesford," I said, turning back to him. "As always, you are invaluable."

"You are welcome, Miss Lee," he said, then added, "If it is not impertinent, miss, may I ask what you may intend to do with this information?"

I caught a certain innuendo in his query, and wondered at its meaning. "If you mean," I said cautiously, "am I going to take this information to the esteemed constable Mr. Poole?" I smiled faintly—the slight increased wrinkle in his brow told me I was correct. "I have no thought whatsoever of bringing this to his

* * *

attention, Mr. Hesford. Quite the contrary, in fact. Mr. Poole did not strike me as, shall we say, a friend to the Irish?"

"Thank you, miss," he said, looking relieved. "You have hit upon the very thing. I shall leave it in your capable hands." He bowed and returned quickly to his station at the door, leaving me to turn away to go back to the High Street.

What to do? I consulted my timepiece and saw I was to be back at Russell House in less than half an hour to meet with John and Ned to compare notes. My first thought was to get back to the Horse and Hounds and interrogate the athletic Mr. McCarthy. But what excuse or ploy could I come up with to introduce myself? I could hardly just approach him and start asking rude personal questions, or blurt out *what a shame it was that Michael Kelly was dead* and see how he reacted. Given what the errand boy had related to Mr. Hesford, it would *appear* that McCarthy and Michael had been friends, but that would require further evidence.

Henrietta Stackpole! That's it! I nearly laughed out loud. I could easily imitate Henry James's inimitable American lady journalist from his most famous novel *Portrait of a Lady.* I could be a reporter for some women's magazine—such as *The Ladies' Companion*, which is the first one that came to mind, perhaps because I'd seen it lying on a table in Lily Millet's parlour.

I darted into a stationery and dry goods store that was happily to hand, and purchased a good-sized notebook of blank paper, and two pencils, which the clerk obligingly sharpened for me. Once more outside, I drew a deep breath and set out for the inn and the Irish party of rugby players.

I began formulating an introduction as I strode purposefully up the High Street, and stopped once or twice to write down innocuous questions that might put him off his guard and give credibility to my pose.

But all of my efforts were to be in vain. As I drew near the coaching inn, I could see Mr. McCarthy standing outside in earnest conversation with another man. They were situated a little to the side of the inn, in an open corridor that led to a sort of garden courtyard in the rear, and were absorbed in serious talk. I halted in my tracks and turned away before I could be seen by either of them.

McCarthy was talking to David Cowan—there was no possible way for me now to approach the athlete as a ladies' magazine reporter. And definitely no way for me to determine if McCarthy had already been aware of Michael's death, for surely David Cowan would be telling him of it.

As I began to walk back to Russell House, I set my mind to thinking how to have a discreet chat with Mr. Cowan and try to find out what his connection with Mr. McCarthy was, and what part Michael Kelly played in it.

THIRTY

7 OCTOBER 1726

At the Olde Swan Inn

"IT'S ALL LIES, DA, CANST THOU NOT SEE THAT?" Bess trembled with anger as she strode back and forth in the tavern. Her father sat at the table where the Squire had sat an hour before. Richard's head hurt from thinking what he should do, and when Bess had appeared at the door, he started talking and it all spilled out.

"Why would the Squire lie about such a thing?" he said. "He said as he'd been there, to that farm his own self, and talked to the real owner." He looked at her helplessly; it wrung his heart to bring her such distress.

"No matter, there's a great trickery going on here," Bess said firmly. She paused in her restless walking to and fro, and stood in front of her father, a fierce light in her black eyes. "It's that Mary Cummings, nasty cow, she's got her hooks somehow into the Squire, and she's feedin' him lies about my Colm."

Richard was completely bewildered. "What has Mary Cummings to do with anything?"

Bess waved an impatient hand. "Ach, it's too long a tale to go into, Da, but thou must trust me, I see what I see, and I know what I know." She softened a bit as she regarded her father, confused and sorrowful as he was. "What else did the Squire say, Da?"

Richard cleared his throat, buying a little time. He hadn't told her everything; she'd exploded with anger at the first mention that Tremayne was a fraud about the farm.

"He said that it seems Tremayne has gone off, been gone near a week, and no word of him," Richard said reluctantly. He ventured a glance at his daughter, but her face was calm, as if this fact did not trouble her. But that suggested to him that she knew a good deal more about Tremayne's whereabouts than she was saying.

"What else?" she said.

"He...he said as how Tremayne is only makin' up to thee so as to take over the inn when I'm dead and gone." He waited, holding his breath, for the storm that was his fiery daughter to break upon his head, but when he looked up again, she had a smile on her face.

"And what would be so wrong in that, if it were true?" she said. "Not that he doesn't love me, because he does," she added quickly, "but who else would take on the inn but me and a husband of mine, I ask thee?"

Richard felt better on hearing this confidence in Bess, but his mood darkened as he thought of the last thing he had to tell her.

"Squire said as he'll have Tremayne arrested and tried for fraud and thievery if he catches him in Broadway ever again," he said.

She drew in breath sharply. "Then I must go to him, and tell him to beware," she said.

"You'll do no such thing!" Richard stood up, facing her. "The Squire was very clear that he considers this man a criminal, and anyone who helps him or gets in the way of the law will pay dearly."

"But he must be warned," Bess insisted.

"And not by thee," her father rejoined. "Dost thou want to see thy old Da in gaol then? For surely they'd take me and not put a lass behind bars," he said in a softened tone.

"Oh, Da, could he even do such a thing? To one who's not done wrong?" Bess said, her eyes blazing, angry and fearful.

"Aye, lass, he's a powerful man, and the magistrate of the county," he said, shaking his head. "He's got a mean streak in him, especially when the drink is telling him what to do."

"And Mary Cummings too," Bess muttered under her breath.

"Wilt thou gi'me thy word, my Bess, not to see him any more, not to try to get to him?" Richard waited, holding his breath, while he searched his daughter's eyes. What he saw did not comfort him.

"I cannae do it, Da," she said. "I cannae let him be taken, even if it means I'll ne'er see him again." She caught back a sob as she said this, and fled the room in tears.

* * *

Bess had gone up to her room, and stood at the windows overlooking the London road as it rose and fell over the hills. Her heart beat fast, and she pondered what to do. Her first thought was to go herself, with a note prepared, to St. Eadburgha's, and leave it under the stone at the old grave. But she knew her father was watching her, and she didn't want to grieve him by running off with no good excuse, leaving him to think she was going to bring down the Squire's wrath on all their heads.

Perhaps she could send Sam? She immediately dismissed the thought, as Sam would of course say something to Tim, and Tim would no doubt tell her father. They all thought she needed looking after!

She settled on Germaine, who was her friend, fearless, and a woman who wouldn't give her away. She sat down to compose the note and write it out. After some thought, she hit upon a way to give Tremayne as brief and opaque a message as possible, and she wrote it with her left hand, awkwardly, hoping no one would ever guess it came from her, or even know what it meant, were it somehow to be carried off by the wrong person.

Jesus rose from his tomb in three days, at break of dawn.

He's a smart man, she thought to herself. *He'll work it out.* She threw a little sand on the paper, blotted it carefully, then folded up the note, dripping a bit of candle wax on it to hold it closed. Then she went in search of Germaine.

THIRTY-ONE

SATURDAY 4 SEPTEMBER 1886

Back to Russell House

IT WAS NEARING HALF PAST THREE as I turned in at the gate to Russell House. I had walked rather slowly, ruminating on all the varieties of clues, half-clues and the utter lack of clues about the strange events of the past two days. Thinking of the original "murder"—the death of the blue bird—effected an altered assessment of that vexing incident in light of the much more serious and tragic loss of the young Irishman's life at the brook. But were they connected or not? And who was behind the shove that sent Alfred Parsons down the ice house steps? The pitchfork holes in John's canvas in the hayloft? I shook my head in confusion—those relatively minor incidents could mean something, or nothing.

Lurking in the back of my mind was the strangely interesting *fortune* that Michael Kelly had seen in the cards last evening. *The Knight of Swords* and the *Queen of Hearts* something bedeviled my brain about whom they might represent, but it was just out of reach.

The courtyard of Russell House was quiet and empty. Reluctant to go into the house just yet, I wandered down the garden path, past the tennis court, and followed a beaten trail under the orchard trees that John had told me led to Abbots Grange. At a break in the trees, I had a clear view of the former near-ruin of the 14th century building that Frank Millet had recently leased and set about restoring, mainly as studio space for the many artists and writers who came to visit. It was large and imposing, built of the glowing golden Cotswold stone, with many roofs and rock walls up and down the property.

I stood in the shade of a large apple tree, the light flickering through the leaves a bit dazzling to my eyes, and drew a deep breath of the flower-scented air. The hum of bees surrounded me, and bird song pierced the drowsy silence. I felt like a wanderer in a fairy story, and silently laughed to think I might come upon a witch offering me an apple or a magic dwarf at a spinning wheel.

What I did see was more alarming than either of those legendary apparitions.

I had leant against the solid tree trunk, feeling the need for a bit of support and rest, and my eyes had begun to close, when a circling wave of cold air wafted around me. The sun had slipped behind some ominously dark clouds, and the dim shade of the apple tree deepened to a dusk-like obscurity. My eyes flew open, and I swear I was completely alert and awake—before me stood a wraith, the figure of a woman with long dark hair, wearing a pale dress with what looked like blood flowing down the front of it. Her lips moved in speech I could not at first hear, and she held out one hand appealing to me, her face kind and grief-stricken.

I leaned forward to hear her words—oddly enough, I felt no fear. Her whisper came to me as all the world fell still around us, came with urgency and insistence: *Save her, do not let her die. Save her.*

"Save whom?" I ventured to ask—although I could not tell if I merely thought it or spoke it aloud.

The dark clouds moved past the sun, and the specter began to fade into the shadow of the tree. The daylight burst through the leaves once more, and she was gone.

Slowly I became cognizant of the birds singing, and the scent of the apples and flowers, and the sound of the rushing brook below me. The world righted itself around me, and I felt myself on firm ground again.

Nothing like this had ever happened to me before—a human ghost appearing, and speaking! I am not given to fits or fainting or wild imaginings, but I dismissed the idea that this time—as I had earlier, hearing the sounds of soldiers and guns in the old barn studio—it was a mere manifestation of an empty stomach. This was real.

Was this the ghost of Russell House? I think I knew whom I would ask first about this—little Kate, who said she had seen the ghost herself. They say children are more approachable by spirits than we hardened, cynical adults, so her testimony might be valuable.

I had stood for several minutes now, lost in reverie, and recovering my nerves, which I admit were somewhat shaken. I gradually became aware of my name being called, and looked up in time to see John striding down the path some yards away, coming back from Abbots Grange, where I recalled he said he was to escort Henry James. He was alone, however, so Mr. James must have stayed behind to sort out his writing room. I hastily composed myself to meet him; I was in no frame of mind to speak about, or even be able to describe what I had just experienced.

"Ho, there, Violet!" he called out. "Odd to see you out in nature, surrounded by trees and flowers," he laughed. "I imagine I'm simply more used to seeing you in a drawing room, or at a museum."

"Fair enough," I gamely answered him, pretending to swat away bees. "*Nature is red in tooth and claw*, you will kindly remember, as Alfred Lord Tennyson has informed us. I prefer the teeth and claws of amusing, intelligent humans, in their native habitat indoors."

"Where you spar with the best of them," John said, looking at me fondly. But he was a keen observer. "What's the matter, my Twin? You look as if you'd seen a ghost."

I stared at him—how had he hit the nail on the head so precisely? But I fended him off. "Perhaps I have," I said, seriously. "May I tell you about it later?"

He looked surprised at my solemn answer, but only nodded as he placed my arm in his and began to walk us back to the house.

"You are about to become initiated in the *Painting of the Garden Picture*," he said, patting my arm. "In about forty-five minutes, we shall all be gathered at the clearing, the Barnard girls dressed in white and posing as if their lives depended on it, the dear things, and I dashing to and fro, splattering paint on everyone and everything, but often to little effect as regards the actual painting."

He was silent a moment, then spoke more seriously. "There is something almost sacred, I feel, in the way the light seems to shine in the garden, at that dusky time of the day, in a kind of cloud—full of scent and brilliance and even movement—it surrounds the children and makes it seem as if their faces, and the flowers, were all lighted from within."

I was silent for a moment, deeply touched by John's unusual (for him) eloquence in describing his painting.

"I am looking forward to it exceedingly, I assure you," I said, making an effort to sound more like my rational self. "Will Mr. James be joining us, or have you  left him quite absorbed in writing, up there at Abbots Grange?"

"Oh, he says he'll be along presently, wouldn't miss it for the world," John replied. I imagined that was not exactly the phrase Mr. James used; he was not given to enthusiasms. We were both silent again for a bit, wending our way back up through the garden, when we both spied Ned Abbey standing quite still, one hand clutching his chin, in contemplation of something he apparently held in the palm of his other hand—in short, he was standing at the top of the ice house steps. We hastened our pace, and John called to him as we drew near.

"Eh? Oh, it's you, John, and Violet," Ned smiled as he spoke, then shook his head. "Come and see, quickly, before anyone else arrives." We hurried to his side, and he held before us his open palm, on which lay a golden lapel pin. I peered at it closely, and saw depicted on it a harp with an angel as part of the frame, holding a banner with the word "Equality" on it, and under it, a ribbon inscribed with *It's New Strung and Shall Be Heard.* We looked at Ned for an explanation.

"I found it on the step, just there," he said, pointing to the second step down from the top, leading to the ice house. "I dare say it's been there since last night, perhaps came off when that scoundrel shoved our Alfred, but it was too dark to see it then."

"What does it mean?" I asked. "What is it a symbol of, with the harp and that interesting assertion of *Equality* and *being heard?*"

"It's the symbol of the Society of United Irishmen," Ned said. "It's long gone now, but started with the Rebellion of 1798. The harp, you know, is a symbol of Ireland."

"But this looks new-made," John said, taking it up and turning it over. He handed it back to Ned, who nodded.

"There are some who would do the same again as was done nearly a hundred years ago," Ned said solemnly. He looked up to see both me and John watching him curiously. He colored, and mumbled an explanation of sorts. "Michael talks of it—*talked* of it, and I was interested."

This, and his embarrassment, prompted me to ask him about Kitty. "Have you learned anything new from her?"

He shook his head. "But she knows something she's not telling us," he said. "I'm sure of it." He looked hopefully at me and John. "Have either of you found anything encouraging?"

I told them quickly about what Mr. Hesford relayed to me about the *two* young men at the brook the previous night, the remarkable similarity between Michael and

Thomas McCarthy, and that I had seen McCarthy and David Cowan in deep conference at the Horse and Hounds inn. John summed up our position easily, but it was of little help.

"Whatever is going on, it involves the Irish," he said. "But it's so very tenuous and out of reach."

Ned grimaced as he agreed, and closing his fingers around the Irish pin, put it in his waistcoat pocket. "Things will come to light," he said. "I feel it in my bones, this isn't over yet."

I looked away, up toward the house, and saw that people were stirring again. Lucia was peering out the back windows at us, and I could hear children's voices at the gate. I alerted our companions that we needed to move and be prepared for the invasion.

"Time for painting!" John said, laughing. "Perhaps a little change of mood will clear our heads."

I nodded, attempting a smile; there was so much I had *not* told my two companions, and the warning of my ghostly visitor still reverberated in my heart: *Save her.*

THIRTY-TWO

10 OCTOBER 1726

At the Olde Swan Inn

TIM WHISTLED SOFTLY UNDER HIS BREATH as he brushed down the horses in the stable. As the night of the full moon drew closer—it was only a few days, it would be on the night of the 15th—he became more and more nervous and on edge. At first, his dreams of marrying Bess, of winning her love, and being truly the son of the old innkeeper, kept him humming merrily, looking at a future he had scarcely ever believed possible. The promise of the reward money grew great in his eyes—it would be the saving of them all.

But soon, and for the first time ever since he'd come to work at the Olde Swan, he avoided running into Bess, and when she called him for some specific request or duty, he answered her as briefly as possible, not looking her in the eye, and scurrying away. But strangely, it seemed, she didn't notice any change in him, or at least she said nothing if she did. He hunched up his shoulders at the thought that she was oblivious to him—*probably thinking of that damned farmer,* he brooded to himself. But Bess seemed moody and distracted, too, and not at all happy—so perhaps she was changing her mind, and didn't want to be involved with Tremayne anymore?

After all, he continued to think, absently brushing the roan mare's flank, *I'd be doing her a favor to be sure, and though she might not think so at first, she'll come round to see it was for the best. Marry a thief? Marry a criminal? Nae, she would see the good of it, and thank him.*

"Hie there, mate!" cried a well-known voice at his ear. Tim jumped and the curry brush flew from his hand, landing neatly into a bucket of dirty water.

"Georgie, daft fool! Look at what thou've made me do!" Tim turned away from his laughing friend and retrieved the brush. "Why come up on a man like that?" he groused, but Georgie continued grinning.

"I've news of the Highwayman," said Georgie proudly, following Tim step for step as he proceeded to carry out his chores in the stables.

"Oh yes? And what is that to me?" Tim answered, though inwardly he feared the sudden dissolution of his dreams, with the thought that someone had killed the thief, or captured him already. He hadn't heard back from Mr. Wells, but assumed the letter had reached the man, and there were plans afoot; he didn't really expect they would inform him or consult him about anything, so he just had to wait.

Georgie ignored him as usual and kept talking. "They say as he's taken down three coaches in the last four nights, each one further and further from here—above Evesham, for certain, then over to as far as Bristol!"

"Bristol! How art thou sure it's the same man?" Tim said, relieved to hear the Highwayman was probably in good health and still plying his trade, whether this was Tremayne or not.

"A'course and he's the same man, ye'ver heard of such another one in the five counties?" Georgie was secure in his information. "He's a master, that one is, and no doubt of it."

"And thou'rt an idjit, no doubt o'that!" Tim rejoined. He looked his friend up and down critically—though always happy go lucky, Georgie was looking pretty run down, his pants patched almost beyond their capacity to hold a stitch, and no socks on the thin feet stuffed into boots too small. *When I run the Swan,* he thought to himself, *I'll give the lad a steady job.* Cheered with this thought, he looked more kindly on his friend, and offered him some lunch in exchange for work.

* * *

When lunchtime came, Tim and Georgie were at the kitchen door, their hands washed (as Germaine always required), and waiting for a dish of stew and a chunk of bread made that morning. Germaine, Tim noticed, much like Bess, seemed distracted and out of sorts—even the genial Georgie couldn't engage her in their usual flirty give-and-take, though she was so much older than him, Tim couldn't figure where the interest was in that game, for his friend.

"Get along now, ye two," Germaine admonished, once she'd handed over their food and a wooden spoon for each of them. "Don't stand gawking about my kitchen, I've more work to do than I can shake my broom at." She saw them out the door, and stood looking across the back to the high road above, on the hill. She fetched a deep sigh and stepped back into the kitchen, shaking her head.

Supplied with their meal, the two young men went round to the front courtyard where there was a little relief from the sun, bright in a deeply blue sky. The air was crisp and had a tang to it, like cider made from green apples.

"There'll be a frost tonight, aye," said Tim, looking askance at the sun. "This deep a sky allwas brings on the frost."

Georgie shrugged, intent on his lunch. The sudden and familiar sound of the mail coach was heard coming a ways down the London Road, and the two hastened to finish their meal and stand ready for the mail. The coach swept into the courtyard with a great noise, and Tim yelled into the inn for Germaine, so that she might bring out any mail they had to give the post.

"Ay and good morrow to ye, young sirs," said the coachman, a hearty fellow with a good word for everyone.

"And to yerself," they said, reaching up for some letters and packets he was handing down to them. "There's one there just for yerself, master Tim," he said, pointing to an elegant white paper letter, folded and sealed with red wax.

"Ye'll be having some post for me to take?" he continued, looking toward the door. Just then Germaine appeared and hailed him as an old friend.

"There ye be, on time as a sunbeam in spring," she called. "Here is our post for ye, then." She gave him a smile, and a little something sweet inside a napkin at the same time.

"Oh, my dear woman," the coachman said. "And sure ye're as sweet a thing as any man ever tasted."

"Oh Lord, how ye go on," Germaine cried, quite pleased but feigning indignation. After a few moment's chat, the coachman doffed his hat and rode off in a whirl of dust and a clatter of hooves on cobblestones.

Germaine turned to see Tim standing quite still to one side of the courtyard, looking intently at an unopened letter in his hand. She had never heard of his having kin elsewhere, and although she knew Bess had been at some pains to teach Tim his letters these last few years, she had never seen him actually write anything. She felt a moment's uneasiness, some woman's eternal sense of trouble, but then recalled she'd left a pie in the oven and it would burn if left another moment. She ran for the kitchen.

Tim's hand trembled as he looked at the letter, with its sender's address of *Edward P. Wells, Stewart Street, Oxford* embossed on the back of the wrapper. He was amazed and confounded—why would that important man be sending a letter to him?

He carefully slid a finger around the sealed end of the wrapper, and unfolded the sheet of heavy paper. It was but a note in length, but its contents were weighty.

To Master Tim Ostler,

Sirrah, thank you for your recent letter. All is in train to be effected 15 October. Stand by, tell no one. The reward shall be yours.

E.P.Wells

Tim's heart nearly burst with pride and excitement. It was all going to come true—and he would be a hero in the village! Surely Bess would love him for that.

He looked up as he noticed Georgie looking at him curiously, and he hastily refolded the letter and stuffed it in his pocket.

"Tim has got a love letter then?" Georgie called, laughing at him.

"Never thou mind, silly sot," Tim said, then thought he might as well go along with the joke, as a sort of cover. "One that's too good for the likes o'thee to hear of." But he smiled a little as he said it, to make it like a secret about a girl, and Georgie just laughed again and made fun of him. They walked back around to the kitchen to turn in their bowls and spoons, and Tim was proud of how he hid his tremendous secret so that no one would suspect.

Bess met them at the door, and held out her hands for the bowls. She smiled because Georgie had such a grin on his face it was infectious, but it faded when he began to talk of the news he had imparted to Tim earlier.

"Ye've heard o'that Highwayman, yes, Miss Bess?" Georgie kept on, not seeing the guarded look that came over her. "Seems as he's goin' further afield than recent times, even o'er to Bristol, they say."

"Oh yes?" she said, striving to appear unconcerned.

"Yes," replied the oblivious Georgie. "And they say as what he struck down three coaches, maybe four, and there was a bag of gold in one, and some ladies' jewels in another, and he fought them all with his sword, and rode away on his black horse, laughing."

"Seems as if 'they' know an awful lot about what no one could rightly know," Bess said with a sniff. "Just gossip it is." She paused a moment, then asked in an indifferent tone of voice. "There's no one sayin' that he's hurt anyone with that sword, is there?"

"No, Miss Bess, not that I've heard," said Georgie, adding enthusiastically, "but if I were such a one, I'd slash away at all the old rich buggers, maybe cut their heads off for a lark!"

"Then ye'd go straight to the hangman's rope," Bess said severely. "Don't ye go idolizing killing and thieving, silly boy, or ye'll end up with a noose round your silly neck!" And she grabbed their spoons and bowls from them, turned and shut the door in their faces. Georgie looked in amazement at the door, then at his friend, as if to say *what was she all about then?*

But Tim, feeling heavy at heart, just cuffed his friend's shoulder and led the way back to the barn. He'd never had so many opposing feelings in his life, and didn't know what to do with them.

Inside the kitchen, Bess leaned against the closed door, and shut her eyes against the tears that would come. She was that worried about Tremayne, she felt she couldn't fit inside her skin anymore. The only relief was in looking forward to the next morning, when she would set out before dawn to meet her lover at the graveyard. Talking to him would set everything straight, and then she would know where they stood and what they should do.

THIRTY-THREE
SATURDAY 4 SEPTEMBER 1886

At Russell House for Tea & Painting

LITTLE KATE MILLET CAME RUNNING out of the house and straight to me, looking pink and flushed with sleep. "Oh, Miss Violet," she said, taking my hand. "I've been waiting so very long to see you again!" I bent down to kiss the girl's cheek. "Dear Kate," I said, "it's barely two hours since I left you after luncheon, but I am happy to see you, too."

Lily Millet followed her daughter at a more sedate pace, arm in arm with Alice Barnard, who greeted me with great friendliness, Lily somewhat less so. "Don't go hanging about Miss Lee and bothering her," she said rather sharply to Kate, who flashed a glance at me.

"No, please, I am delighted to have her nearby," I said at once, and meant it. Not only was it true, but I also wanted to inquire about the little girl's experience with the Ghost of Russell House, and having her cling to me provided appropriate opportunities.

The Barnard girls trailed behind their mother, dressed in the white costumes that I had seen in the Garden Painting—the heat of the day was cooling slightly but the light garments were perfectly suited to the place and time.

* * *

Finally Lucia stepped out of the doorway, also dressed in white, but to my eye, looking a trifle wan and weary. She was accompanied by Frederick Barnard, looking rested and content. He nodded in my direction, and came over to chat a moment, while his daughters raced over to where John was chatting with Ned.

"Mr. John! Mr. John!" The girls called out excitedly, and he knelt down on one knee as they approached him to be scrutinized for their readiness to pose for the painting. They twirled round and struck poses as he regarded them thoughtfully, pretending to frown and be doubtful.

"You are both delightfully perfect!" He declared at last and stood up, brushing at the knee of his trousers. He clapped Ned on the shoulder. "Give me a hand with the canvas, eh, Ned?" The two of them went off to the Tower room to gather the canvas, and at a glance from John, I saw Lucia hurry over to them—perhaps she would carry out the paint box, I imagined.

Mr. Barnard leaned toward me and spoke, as in a confidential manner, "Now you shall see what fun we have here in Broadway, Miss Violet. What fun, what fun," he repeated in his curious way.

"And are you currently doing any illustrations whilst you're down here, Mr. Barnard?" I asked.

"Oh, yes and no, yes and no," he said, which I found somewhat enigmatic. His wife then called to him for assistance, and he bowed to me again and was off.

Everyone was involved in one way or another. Alice Barnard had gone to fetch a large bag from the garden shed, from which she and her husband pulled several Japanese or Chinese paper lanterns, collapsed into round circles. Setting them all on a table, she, Mr. Barnard and Lily began pulling them up into their beautiful rounded shapes, and setting inside the little candles that would light them. I drew near the table, Kate still holding my hand tightly, and watched the procedure.

"You see, Violet," Alice said, "we are quite the artists' colony at Russell House, everyone has his or her duty to forward the great works that are created here." She glanced at me, smiling. "You have seen John's canvas? Do you like it?"

I nodded. "Oh, yes, it's quite wonderful!" I chattered on, mostly to obscure my dark mood. "And to think that he worked on it last year, and now after several months of interruption, he's ready to take it up again! I don't think I could do that, for instance, with writing—I have to push it all out at once, or I fancy the idea will wither and die if I leave it for too long."

Alice smiled sympathetically, and Lily looked as if she were going to make some kind of sarcastic retort (or maybe that was only my spiteful imagination). Mr. Barnard spoke up. "Yes, yes, once I begin a drawing, you are quite right, I must go at it til it's done, or I lose the inspiration, I quite understand you, Miss Violet."

John and Ned were seen returning with the canvas, newly bound to a stretcher after having been cut down to its square shape, and were carrying it down the lawn. Lucia did indeed have a paint box in her arms, and there was Kitty, much to my surprise, with David Cowan, together bearing two large wooden props for the painting to rest upon. Our little group at the lantern table jumped to attention, gathered up all the items—Kate and I helping where we could—and followed along in the parade to the clearing.

The afternoon sun was moving behind the tall trees and the hillsides, but the sky was clear.

"We have to move quickly," Alice explained to me as we hurried along. "It takes a bit of time to set it all up, and this is the first time we've done this since last Fall, so we have to be sure to put everything in its place, according to what's on the painting." She glanced up at the sky. "This looks perfect," she said approvingly. "Dusk will come swiftly, however, and John will only paint while the light is 'just so'—and that only lasts about twenty minutes!"

"Goodness," I said. "Quite a production for twenty minutes!"

"Oh!" said Alice. "One gets very used to it, as it will happen every day at this time for several weeks now."

"Quite a production, quite a production," her husband chimed in, laughing.

Lily spoke up at this point. "John is so very diligent," she said, admiration clear in her voice. "Last year, he worked right through most of October, and the poor girls had to wear dresses and sweaters underneath their frocks—they looked like fat little sheep!" The two women laughed at the memory, and I just shook my head in wonderment.

When we came to the clearing, I stood off to one side, with Kate, and let the others manage setting up the site. It was done admirably, with Lucia stage-directing the set, so to speak, and Alice helping her daughters to stand in the exact poses depicted on the canvas. Lily and Kitty hung the lanterns from the branches of rose bushes, with many blossoms still full, and David and Ned carried over large pots of gorgeous lilies to the area of the clearing that was the stage, to complete the scattered garden atmosphere. Carnations also grew in profusion at the sides of the clearing.

"Sing the song now, do, please Mr. John!" the two little models called out. "And Mr. Ned, too, please, we want to hear the song!"

"Yes, the song, please!" Kate piped up at my side, with a little squeal of excitement.

All the women started laughing and teasing the gentlemen about their singing. "Shall I run get my pitch pipe?" Lucia asked as she helped John set up his paints.

He shook his head, laughing. "I expect Ned and I can start at the right place," he said. And looking at Ned, he gave a nod, the two of them hummed for a bit to find the right pitch, and began. Mr. Barnard also joined in, his voice a pleasant baritone.

"Ye Shepherds tell me, tell me have you seen, have you seen my Flora pass this way?"

It was a charming little ditty, and I was reminded of the Italian peasant airs I had written about a few years ago—it seemed but a dream now when I had been there, in Tuscany, so untried an author then. I shook my head to clear it of vaguely regretful thoughts, and was greeted with the whole group, children and adults, singing the most significant (to the present purpose) lines in the song:

"A wreath around her head, around her head she wore, Carnation, lily, lily, rose, And in her hand a crook she bore, and sweets her breath compose."

Applause burst out, and everyone laughed again, and then John called the two models to order, and everyone settled down. Kitty simply sat in a low chair, her hand shading her eyes, as she absently watched the scene, and Ned stood attentively just behind her, leaning over now and then to murmur something.

David Cowan had, apparently, left the garden, as he was nowhere to be seen.

Lucia had seated herself near her sister-in-law, some piece of sewing in her hands. Alice and her husband stood off to one side, giving encouraging glances to their daughters, with Alice now and then giving a twitch to a fold of cloth, under John's direction. It was a picturesque group!

Lily now had charge of her small son, Laurence, whose nursemaid had brought him out to join the group—to my untrained eyes, he looked to be about two years old, sturdily attempting to walk and run about and make all kinds of mischief. His older sister, my little Kate, still stuck by my side, and I thought this might be as good a time as any to query her about the ghost.

"Dear Kate," I said, "shall we take a turn about the garden?"

"Oh, yes, Miss Violet, I would like that," she said, and we slipped away from the others and, hand in hand, walked on the flagstones that led to the garden area just below the tennis courts, and above the brook.

I spied Henry James making his slow, cautious way down the path from Abbots Grange and, not wishing to encounter him, I guided Kate to a different path in the opposite direction. We were soon far out of earshot of all the others.

"So, my dear, you have seen the Russell House ghost," I said. "I am very interested in ghosts and all that sort of thing—for my story writing, you see," I fibbed only a little, as I had actually started thinking about "ghost stories" in light of my current experiences. "Can you tell me what you think—what you saw?"

Kate nodded solemnly, and as we had come to a little stone bench in the curve of the path, we seated ourselves and sat looking down at the brook rippling smoothly a few feet away.

"I saw her in the hallway, at the top of the stairs," she said, looking up at me a trifle warily, as if fearing I might laugh at her.

"So it's a woman?" I asked, my heart quickening.

"Yes, a very lovely woman, with long black hair, all undone, and she was wearing a white dress, only she seemed to have spilled something on it, something dark that messed the front," Kate said, and I was glad that she had not interpreted the dark stain as blood.

"What did she do?" I asked carefully. "Did she say any-thing to you?"

Kate considered this. "I saw her lips moving, like she was talking, but I couldn't hear anything. She didn't really seem to see me, if you know what I mean." She looked up at me, fully trusting I would understand her.

"You mean, she didn't really look at you standing there? Perhaps she was looking around, as if to see someone else?"

"Yes!" Kate agreed readily. "That's just it, exactly. She looked like she was trying to find out someone, looking this way and that, but then she looked very sad, and went back into her room."

"*Her* room? Which room is that?" I shivered with a sudden sensibility.

"The room at the front of the house, the second door on the left from the top of the stairs." The child looked at me with puzzled eyes, and added, "That is, I *think* it is her room, because it's the one she went into."

The chill in my heart increased—that was the guest room in which I was going to sleep that night. I commanded my feelings to stillness; I didn't want to frighten poor Kate.

"And was that the only time you saw her?" I asked.

Kate shook her head decidedly. "Oh no, I saw her again, in front of the door to her room, and one other time, downstairs, very late, although there were some visitors in the drawing room singing and talking very loudly. I was waked up by the noise and came downstairs," she explained.

"What was the lady doing?" I asked.

"She was holding a lantern, and looking out the front window. She stood there for ever so long, then, when I blinked my eyes, she had gone."

"Did you not feel..." I hesitated. I didn't want to put ideas into the child's head.

"Afraid?" She filled in the word, and shook her head again. "Not at all, I felt sorry for her, she was so sad, and she looked so kind. I think she was very young, even younger than you, Miss Violet." And she put up her hand to touch my face, which was very sweet, and which prompted me to give her a kiss, and thank her for telling me all about the ghost.

"Do you think you might write about the ghost in one of your stories?" She asked this as we stood up to go back to the painting party in the clearing.

"One never knows, with writing, my dear," I said, as she took hold of my hand for the walk back. "It may depend upon what the ghost has to say to me."

THIRTY-FOUR
11 OCTOBER 1726

At the Olde Swan Inn

IT WAS NEARING DAWN, and the hoarfrost lay on the land, limning every remaining brown leaf and branch, roofs and barrels and wooden sheds. The far eastern light glimmered in a clear sky, still night across most of the land, with deeper blue shadows at the foot of the hills, and the palest of shimmers on their crowns.

Bess had on her warmest cloak, and two pairs of stockings, and a scarf around her head and throat as she slipped noiselessly out the back door. She'd had to unlatch it, but she hoped she would be back safe inside before even Germaine began stirring—she just needed to be with Tremayne long enough to kiss him and plan what they would do next.

There was a path through the orchards and fields behind the Inn that was a straighter way to St. Eadburgha's than taking the road roundabout, and Bess could walk that path like she could walk through the inn itself, even in the dark. She heard the rippling brook, still low and waiting for the melting snows of the highlands in time, and knew she could easily skip across its shallows. The small birds were awakening and trilling their morning prayers as she stepped onto the wide path known as Snowshill Road—

* * *

just a beaten dirt path at this stretch—and the church was barely a ten-minutes' walk now.

Her heart beat hard, and her throat felt closed up. She  didn't know for sure he would be there waiting for her. What if he hadn't looked for a note? What if one of his coach raids had ended in disaster for him—taken, or killed? Wouldn't she have heard of that, though, with all the interest everyone took in the Highwayman's adventures? Her mind buzzed with questions as she trod softly on the earth.

The ancient tower of St. Eadburgha's was soon in view, although tall oaks concealed the church from a distance. The first few tombstones started to appear through the mist on the ground, the newest ones those farthest from the church, the succeeding generations of the dead of the parish buried in concentric circles around the church. Her own mother's grave lay in one of these outermost circles, she having died near this time last year, after Harvest. Bess felt a pang; her mother had been a friend, had listened to all her little troubles and woes. She felt sure her mother would be sympathetic to her love for Tremayne, and mourned her absence more than ever. She crossed herself as she felt a moment's guilt for deceiving her father, or as good as doing so, in slipping out to meet with her young man.

All in and around the church was quiet; the sexton would not yet be up nor lighting any candles for some hours. Bess crept close to the church door, and by the growing light of dawn, saw the tombstone of Cwynedd Bowhill just beyond the door and off to the side. Germaine had told her precisely where the loose stone was, and she trembled as she reached for the stone—she grasped it, put it aside, and with great relief, saw there was nothing under it—so he must have gotten the note! She quickly put the stone back, stood up and looked around.

She heard a low whistle, fragments of an Irish tune, and knew he had come. Another moment and she was in his arms, strong and warm about her, with his lips full on hers. He drew her into the shelter of the church door, where they might be better hidden from any traveller on the road.

"Dear love," he said, pulling back her scarf so he could kiss the fragrant waves of black tresses that tumbled forth.

Bess felt her heart racing, and she ached to just run away with him at that very moment, but she remembered her father, and quelled the thought. She pulled herself away from her lover—they had little time.

"The Squire," she whispered, looking up into his dark eyes, "he says he'll arrest thee if thou show in Broadway."

Tremayne looked more annoyed than fearful. "And by what right does he say that I'm to be arrested? These damned English!"

227

Bess looked down, and spoke. "He says thou'rt a fraud, that thou donnae own the farm, and thou've taken money from the old man that does own it." She held her breath, and once again looked in his eyes.

Tremayne's face darkened in anger. "Dost thou believe that o'me, my Bess?"

She shook her head. "It must all be lies, my darling."

He kissed her soundly. "Thou'rt that true, i'faith. The old man—I'm like a son to him, and he has made me his heir, and the farm is promised to me alone." His mouth twisted in a sarcastic smile. "And as for bein' a thief, well, I've ne'er taken anything from the old man," he said, "just the rich English who've taken the bread from the mouths of my people." He caught the question in Bess's eye, but only said, "The trouble with being Irish is the land ne'er lets thee go." He formed a fist and held it over his heart. "I do what I can to help the cause of freedom, but...." His voice trailed off, and he embraced Bess even more tightly. "With no kin o' me own, I long to have a family to work for...to die for, if needs must." He looked at her tenderly. "My own love" he murmured, and kissed her sweetly.

The sound of a horse and rider was heard at a distance, coming up the road, and the two squeezed back further into the doorway, waiting until the traveller had passed on by the church. But it served as a grim reminder they had no time left.

"I'm after a prize in the coming nights," he said, "then all this will be done, and we can be together."

"But thou cannae come to the inn by daylight," Bess told him, "as we thought to do, or show thyself at all in the village. The Squire will take thee."

Tremayne brushed back her fallen locks with a gentle hand. "Then look for me by moonlight," he said. "Watch for me by moonlight, on the fifteenth, at midnight—I'll come for thee, be ready, we'll go off together, to Ireland."

Her heart leapt at the thought, and she couldn't help herself from agreeing to whatever he wanted. "Yes, yes, my dear, I'll be ready."

"One more kiss, my bonny sweetheart," he said, and they kissed as if it would be their last embrace. He stepped away from the door, cast a look around to see the way was clear, then turned back to speak once more.

"I'll come to thee by moonlight, though hell should bar the way."

THIRTY-FIVE

SATURDAY 4 SEPTEMBER 1886

Teatime At Russell House, and Mr. Millet Returns

KATE AND I RETURNED TO THE CLEARING where the painting was still in progress, but about to cease for the day—the sun being clearly past the treeline, and the special light in the garden that John wanted to capture, quite waning away. We joined the group as everyone began rising from their places, plucking the lanterns from the bushes (it wouldn't do to leave them in place, I learned, as the morning damp would cause the paper lanterns to melt away) and began the task   of carrying the canvas and poles back to the Tower House.

As our gypsy parade wended its way back up the lawn and through the garden, the sturdy, compact form of a man appeared at the top of the small rise leading to the house.

"Frank! Oh my dear! You've come home!" cried Lily, who gathered her skirts in one hand and ran to greet her husband. I couldn't help but wonder if she found this as surprising an event as she seemed to express—had there been some uncertainty as to whether he would return? Others of the group called out cheerful greetings, and little Kate let go of my hand to run to her father. I was gratified to see that he greeted her with great affection, swinging her up in his arms and kissing her again and again, whilst Lily hung on his arm and looked up at him with adoring eyes, shiny with tears.

"John, I say, John, the painting's coming along splendidly," said Mr. Millet, as John and Ned, carrying the canvas, came near. He planted another kiss on Kate's head, turned to kiss his wife on her cheek, then carefully disengaged himself from their embraces. "But what's this, then?" he said, coming closer to the painting. "It's a different size, isn't it? You've made it square? By golly, I do like it!" His manner was American to the utmost, jovial and free.

John, mindful of propriety, had Ned continue to hold the canvas whilst he turned Mr. Millet in my direction. Near to him now, I saw that he was only a few inches taller than I, but compactly built, with brown wavy hair, a full upturned moustache, and merry brown eyes. As an admirer of his paintings and literary works, I was eager to meet him, and to see in what way his American-ness would unfold upon me. I was soon to find out.

"Frank, you must meet Violet Paget—rather, Vernon Lee as you must know of her, to be sure! Violet," he said, presenting his friend to me, "this is Mr. Frank Millet. Frank, this is almost my oldest friend in the world, Violet Paget."

"Vernon Lee, God bless me!" exclaimed Mr. Millet. "Do you prefer that cognomen, my dear woman, or shall I call you Violet?" Without waiting for an answer, he immediately turned to his wife. "Lily, my dear, what am I supposed to call this amazing, intelligent and famous person? I am envious," he continued, smiling at her and then at me, "that you all have had her company for some days, and now I have to catch up with you, and take her off so we can have a proper conversation, just the two of us." At this, he took my hand in his own and with a noticeably strong grip, shook it enthusiastically. I observed that Lily, oddly enough, didn't seem a bit disturbed by her husband's attentive attitude toward me, but continued beaming at him with great affection.

"Violet suits me perfectly well," I said, asserting myself before Lily had an opportunity to say anything. I withdrew my hand from his grasp, trying not to wince as I flexed my fingers after his muscular grip. "I am delighted to meet you as well, Mr. Millet, and I look forward to some pleasant conversation with you."

"If you don't call me Frank right off, my nose will be quite out of joint," he admonished me. "Well!" he said, looking around happily at the group. "Well! And what do you think I've gone and done, Lily?" he said, turning once more to his wife. "Having been set down at the Horse and Hounds, I ran into that famous rugby player, McCarthy, and invited him straight off to come to dinner tonight! He's to play an exhibition game tomorrow, on the field south of village, and we're all to go as his guests."

The children, hearing this, cheered at the idea of a day out watching the games, although I noticed that both Lucia and Henry James (who was helping to carry the bag of lanterns in) looked rather uncertain about the pleasure involved in such an outing. Mr. Millet continued chatting with his wife and children as the whole group made its way to the house, he declaring that he must see his son Laurence, this very minute. As the nursemaid was standing close to Lily, holding the infant, his wish was gratified almost instantly. I don't know why I was so pleased to see him so very much attached to his children; little Kate still clung to his pants leg, worshipping him with her eyes, and Lily seemed quite a different person in his presence. It was a fine family tableau, and gave me what I felt was an insight into the genre of paintings he created—homey scenes in quaint parlours and cozy inns.

I dropped a little behind, feeling quite fatigued after the many events and twists of the day—it was nearing five-thirty now—when Lucia came alongside me, linking her arm familiarly in mine as we walked slowly to the house.

"I have a social call to make, Violet," she said. "I have been invited to take a late tea today with an ancient resident of Broadway, who lives not too far away, a Miss Marshall, a remarkably active old lady, eighty-six years old! I have been quite anxious to get at her for some time as I have heard wonderful tales of the old gowns in her possession, as well as her memory of times past in Broadway—quite the antique bard of old, apparently, knowing all the local legends and stories." She paused for a moment. "Would you be so kind as to accompany me, please?" Her voice, warm and inviting as always, held an extra note of particular pleading, and I could see the same in her eyes as she watched my face for a response.

* * *

"Of course, dear Lucia," I said. "It sounds delightful," I lied; I was much more interested in the coming visit of the rugby player McCarthy at dinner this evening. But then I had a thought that helped me comply more sincerely. "Perhaps she may know the story behind the Russell House ghost?"

"Oh yes, I'm sure she does!" cried Lucia. "She knows everything about anything that has ever happened in Broadway. Thank you, Violet, thank you so very much!" And she heaved a little sigh, and patted my arm. "You can have no idea," she said after a moment, "how delicious it will be to be away from Russell House for even a short time."

"I can imagine it," I murmured. She glanced at me sideways, and gave a little rueful laugh.

"Oh, I'm not complaining," she said, and then laughed again. "At least, not very much! But now that Frank is suddenly back, Lily will be full of energy, and able to manage beautifully for tea without my help," she said. I wondered at her remark, but asked no questions; it seemed to confirm my own observations. We caught up with a few other stragglers, including Henry James, who joined us as we walked across the garden pavement.

"Quite an interesting production," he said, as he opened the door and stood aside to let us in. "I am always interested in seeing an artist at work."

"Yes," I said, and added, "but I think it's quite a shame that one cannot observe so easily the *mind* of an artist—say, a writer—while he or she is at work. What an interesting array of ideas, fancies, discernments, rejections and so forth, one could watch as they flit across a writer's mind during the creation of a story, or an essay."

Mr. James seemed struck by my idea. "What a remarkable notion, Miss Lee," he said, and stood quite still, holding open the door, as he thought upon it. "Watching an intelligence at work!"

I smiled. "Perhaps some day, Science may be able to show us the workings of the mind—or rather, the brain I suppose, which is the mind's physical component, don't you agree?"

He contemplated the idea, then nodded slowly. "The mind is indeed more comprehensive than the brain, but yet must be considered to be housed, as it were, in that organ." He bowed as I went before him into the house. "And you, if I may say so, Miss Lee, are certainly a person whose mind would be delightful and instructive in the extreme to observe as it is working."

I stared at him for a moment, but he seemed to be perfectly serious, so I thanked him, and we went into the house. He continued down the hallway to the drawing room, while Lucia and I stopped at the foot of the stairway.

"When shall we go to see this remarkable old lady?" I asked. We consulted the hall clock, and agreed to meet at the kitchen door in twenty minutes. I assured her that was sufficient time for me to do whatever tidying up of my person and dress needed doing, and we parted at the top of the stairs, she to her room farther down the hall, and I to the dubiously restful chamber of the ghost of Russell House.

But there were no spirits or gloomy visions inside the cheerful, sunlit room, and I was able to prepare for our visit in ease and comfort. Nonetheless, I felt it in my bones that the dire warning from the ghost was very much connected to Michael's death, and learning more about her legend from this Miss Marshall couldn't help but throw more light on the case.

THIRTY-SIX
14 OCTOBER 1726

At the Squire's Estate, and the Olde Swan Inn

BESS HAD RETURNED TO THE INN, on the day she met Tremayne at the churchyard, well before anyone else rose, and so was able to appear to her father that she was trying to abide by his instructions, staying at home the rest of the day and the next. Thus he only gave her one quick look when she said she had to go into the village for supplies, and merely nodded his approval.

Truth be told, she was actually going to see Squire Robert, and confront him about his lies regarding Tremayne. It seemed to her there was no hint in what the Squire had said that he knew anything about Tremayne being the Highwayman, which was a great relief, but she wanted to try her luck in persuading the man to drop his persecution of her betrothed. With her courage high, and love in her heart, she set off across the fields and up Snowshill Road to Oakehurst, there to meet the Squire. If she could only catch him when he was sober, she thought she might be able to bring him to reason—he was not altogether a bad man, she thought, just too inclined to drown his better self in drink.

She was met at the door by a very different sort of person—Mary Cummings happened to be in the grand hall when the butler opened the door, and she walked forward in haste, to prevent Bess from entering.

"What business hast thou here, Miss Bess?" she said, sneering a bit. She was robed in high style, in a deep green dress that favored her blonde looks; her hair was all in ringlets, the latest fashion, and she stood in the doorway very much like the lady of the house, even dismissing the servant with a cool look. Bess wondered again what on earth could be the attraction for the Squire in such a woman?

"I've come to talk to Squire Robert," Bess said evenly. "On a matter of personal business."

"*Personal* business, is it?" Mary echoed, raising a well-shaped brow. "And what kind of personal *anything* can a creature like thee have to discuss with the Squire?"

The two women were a match for each other in spirit, and they both just stared full face, neither one blinking. Bess knew that Mary ultimately held the upper hand, but that wouldn't keep her from trying to see the Squire.

"Could ye please let Squire Robert know that I am here, and would like to speak to him?" Bess said with forced politeness.

• • •

Mary tossed her head. "He's not here just now," she said. "He's out looking over his estate, so much is demanded of him." She smiled spitefully. "He has little time for petty problems that people like thyself are always bringing him."

Bess realized there was little she could do but leave a message, but she knew any message she might leave would never reach the Squire. Biting back all the insults and recriminations she longed to hurl at the woman, she merely smiled. "Then I'll come another time," she said.

"Oh, well," said Mary, her hand on the door and starting to close it. "I doubt whether he'll ever be at home for thee."

Bess turned and walked away without another word; she heard Mary laugh as the door closed. Angry now, she swatted away some low-hanging branches that were in her way as she took to a path across the fields, a shorter way back to the Inn than the road.

She had gone some half mile or so when she spotted him—the Squire, leading his horse by the reins and coming down the common path. The animal appeared to be a bit lame, favoring its rear right leg. With her heart thumping hard, she waited on the path until he should draw nearer and see her; he seemed to be lost in thought, his head hanging down as he walked slowly toward her. She thought she'd better say something, so as not to startle him.

"Good day to ye, Squire," she said, raising her voice a little, and trying to smile.

He lifted his head at the sound, started slightly, but came forward with a firm step. He stopped a few feet in front of her, and made her a short bow.

"Mistress Bess," he said.

Bess curtsied slightly and drew breath to speak, but Robert was before her.

"You see my horse has thrown a shoe," he said, patting the animal on the neck. "So I'm forced to walk across the field like everyone else." He half-smiled. "Tis a good way to see the world, planted on the ground."

Bess was encouraged by his manner, and determining that he was sober, she took heart and spoke to him.

"I've just come from Oakehurst," she said. "I'd hoped to meet ye there, but was told ye were not at home. I would have some talk with ye, sir." She thought she couldn't lose anything by being respectful, but felt a twinge of resentment that there was such an imbalance of power between them.

"And what is it that you need to discuss with me?" Robert said it lightly, but she saw a flash of wariness cross his face. *He knows he's been lying, of course,* she thought, and it gave her strength to confront him.

"Why did ye lie to my Da?" she burst out. She continued in a rush. "Did ye not know that Tremayne is heir to that farm? He's no fraud! The old man loves him as a son, and he's nae a thief either!" Her black eyes blazed with passion, and he thought he'd never seen her so beautiful and proud. She caught her breath as she took in the expression on his face, and watched him carefully, as if in the presence of a wild animal. Around them the bees buzzed, and the little birds twittered in the dry grass, and

● ● ●

the sun shone down through high clouds. A sudden burst of wind whispered over the long grass, and it seemed then that everything in the field held its breath.

Robert felt a pain in his chest, as if something were cracking. He was not a bad man, and he knew he'd done wrong. He knew he needed to make up for his lies. He had looked down after a moment, but now lifted his eyes to look at Bess. She was surprised to see sorrow and humility in them now, and it struck her kind heart so, that she stepped nearer to Robert, and laid a tentative hand on his arm, to encourage him to speak.

"What would you have me do?" he asked her, looking all the world like a young lad caught in mischief and realizing he'd caused trouble to a dear one.

"Say ye'll not arrest Tremayne should he come to Broadway—say ye were mistaken about his situation with the farm, that he's a good man," Bess said. Then, with a sudden surge of anger, she added, "And tell that Mary Cummings the same, and that she's not to be spreading rumours and trash about Tremayne anymore."

He nodded slowly, his face taking on a harder look. "I shall see it done." He made as if to move along, and Bess stepped aside so he and the horse could pass by. He looked long at her as he passed, but said nothing more. She stood and watched him walk away until he was around a bend by the brook and she could see him no more.

With a lighter heart, but one that nonetheless felt a deep pang for the Squire, alone save for that awful Mary Cummings—perhaps he would see how wicked she was, and turn somewhere else for comfort—Bess walked slowly back to the Inn, thinking with delight how tomorrow at midnight when Tremayne showed up at her window, there would be no need for them to flee, to elope in secret and go to exile in Ireland. They two could take their place with each other in the full and beautiful light of day.

THIRTY-SEVEN

SATURDAY 4 SEPTEMBER 1886

At Miss Marshall's House in Broadway

"A VERY SUBSTANTIAL TEA OFTEN TAKES THE PLACE of a formal dinner at Russell House," Lucia was saying as we walked up the High Road toward the village. "We Americans are much more casual about dining than the English, I think."

"And what about guests, such as this rugby player McCarthy, who's been invited to dine?" I asked. "Do they join in the bohemian fun of Russell House?"

"Oh, my yes," Lucia said. "I've rarely seen anyone who does not easily fall into the spirit of the house. Even Lord and Lady Elcho, over to Stanway Castle, if it *is* a castle, I have yet to see it—he's an Earl, I believe—even they, when they've been here, have been seen to put on paper hats and sport flowers in their buttonholes, and eat cream pies and apple-and-cheese sandwiches for dinner right along with the rest of us!"

The dusk of the autumn day was delightful: warm but not too warm, bright but not sunny, and quiet with the soothing quiet that is a small village closing up at the end of a busy market day. Saturday night would see everyone in their own homes, enjoying their families, and preparing

• • •

for church on the morrow. I thought to ask a rather impertinent question—I laughed to think I was acting like an American!

"Does anyone at Russell House, or the people who visit there—are any of you churchgoers?" I pointed to a large edifice of the ecclesiastical genre, high on the hill up which we were walking. We had turned to the right when we reached the green, and were mounting a not inconsiderable incline to the west.

"Oh, dear me, not very," Lucia responded; she didn't sound very concerned about it, though. "We were all

Episcopalians at home, so that would naturally lend itself to our attending Anglican services here, but what with one thing and another, we don't visit much—Christmas and Easter, of course, if we're here, we wouldn't miss!"

We reached the summit of the hill in a few minutes, and paused to catch our breath and gaze up at the imposing church of St. Michael and All Angels.

"They call this one the 'new' church, I understand," Lucia said. "It was built about forty years ago or so."

"And the 'old' one?" I asked.

"St. Eadburgha's," Lucia said, and pointed north. "It's about a mile past Russell House, and a little way west. It has an extraordinary churchyard, and the main part of the church itself dates to the 11th century."

"I must go visit it," I said. "Nothing religious in the visit, of course," I added quickly, "but I do adore old churches and graveyards."

"You and I shall go," Lucia said promptly. "And we'll get Henry to go with us, he loves old churches too, especially ones that used to be Roman Catholic." She chuckled, and added, "I do believe that the Irish side of Henry James, though presumably Protestant-raised, tends much more to the pomp and mystery of the Roman Catholic Church."

I thought about that a moment. "I think I agree with you there," I said. "Let's do ask him to join us."

We were silent for a few minutes, and then Lucia announced that we had gained Miss Marshall's house, a charming two-story stone cottage, with a neat garden and a pear tree in a stone pot at the front steps. We entered at the gate, and proceeded to the door, a sturdy oak studded with iron nails and curved at the

top, just as we heard the "new" church bells sounding six o'clock.

Miss Marshall was a very tiny and spritely old woman, who opened the door of her cottage herself, and ushered us in with great friendliness and attention. Her voice was high and thin, but not unpleasantly so, and she was dressed in the style of clothing from at least fifty years past, with more frills and bows than ladies seem to sport nowadays. Her white hair was soft and abundant, though carefully folded under a mob-cap of ivory silk, and she made light use of an ivory-headed cane to steady herself.

"You are very welcome, Miss Lucia Millet," said Miss Marshall. She smiled at Lucia, and with a little blush, said, "I do believe I have never met an American before."

Lucia laughed. "We are not so very strange a race, ma'am, you will find." Then she turned to introduce me. "This is a dear acquaintance of mine—*not* an American— Miss Vernon Lee, whom I have taken the liberty to bring with me to visit you."

Miss Marshall said all that was polite and obliging—I do not believe that my *nom de plume* meant anything to her—and led us into the cottage. We entered a large room that appeared to encompass both dining and sitting rooms, with a large, glowing hearth at one end. She rang a little tinkling bell as we seated ourselves at a small table near a bow window, and a nicely uniformed maid appeared almost instantly with a tea tray on a wheeled table.

"Do please help yourselves to such pastries and things as you prefer," said Miss Marshall. "However, Sally makes by far the best cucumber sandwiches I ever et, and I pray you to taste them." Her quaint way of speaking was of another era, like her clothes, and, as I looked around, I saw that the furnishings of her cottage also came from the last century. An ancient oaken sideboard stood against the wall at one end of the table, filled with blue and white Dutch pottery; the sofa was barely visible under a mound of small, tatted pillows, and the walls were decorated with plain paper. At precise intervals, brown etchings of "Village Life" scenes in elaborately carved wooden frames broke up the solid ivory of the walls nicely. Facing East, the windows let in only reflected light at this time of day, but the effect was warm and soothingly dim.

"Well, then, Miss Millet, would it please you to tell me a little of the Americans at Russell House?" Miss Marshall raised her bright, inquiring eyes from her teacup, which Sally had just filled, and smiled at Lucia.

"It would please me indeed," Lucia said, and proceeded to enumerate the artists and writers who came to visit them, dwelling on the production of the many illustrations and paintings, literary works, poetry and murals they created.

"So you see, ma'am," she wound up, "We are constantly living in different centuries and decades at Russell House, due to everyone wearing costumes and clothing from times past—it is quite like travelling back in time to see history in the flesh!" I could tell Lucia was leading up to her main objective—that of seeing what ancient costumery Miss Marshall had hidden away in her closets and wardrobes. She was immediately gratified in her quest, therefore, when Miss Marshall brought up the subject herself.

● ● ●

"Why, if t'would be of any use to you, my dear, I have wardrobes filled with my mother's and grandmother's apparel—and indeed, some of my father's as well—that go back a century or more—ye're welcome to them, in the cause of art, I say." She sipped at her tea. "You must come along soon again, in daylight, so to see them all the better."

Lucia was effusive in her thanks, and gave me a triumphant glance. But Miss Marshall was more up on modern times than I expected, as shown by her next question, posed to me.

"And Miss Vernon Lee, you are a writer of histories and stories, are you not?"

"I am indeed," I said, and added, smiling, "I did not expect that you would know that, ma'am."

"Oh, my, there is not much that gets by me," she said. "And what particular idea are you pursuing, in coming to see an old lady like me?" There was a twinkle in her eye as she said it, and it made me smile again.

"There you have got me, Miss Marshall," I said. "You're very perceptive." Then I grew serious, and putting aside my teacup, I leaned toward her.

"I am come about the ghost of Russell House, ma'am," I said. Her face became tinged with sadness as I spoke. "I have reason to believe that the ghost is very much connected to some strange...events...that have lately visited the place."

"You are referring, I take it, to the passing of the poor Irish lad," she said softly. *Small village indeed*, I thought. I nodded agreement, and waited for her to speak again.

* * *

"Russell House, as you may know," she said, with a nod to Lucia, "was a coaching inn, time out of mind, going back three or four centuries. 'Twas called the Olde Swan, and had a good reputation, though it vied for trade with the White Hart—that is now the Lygon Arms, after that odd man, but that's neither here nor there—my father knew him but didn't like him." She waved away her memory of Mr. Lygon, and continued. "My great-great grandfather was alive at the time, early in the 1720's, and my grandfather heard the tale from him, and I from my own father." Then, like a bard of ancient times, she began the well-known tale, seemingly recited and handed down through generations. We sat back and just listened, entranced.

"There was in and around Broadway, at one time, in the reign of King George the first, a rascal of a Highwayman named Tremayne. Irish he was, and a joyful, mannerly thief of the High Road, dressed in tall boots, with lace at his throat, and a cavalier's feathered chapeau and sword.

Now at the time, the Olde Swan inn had a landlord with a jewel of a daughter, Bess her name, for our good Queen Bess—but black of hair and black of eyes—the apple of her father's eye. She loved the Highwayman with her whole heart, and he pled his troth to her, and swore they would wed after he'd gathered the gold, to take her away and live as man and wife.

But betrayal came in the form of a jealous stablehand, who wanted Bess for his own, and he told the King's men how to find the Highwayman, and bring him down like a dog in the road."

At this point in the tale, Miss Marshall, whose eyes had closed while she softly told the story, ceased speaking and seemed to have fallen asleep. Lucia and I looked at each other, wondering what we should do. Just then, Sally the housemaid returned, and seeing her employer sitting with closed eyes, she smiled a little and whispered to us, "She does this, poor dear, more and more these days." She motioned for us to quietly rise and follow her out of the room.

"Will she be all right, sitting in the chair?" Lucia asked.

"Oh, yes, miss, she remains upright, even in her sleep, it's such a marvel, that," said the girl. "She'll sleep for p'rhaps an hour, then wake and want her tea." She handed us our wraps, and saw us quietly out the door.

"Well!" I said, as we walked back down the hill to Russell House. "How I wished she had finished the tale, but what she did say was enough..." I stopped abruptly, seeing Lucia's quick, interested glance at me, and realizing that of course I had told no one about the visions I had encountered, nor had we included Lucia in our investigation of Michael's death, so it was no wonder she was curious.

"Enough for what, Violet?" Lucia said, and paused as we arrived at the bottom of the hill. There was a determined look on her face. "I know there's more going on—with you and John and Ned all whispering in corners and going off together—do please, I beg you, tell me what you are about, the three of you—and if the ghost of Russell House has any-thing to do with it, too! Please, I want to help."

* * *

THIRTY-EIGHT
14 OCTOBER 1726

At Oakehurst, and Later, At the Olde Swan Inn

A STORM WAS BREWING AS SQUIRE ROBERT neared his estate of Oakehurst, with dark clouds and winds coming in from the north, whipping the trees into frenzy. He handed the reins over to a stableboy who'd seen him walking up the drive and came running to help, and after some instructions for the lad and his father, the ostler for the estate, he trudged his way up to the house.

All was silent, and darkening with the gathering clouds. He called for a lamp, and a footman came on the run with a light, and to take his cloak and dirty boots. Robert thanked him—which made the boy stare a moment, then bob his head and dash away—and he leaned back in the tall chair in the main hall, where he had sat to take off his boots. A fire was burning in the hearth, but the hall was so high, and there was so much stone, that even such a grand fire as it was could not take the chill from the room. He stood up with a sigh, rubbing his eyes and face—he couldn't erase from his mind the soft, kind look on Bess's lovely face as she tried to soothe his spirit. *Where can I find another such a one?* he asked himself. *It's kindness I need, and a pure, simple love.*

* * *

He'd had that love, near enough, with his late wife, but they had not been together even three years before the sickness took her. There had been no children, and he grieved for that as well. He shook the wool from his brain, and made his way to the stairs, up to his own room, his study, which faced the rear of the estate, looking out onto gardens and forest, toward the West. As he climbed the ornate carved staircase, he heard the rain begin pelting against the glass of the windows high above, and he hoped that Bess had made it home before the rain began.

He opened the door of his study, and saw the fire was lighted there as well, and all was warm and quiet. Then he saw that he was not alone, as he had wished. On the sofa, Mary Cummings lay asleep, but as he drew near and carefully observed her face, he could see, even in sleep, the hard lines of scorn and anger etched in her face, and the lips pursed as in some pouting fit of temper. His heart rose up and castigated him—how could he have thought such a creature would suit him? He was outraged that she felt so familiar as to take the liberty to sit in his very own study without his permission.

He would have no more to do with her.

But he couldn't bear to confront her; the thought of it made him ill. He didn't want her angry features replacing his memory of Bess's charming smile and kind eyes. He quietly retreated from the room, and went to the kitchen to find his housekeeper.

"Mrs. Reynolds," he said, standing at the open door of her tiny sitting room, off the kitchen. She was startled awake from a nap in her rocking chair, and nearly upset a small table with a tea cup and saucer on it as she struggled to her feet.

"Squire! Sir, you startled me so, dear me," the flustered woman said. She righted her cap, which had come askew, and tried to recover her dignity. "What may I do for you, sir?"

"I want you to call the carriage, and have Miss Cummings taken home, immediately," he said. Her eyes widened in surprise. "You'll find her asleep in my study." He eyed the older woman for a few moments. "And please convey to her my thanks for her help, but tell her it—and she—are no longer needed at Oakehurst, and that she should never come here again."

"Squire!" Mrs. Reynolds couldn't help herself from bursting out in protest. "Why, what has she done!"

He looked at her coolly. "Nothing good," he said at last. "And I want no more of it. See that she's gone within the hour." He turned and left the room, trusting the housekeeper would carry out his commands.

He retreated to his library, closing the door, and thought that would be an end to it. But not much time elapsed before he heard a woman's angry voice in argument with the softer tones of his housekeeper. The voices drew near, and suddenly the library door was thrown open without warning, and Mary stood in the doorway, her face white but her eyes fierce, as she seemed to be attempting to compose herself.

"Mrs. Reynolds has just had the temerity to dismiss me from this house," she said. The housekeeper hovered behind her but said nothing, only looking beseechingly at the Squire. Mary walked further into the room, her head high. "Surely there must be some grievous mistake, after all the hours I have given over to your care, and all the trouble I have taken to help you in your time of need." Mary took a cautious step closer to where Robert sat in a big leather chair by the fire. "Robert? Surely you don't mean me to go?" Her voice had softened, and Robert felt nothing but revulsion at her tone of voice, and her false concern.

He looked down at his book, placed the ribbon on the page and closing the book, stood up slowly.

"You have led me to betray my own principles," he said in a quiet voice. He made a deprecatory gesture with one hand. "Not that I've been a model of principle for some time now, but that is all done with." He glanced at her, and saw a look of contempt on her face, which hardened his heart more fully. "You have lied to me, and caused me to harm one who was innocent of wrongdoing, and I cannot bring myself to consider you welcome in any fashion here at Oakehurst."

He glanced at the housekeeper, still hovering at the door, and nodded to her. "Mrs. Reynolds was only carrying out my orders, and I wish to have no further interaction with you here, or anywhere."

Mary opened her mouth to speak, but stopped when the Squire held up his hand. "Go, now," he said. "And try to be a better woman than you have shown yourself to be." He turned his back to her and walked to the far window; it was some moments before he heard the door close, but she was gone at last.

Later that night, at the Olde Swan Inn

The storm raged and blew, but all inside the Inn was quiet and warm. There had been no travellers for a day or two now, and the storm kept the local folks away from the tavern, so it was just Richard and Germaine and Bess at the inn, with Tim at the stables, and Sam home with his own mother and father and siblings.

Bess sat with the two older folk at dinner, a thing that happened rarely, as they usually were all busy looking after guests and customers in the tavern. She longed to tell her father and Germaine, who kept looking at her with worried eyes, what she had said to the Squire, and what his response had been—but she wanted to tell Tremayne first of all, then they could give the happy news to the rest of her family. Nothing ever need be said about him being the Highwayman—he would be all done with that life, as he told her he would, and they could live happily, here in Broadway.

Lightning streaked across the sky along with a tremendous crash of thunder that rattled the windows, and Germaine jumped.

"Lord!" she cried. "This storm'll be the death of me, it scares me so!"

"There now, lass," said Richard, laying a soothing hand on her arm. "It's just noise, isn't it? Calm thyself, all is well indoors."

Just as suddenly as the lightning and thunder had come, the rain ceased, the wind died down, and a stillness came over the world outside.

"We're in the eye of the storm, then," said Richard sagaciously. "Another few minutes, and it'll all start up again, on t'other side of it." The three got up from the table and went to the front windows to look out at the late evening sky. There were purple clouds, torn by winds higher than anyone on earth could feel, flitting across the sky.

"It's like the whole world is holding its breath," Bess said in wonderment.

Then they heard it, faint but clear—coming down the London road, the sound of marching, singing soldiers. Bess ran to the door and flung it open, and the voices were louder and coming close. They could make out the words now, the end of a rough but well-known song:

For I know that the gallows are waiting for me.
Young friends, you had better be starved by your
nurse,
Than live to be hang-ed for cutting a purse!

Bess felt fear like a spike to her heart, and she clutched at her father and Germaine, who looked with wide eyes at the small troop of King's men who were now marching into the courtyard, their red coats drenched and bedraggled but their spirits high and ready for action.

THIRTY-NINE

SATURDAY NIGHT, 4 SEPTEMBER 1886

Back to Russell House and the Rugby Player

WHAT COULD I DO BUT ANSWER LUCIA'S DEMAND? Spying a bench at this end of the green, I invited her to sit down with me. The church bells had just tolled the quarter hour past seven. The sun was setting, the air was warm and pure, and we could surely, I thought, spend another fifteen minutes here in this quiet space before returning to the undoubted clamour of Russell House. I rapidly told her all of our suspicions about Michael's death, at which she exclaimed greatly.

"But are you sure, Violet?" she pressed. "Are you sure it was murder?" She put a hand to her throat, and her eyes filled with tears. "That poor, poor boy! What on earth..." her voice trailed off, the thought unspoken. She leaned closer to me and said in a low voice, but vehemently. "I want to help you find his murderer," she said. "You must let me help you." A gleam came into her eyes. "I shall take it upon myself to find out more from this Thomas McCarthy, all right?" She stood up, in her haste to be doing something. "He's probably at the house even now, come, we must hurry!"

"Wait just one moment, though, Lucia," I protested, and she sat back down again. I wasn't sure how to tell her

* * *

259

about my ghostly experiences, so just started in. She gaped at me, aghast, as I told her what I had experienced, but she did not laugh, as I had feared.

"Do you think that what you felt in the old barn room—the noise of soldiers and gunfire—could that have been a memory of when the King's men came to capture the Highwayman, as Miss Marshall was just telling us? The ghost's memory, perhaps, which she somehow translated to you?" Lucia was intrigued, I could tell, but not fearful.

I nodded. "Yes, I believe so," I said.

"And little Kate, God bless the child, she corroborates the vision, as you saw it in the garden?"

"Yes, most remarkably—we both have seen the ghost—we have seen..." I hesitated, then forged ahead. "We have seen Bess, the landlord's daughter, black of hair and black of eyes, as Miss Marshall described." I did not tell her about the Queen of Hearts, who is *"both here and not here"*, as Michael saw in the cards, and *"whose love calls out through Time to be heard."* Who could it be but Bess?

"Oh my goodness, Violet, this is amazing," cried Lucia. Then, with determination, she put her hand on mine, as if swearing an oath. "We *will* find out whom she means you to save, we must! Have you any notion at all whom she might mean?"

I had my own idea of this, but I was not prepared to say just yet, so I only shook my head. I placed my other hand on top of hers, and thanked her for her interest.

* * *

"Now," I said, standing up from the bench. "Let us go to Russell House, and see what our Irish athlete may be able to tell us that will help us solve this wretched puzzle."

* * *

We returned to a surprisingly sedate company at Russell House—the children had been given their sumptuous tea, and were bathed and tucked into their beds, and all the adults were still gathered in the dining room, finishing up stray bits of bread and cheese and fruit.

Lucia and I divested ourselves of our light wraps and entered the dining room to a hearty outcry and welcome. I paused at the door as Lucia responded to the many inquiries directed at us, and observed all the personalities gathered for dinner: Frank Millet at the head of the table, as was appropriate, and on his right his wife Lily, then dear John and Ned, Alice Barnard, then her husband Frederick at the foot of the table. On the other side, Henry James on Frank's left hand, then the guest of honor Thomas McCarthy; next to him was Kitty, then David Cowan. There were numerous candles in the candelabra on the table, spreading a warm glow over the company, and imparting a rosy, softening tinge to everyone's features. John was pouring out the remains of what looked like the last of several bottles of wine.

"Lucia, my dear sister, thank God you've come!" cried Frank Millet, rising to kiss her cheek. "And Miss Lee as well, we are sadly in need of more genteel company than these rough male types you see here gathered," he continued, then at Lily's protest and Kitty's seconding her indignation, he bowed to both of them, and nodded to Alice at the other end of the table, apologizing. "It's not, dear ladies, that I would fault your presence or your femininity, but just that the overabundance of male company needs more balance—and now we have got it!"

I had the oddest feeling that "the gentleman doth protest too much, methinks", to borrow from *Hamlet*. How often does Shakespeare supply the exact phrase to express our own feelings and observations, still apt some three hundred years on!

Frank Millet

Lily Millet

John Sargent

Violet Paget

Ned Abbey

Alice Barnard

Henry James

Lucia Millet

Thomas McCarthy

Kitty O'Byrne

David Cowan

Fred Barnard

John moved his chair, obliging Ned to do the same, and directed me to sit between them, across from Kitty and McCarthy, which suited me just fine. Lucia was invited to be seated next to Henry James, and a chair was vacated for her, with McCarthy, Kitty and David Cowan all moving down a space to fit her in, thus she was seated next to the rugby player, and she gave me an amused glance at the serendipity of her seat. Musical chairs with a vengeance! and to my mind, so exactly a metaphor for not only the atmosphere at Russell House, but the ever-changing perspectives that surrounded the sad death of Michael Kelly.

Frank had swallowed down the last of his glass of wine, and now rose, declaring he'd go to the cellar for more. Lily put a hand on his arm, as if to stay him, and he leaned down to hear her whisper. Her request was clear from his answer.

"Nonsense, my dear, enough is never too much! And we've not had nearly enough!" He kissed the top of her head, and negotiated around the small space between a large cabinet and his chair. He moved easily and with grace, and laughed as he said, "Besides, our dear Henry here has barely had three glasses of this excellent claret, and I've no doubt he'd like more. Eh, Harry? Shall we go together to choose another?"

I saw with amusement that "Harry" appeared to be somewhat intoxicated—I wondered if it would loosen his tongue at all, and cause him to open just a crack those shutters behind which he hid—and from which he observed all the rest of the world with those unruffled but piercing grey eyes. Everyone quieted down when he rose, purposefully, as he appeared to ready himself to address the company. Raising his almost empty glass, he spoke with deliberate enunciation—which proved to me he was more than a little drunk.

"Good wine is a good familiar creature," he said, and burped slightly. *"If it be well used."* He looked around the group with a questioning lift of his eyebrows.

"Othello!" cried Ned and Frank at the same time. Henry tipped his glass to them, and drank the dregs. "Mr. Millet," he said, his manner formal, "I shall be pleased to

accompany you to the wine cellar." Frank, laughing, drew Henry's arm under his arm, and the two of them walked off.

Ned got up and went into the room adjacent to the dining room, and we soon heard some quiet music as he practiced playing a Spanish guitar, which was a soothing background for those of us left at the table, whether we wished to converse or not. John, looking toward Alice Barnard, rose quickly and, taking a large sketchbook which he always had to hand, took another seat a little distance from her and began to sketch her as she languidly held up a wine glass to the candlelight. Mr. Barnard excused himself, saying he wished to retrieve some cigars to bring back to the table, if the ladies would allow it. No demurs were heard—I even thought to myself that if the cigars were small enough, I might join in! Lily sat, seeming a bit forlorn, then rose and began taking some of the dishes back to the kitchen.

Lucia was engaging Thomas McCarthy in playful conversation, so I casually turned my attention to them, noticing first that Kitty was trying to hide her displeasure at Lucia's monopolizing the guest of honor. David Cowan appeared somewhat gloomy, and stayed silent, occasionally watching John as he sketched Alice Barnard. He appeared to me to have been drinking steadily, and heavily.

I mused again on how alike McCarthy was to the late Michael Kelly, although on closer inspection, the rugby player's dark curls made him look more youthful than he was—there were lines about his eyes, and a more grizzled look about his face that spoke of some years he had on the much younger Kelly; his muscular frame, too, though graceful, held a coiled strength that the young actor had not had. But I could see that from a distance, and in dim moonlight, one might be mistaken for the other.

The name "Michael Kelly" had just been spoken, by Lucia, and I was alert enough to catch a passing look on McCarthy's face—one of sorrow or guilt? Or both? He had cast his eyes down, and was answering Lucia. I paid close attention, but fiddled with my wine glass and a piece of bread to cover my interest.

"Aye, I know he was a friend of David's," McCarthy said, nodding in the older model's direction. "Did ye know him well, ma'am?"

Lucia shook her head. "He was new to Russell House," she said, "but he'd been here a fortnight at least, he came down with Kitty, and we all grew to like him—he was such a lively lad, with a good sense of humour." She sighed, and I knew she wasn't pretending. Then she cocked her head and looked at McCarthy. "You look like him, you know," she said. "You could be his brother."

I saw Kitty make a sudden small movement of her hand, and she almost knocked over her wine glass. McCarthy turned to her, and she righted the glass and smiled unevenly.

"Brothers of a sort, don't you know," she said pleasantly. "We Irish find our family in all our folk that are far from their own land, do we not, Mr. McCarthy?"

"Brothers in arms, more like!" David Cowan spoke up, a little loudly, from his end of the table beyond Kitty. "We fight for the family, we do, and the Harp, to take back

Eire for ourselves! We die as we must along the way." I could see the tears forming in his eyes.

McCarthy frowned and started to rise, but Kitty laid a quick hand on his arm, though she, too, looked alarmed. "David," she said soothingly, turning to the man, "I'm wondering if you could come with me a moment now, I've some costumes to show you that Mr. Frank would like us to pose in tomorrow—can ye do that for me now, David?" And so saying, she rose and waited for him to stand up, unsteady as he was, and walk with her.

I did not fail to notice the look exchanged between her and McCarthy as she took David's arm and went in the direction of the studio. It was one of guarded relief, and warning. I looked at Lucia, whose eyes were wide with interest and speculation.

Frank and Henry came back with more wine just then, and began filling glasses once again, and little by little the atmosphere grew cordial once more, and everyone who was absent returned to join the party, except David Cowan.

And I treated myself to a cigar, much to everyone's amusement, and Lily's noticeable disapprobation.

• • •

FORTY

15 October 1726

At the Olde Swan Inn

THE CAPTAIN OF THE KING'S TROOPS stood straight and tall, but weary, before the doorway of the Olde Swan. His eyes were old in a young face, bearded and lined from responsibilities beyond his years. He gestured to his men—there were nine of them—who stood at attention silently, dripping wet from the march through the storm.

"You are the landlord here?" he asked Richard, his eyes briefly scanning the two women who stood behind him.

"Aye," Richard said, wary but not unwelcoming.

"Is there anyone staying at the inn at this time?" the captain asked, wiping his wet cheeks and beard. His color was high, and Bess, peering at him from behind her father's shoulder, thought he looked feverish.

Richard hesitated, and it was too long for the impatient officer.

"Come, man, tell me! Are there others here?" he barked it out.

Richard shook his head. "Nae, no lodgers here tonight," and at the look on the officer's face, he hastened to add, "and none expected, not in this storm."

* * *

The captain nodded curtly, and motioned to his men to file into the inn. "Then we will lodge here tonight, and tomorrow," he said. "You are to turn away any who come to the door."

Bess spoke up, protesting. "We cannae turn away those who come to the Inn for shelter," she started to say, and the captain turned his weary eyes to her, and cut her short.

"Put a sign up that says you are closed due to sickness," he said, and gave a humourless smile. "It works every time. Everyone thinks it's the plague, and runs away fast." He took another step closer. "Now move aside, my men need warmth and shelter, some food and drink as well."

Richard saw quickly it was no good to protest further, and he held his arm out to move Bess and Germaine back, and shield them, however ineffectively, from the leering glances of one or two of the soldiers, though most of them entered quietly, fixed only on getting out of the cold.

Moments later, the skies opened up and poured down rain as if it were the Great Flood come again, and Richard hastened to close the door behind the last of the soldiers, tramping mud and water into the inn. They made directly for the tavern. With a nod to Germaine and Bess, Richard sent them off to the kitchen—*out of harm's way,* he thought to himself—and walked into the tavern to manage the lot as best he could.

One bold soldier, more ragged and dirty than the others, had gone behind the bar and was pulling the tap, filling up cups of ale, and setting them, splashing, on the clean polished surface of the bar, where the others eagerly gathered to grab a pint for themselves.

"Here now," Richard said, and seeing the fight in the dirty soldier's eye, amended his speech. "It's my job to serve ye, is it not, gentlemen? Sit ye down, and be comfortable, there ye go," he said, as the soldier, satisfied he had cowed the innkeeper, left off pouring the ale himself. "We'll have some hot food and bread up for ye in good time, and I'll serve ye myself, there, go sit by the fire and warm yerselves."

The captain had removed himself from his troops by turning off into the snug adjacent to the tavern, where he already lay weary on a bench, on his back, one foot on the floor and an arm flung across his eyes.

The men were, for the most part, barely past their first youth, although the 'dirty one' as Richard named him to himself, seemed older and more hardened. As the soldiers drank, he got louder and more belligerent, bullying the others by calling them names and questioning their manhood if they failed to drink a proper amount of ale. One of the younger soldiers, however, stood up to him and was able to appease the man's ire.

"Come now, Potter," said the younger soldier. "You know as Curler 'ere 'as got the sickness on 'im, and if 'e drinks more, 'e'll just upchuck it on the rest o'us, yes? Waste o' good ale, that!"

Potter guffawed at that, and let off razzing the poor soldier. His attention drifted back to Richard.

"When the damnation will we be getting any food, eh? That slut of a girl and the older slag surely have done their work by now, yes?"

Richard's hands clenched into fists at these slurs, but he checked his temper as best he could. At least the women didn't hear them. Potter laughed and drank some more, turning back to badger some of the other soldiers, who mostly ignored him and kept to themselves.

Bess and Germaine soon arrived with fresh bowls of chicken stew with potatoes and apples, and bread with fresh preserves. Germaine doubted they would actually be paid by these rough men for their room and board, but she bit her tongue and served them. Two or three of the younger soldiers looked at her with timid smiles, and mumbled their thanks as she placed the bowls in front of them. *Why, they're just boys*, she thought, and patted one on the shoulder when he said aloud how good the stew was.

Beth was unfortunate enough to be the one serving the scurrilous Potter, and he wasn't slow to throw an arm around her waist and pull her to him. But Bess still had a bowl of stew in one hand and (apparently) lost her balance, dumping the hot brew into his lap. This provoked great hilarity on the part of the other soldiers, and Potter rose, cursing and flailing at the food on his trousers. He seemed about to grab Bess and punish her, but a sharp command from the captain brought the room to a halt in sudden silence.

"Potter, you villain! Clean yourself up and act like a King's soldier for once," he said. The captain swayed slightly in the doorway, and Bess could see clearly that he was ill. Glancing at her father, who nodded, she approached him with care.

● ● ●

"Sir," she said. "I have some medicines that will help ye with this fever, I can see ye're not well."

The captain at first just glared at her, then with a quiet sigh, he collapsed and would have fallen to the floor but for Bess catching him in her arms. Richard hastened over, as well as the young soldier who had stood up to Potter, and together they carried him back to the snug, where Bess made him comfortable on a low couch with pillows and blankets.

"Thank'ee, miss," the young soldier said. He had bright eyes, dark brown, and a shock of blond hair that fell into his eyes from time to time. "Captain's been that sick a day or so now, we was worried so about 'im."

Bess took a chance, and leaning toward him, whispered, "Why are ye here? Is there something we need to know?"

The young soldier looked uncertain a moment. "Captain ain't told us much, we're just blokes wi'muskets, see?"

Potter came to the door of the snug, and smirked. "If the Captain is out o'commission," he said, "I guess that leaves me in charge, don't it?"

Bess could feel the young soldier stiffen at this statement, and he left her side without another word. She turned back to the unconscious captain, and prayed that his fever would soon break, and the troop would be on its way. It had crossed her mind that they were here for Tremayne, but how was that possible? No one knew he was coming tomorrow, only Germaine, and Bess trusted her with her life. But if he came tomorrow at midnight, and they were still here....? She shuddered to think of what

* * *

273

might happen, and her mind was busy thinking about how it might be possible to get word to him before tomorrow midnight.

Potter still stood in the doorway, watching Bess with a hungry look on his dirty face. Richard, who was still in the room, came over and stood before him, his considerable bulk more than a match for the younger man. Potter took a step back, then with a bit of a swagger, said in his loud voice, "So, where's that ostler fellow, that stableman of yours who's been so helpful to the authorities? I need to talk with him about a certain Highwayman."

Richard was dumbfounded, and couldn't find a word to speak. Bess felt her heart sink into a dark pit, as the stark truth behind the man's words became crystal clear to her. Tim, somehow, had betrayed her, and brought the soldiers here to capture Tremayne! It was all she could do to keep from fleeing the room that instant, out into the storm and the night, and find Tremayne and warn him.

FORTY-ONE

SATURDAY LATE NIGHT 4 SEPTEMBER 1886

Nightime at Russell House

FRANK MILLET OFFERED TO WALK the famous rugby player back to his hotel, and after a pointed look from me, John volunteered to go with them, saying he needed a turn in the fresh air after all the cigar smoke and port, and Ned eagerly joined in, saying he needed the same. Henry James was also to be of the party, of course, and he looked as if he could use an escort to the hotel, if only to keep him upright. John and I had time for a short exchange while everyone was busy departing the dining room and going their separate ways.

"If someone mistook Michael Kelly for McCarthy," I whispered to John, "it would be best if he travelled with a group, don't you think?" John concurred and added, with a wink, that he would keep an eye out for Mr. James as well, to insure *his* safe arrival at the Lygon Arms. It was nearing eleven o'clock; the Barnards had left some time before, walking arm in arm to their large house nearby, where the nursemaid, Alice said, was probably waiting up for them, and they didn't like to keep her longer from her bed.

It had been reaffirmed at the dinner that the whole party were to be present at the rugby exhibition the next afternoon, and though I am no sporting fan, I was eager to be there, in the hope that scanning the crowd might bring forward any person intent on mischief or harm to McCarthy.

The men were off within a few minutes, and we remaining women made our way up the staircase and to our separate rooms. Lucia, indeed, tarried a moment at my door whilst her sister-in-law and Kitty went to their chambers. She gave me a quick hug, and whispered, "Now, Violet, I hope you will not be fearful of sleeping in that chamber," she said. I had told her what Kate said about it being "*her* room", the ghost's, and Lucia had verified that it certainly was in the oldest part of the house, and doubtless had been *someone's* bedchamber for much of the last few centuries.

I returned her embrace, and said stoutly, "Oh, like Kate, I don't think I am at all afraid of the poor ghost, but feel a kind of pity and compassion for her."

Lucia kissed my cheek and bade me good night, and I turned, candle in hand, to open the door and step inside. The fire in the grate was banked for the night, and gave only a feeble glow, which my candle did little to augment. Luckily, the warmth of the day had sufficiently heated the room so that I felt comfortable changing into my nightclothes without a fire to warm me. As I was on the upper floor, I decided to leave the curtains open, with the rising moon to shed a little silver light on the floor.

Outside all was quiet, and I could see the coach road pale and broad under the moonlight as it shimmered its way across the soft Cotswolds hills. I slipped into the cool sheets, plumping the pillow beneath my head, and reflected on the events of the last three days—it had really been only three days, nay, two and a half!—since I arrived on Thursday at Broadway Village. And long days they had turned out to be. Images of all the many people I had encountered in that short time swam in my head—I believe I started counting them, rather like sheep, and before I knew it I was fast asleep.

* * *

A soft, murmuring sound woke me, and I saw in a gleam of moonlight a figure in white standing at the window, looking out onto the London road. It was Bess, with her long black hair streaming down her back, her hands clasped, perhaps in prayer, and her lips moving with words I could not discern. I sat up slowly, moving the blanket aside, and tried to distinguish her form from the white curtains that seemed to be blowing around her, as if the windows were open.

In the utter stillness of the night, I heard the sound of a horse, *tlot tlot, tlot tlot,* coming down the road toward the inn. Bess clutched her throat with fevered hands, leaning toward the window, her mouth open as if crying out a warning to the one who was riding closer and closer. I felt rather than heard a concussion, as of a musket shot, and the ghost seemed to shudder and faint. But she turned her stricken face to me, and though I did not hear an actual voice, I heard the words, "Do not let her die!"

* * *

Well, needless to say, I didn't get much sleep after the visitation, although I must have ultimately dropped off, as I was awakened by the sound of footsteps in the hall, and people hastening up and down the stairs: morning had come again to Russell House, and its denizens were stirring.

* * *

Breakfast was a desultory affair, with John and Ned the only gentleman up and dressed for the meal, which, I must say, was early by almost any standards, with the table set and food brought out by half-past eight! I deduced that it couldn't be on account of the children, as not even Kate Millet was present; her baby brother was doubtless in the nursery, probably with Lily in attendance on him, as she was not downstairs either; the Barnards, I assumed, were in their own home down the road. Kitty looked wan but calm as she spooned eggs onto her plate, and Lucia passed in and out of the dining room with food and coffee. Both Ned and John were cheerful and bright, looking as if they'd both been up and about some time already, and as Ned immediately engaged Kitty in some talk about posing for this or that sort of illustration, I assumed his, and John's, eagerness to be working—even on a Sunday—was partly to blame for such early doings.

Lucia gave me a hopeful smile as she brought in platter of scrambled eggs and a rack of new-made toast.

"Did you sleep all right, dear Violet?" she said as she carefully placed her burdens on the sideboard.

"Oh, well," I stumbled a bit for an answer, then said firmly, "Yes, very well, thank you, Lucia."

John sat down next to me; he had a large cup of coffee, which smelled so lovely and aromatic that I couldn't help exclaiming.

"That coffee smells deliciously of hot sun and a bit of cocoa," I said, and he immediately offered to get me a cup, but Lucia forestalled him.

"I'm just making up some more," she said. "I'll brew one for you and me as well." And she swept off to the kitchen. I looked at John thoughtfully.

"You were right when you said Lucia is the one who keeps this house running," I said, leaning toward him and speaking in a low voice. But we were at one end of the table, almost alone, so there was no one to overhear.

"She's a marvel," John agreed.

"I have told her all our thoughts and suspicions," I said, nodding toward Ned, who was engaged with Kitty. "She is most keen to be helpful, and luckily was able to draw out Mr. McCarthy a bit at dinner last night. Although it was Mr. Cowan who gave voice to an interesting possibility."

John nodded, and answered softly. "That there is something more to his athletic association than meets the eye?" His face became a little grim. "I for one favor having the Irish have their Home Rule," he said, and glanced quickly at me. I nodded my agreement, and he went on. "I would wish it done with less violence, but their grievances are great, and of long standing." He sighed and shook his head. "They cannot be punished for speaking out, at the least."

We both sat silently, picking at our breakfasts, thinking about the fraught political situation—which seemed to have become rather personal, here in little Broadway.

"Are you going to go to the rugby exhibition match this afternoon, Violet?" he said then, and laughed when I rolled my eyes. "I know you are no sporting fan!"

"Nonetheless," I said decisively, "I will be there to cheer on Mr. McCarthy and any other worthy athlete. But mainly," I continued, "I want to be there to keep my eyes upon the crowd, and see if I can spy out anyone who looks to interfere in any way with Mr. McCarthy."

John caught my meaning immediately. "You are convinced, then, that McCarthy was the real target, not Michael Kelly."

I nodded slowly—I had not said it aloud before, but hearing it put into words somehow had the effect of certainty.

"We shall all keep watch," John said. He finished up his coffee as Lucia came through from the kitchen with a tray and two cups, and he stood up to make room for her. "I'm off to some work for a bit," he said, politely pulling out a chair for Lucia to sit upon. "I take it we're to gather here at half past one in order to all walk together to the match at two?"

"Absolutely," Lucia said. "I am looking forward to a fresh air walk and a good deal of cheering and shouting. I had it from Henry James himself that he intends to go along with us, although," and she smiled more broadly, "whether he'll remember that promise this morning remains to be seen." She looked from me to John and back again; a smile gleamed in her eyes. "And perhaps there will be opportunity for some sleuthing as well, I take it?"

John merely smiled, bowed and took himself off. Lucia and I applied ourselves to adding cream and sugar to our coffees, and sipping the delightful brew. I felt instantly alert after the first few sips.

"What an anodyne is here," I said, gesturing to my cup. "You have perfected the art of this brew, Lucia, and I must say it is quite a restorative, after the trials of yesterday and the day before."

Lucia looked at me with sympathetic eyes, and leaned in a little closer. "Was your sleep truly untroubled?" she asked, and after a moment, I shook my head.

"The ghost made an appearance," I said softly—I truly did not want anyone to overhear—"and implored me once again *Do not let her die*." I shuddered as I said the words, and Lucia put her hand on my arm.

"Have you *any* idea whom she might mean?" she asked. I hesitated, then as at the other end of the table, Ned and Kitty were rising to be off to work, I caught my breath as Kitty turned and looked at me intently. There was a fierceness in her eyes I had not seen before, and it seemed to darken the red of her hair and make her white skin glow, so that she looked like some long-ago Irish maiden-warrior. Indeed, all she needed was a sword and a shield to spring into battle. The moment passed and then she was just Kitty, laughing at something Ned whispered to her.

But Lucia had caught the look too, and as the two of us exchanged glances, I think we both knew that Kitty was going to put herself into the center of trouble at some point, and would be in great danger in doing so.

* * *

FORTY-TWO

14 OCTOBER 1726

Late at Night, at the Olde Swan Inn

THE NIGHT BROUGHT NO ABATEMENT of the storm, although the wind was less, but the rain was relentless. Bess stayed in the snug to tend to the captain, sleeping peacefully now after a draught of willow bark tea, Germaine's recipe to reduce fever and inflammation.

"Bess, canst thou leave the captain, and get thyself to bed now?" Richard had tiptoed into the sick room, and spoke in a low voice. He glanced toward the tavern, where the soldiers still ate and drank. "I'll be stayin' up as long as that lot are awake, no need for thee to be here." He looked down at the sleeping captain, who looked years younger at this moment, a young man stressed beyond his powers. "I'll keep an eye on him."

Bess could see the latent fear in her father's eyes; she felt it too, but tried to quell the chaos inside that threatened to overwhelm her. "Aye, Da," she said, rising quietly from her seat at the captain's side. "Perhaps I should do."

The two walked back into the hallway, and Bess kissed her father goodnight, then turned to go up the stairs to her room. From her chamber windows, she could usually see the London coach road clear across the hills, but the incessant rain made everything a blur. *Please,*

please God and St. Eadburgha, keep my love safe from harm, make these soldiers leave us!

Downstairs, Potter approached the innkeeper and renewed his demand to see the ostler.

"Cannae ye wait til mornin?" Richard said amiably, drawing another pint for the soldier and placing it on the bar. "No one's goin' anywhere in this storm, ye can see him in the morning, yes?"

Potter took up the pint, drank, then shrugged and walked away with a loud burp. He rejoined the other soldiers, but began giving orders to the young men.

"You two," he said, pointing to the lad who'd been sick from the drink, and the one who had defended him. "You stay here, on watch, and be on the alert for any goings-on." He glanced back at the innkeeper, then returned to glare at the soldiers. "Make sure no one leaves, and no one comes in, you hear?" They nodded sullenly.

"The rest o'you, off to bed, upstairs," Potter said. Germaine appeared at the door, and motioned that she would show the soldiers where they could bed down. Potter left instructions with the two on watch to wake them all when the sun rose. He had a final word for Richard as he joined the move upstairs.

"Have that stableman of yours here first thing," he said, and nodded curtly when Richard said he would.

* * *

The morning of the fifteenth of October, the feast day of St. Edward the Confessor, broke clear and bright, bringing the light of an autumn sunrise early into the courtyard. The two soldiers who had kept watch had been given some breakfast, and were upstairs sleeping where their mates had slept during the night.

Germaine and Bess had both gotten up before dawn to make things ready in the kitchen.

"Didst thou even sleep at all?" Germaine asked Bess, and frowned as the girl shook her head. "And nor did I, my child." Her face looked like an old woman's from fatigue and worry. "I dinna ken what this lot are here for, but it's for no good," she added, looking closely at Bess.

"I'm that worried," Bess admitted. She didn't think Germaine had heard what Potter said about Tim, so she didn't want to bring it up. The effort to keep quiet, though, made her want to scream aloud, and she shut her lips firmly to keep it inside. The two women worked silently in the kitchen, lighting the fire, preparing breakfast and bread for the oven. Germaine left briefly to administer some beef broth to the captain, and reported that he seemed a little better, but very weak.

Richard came in about an hour later, and just stood looking at them. When they noticed he was there, he simply opened his arms, and both women drew near to be enfolded in his warm grasp. "All will be well, my dears, thou'lt see, all will be well."

But none of them believed it.

* * *

Tim stood trembling in the doorway of the tavern, his head down, refusing to meet the eyes of Richard, Bess or Germaine, who hovered in the background.

"Here, you!" Potter shouted to Tim from where he sat near a window overlooking the courtyard. The rest of the soldiers were at another table, nearer the fire, and were finishing up their breakfast. "Are you the ostler, the one who got us here?" Tim heard the women gasp behind him, and he could easily picture the fire in Richard's eyes at this revelation.

Potter motioned for Tim to come forward and sit down at the table, then leaned in to talk to him more confidentially. Richard walked casually to the farther end of the bar and started cleaning up some glasses, but though he strained to hear, he could only catch a few words here and there, as Tim was mumbling so. But Potter started becoming impatient, and his voice rose with his ire.

"Are you saying you don't know now whether this rogue is coming here today?" The soldier cuffed Tim roughly on the shoulder. "Come, man, you were clear enough for that magistrate to send us, so buck up and say it true now, or you'll be whipped for wasting the King's men on a false mission."

Tim muttered something then, and it appeared to satisfy the angry soldier, who then looked up to see Bess standing in the doorway. An evil smile distorted his lips. He barked an order at his men.

"You, go and take that girl into custody, she's not to leave the inn under any circumstances," he told them. Bess stood paralyzed, and Richard started to protest, but Potter warned him off with an angry look. Tim rose from his seat and spoke up in a loud voice.

"Ye're not to touch her," he shouted. "There is to be no harm come to her, or her father, or any of us!"

Potter answered him with his fists, punching Tim in the stomach and head, then when the ostler fell, gasping, he kicked him several times. Breathing heavily, he gave more orders to his men. "Take this one out to the barn and bind him fast, make sure he goes nowhere." Two of the soldiers rose and got Tim up from the ground and took him away. Three other soldiers had surrounded Bess, and looked to Potter for more instructions.

"Take her upstairs to the room above," he said. "The one that overlooks the courtyard, and the coach road. Tie her up and keep watch." He pointed to Germaine. "You, woman, get behind the bar with the innkeeper." Germaine moved slowly to stand beside Richard.

Bess was wide-eyed with anger, grief and fear. Richard started toward her, but Potter drew his sword and barred his way with it. "No one is to interfere," he said. "And no one will get hurt." The glint in his eyes showed the innkeeper that 'interference' would be broadly interpreted, so he kept still.

The soldiers brought Bess upstairs, and bound her with ropes to the foot of her bed, facing the window where she could now clearly see the London coach road. They checked and re-checked the knots, and all seemed secure.

When Potter came upstairs some time later, he had an evil addition to Bess's bondage—he primed a musket and set it upright on the floor next to her, bound to her body, with the muzzle just below her right breast. "If you try to wriggle free, my pretty lass, this will go off and blast you away." He was lying, but he assumed Bess wouldn't know anything about how muskets worked. When one of the soldiers tried to protest, Potter silenced him with a curse.

"Stay at the window, stay low," he told the soldiers. "He's supposed to come at the full moon, down that road," he said, pointing out the window. "Wait til he's in the courtyard, and we'll give him a fine welcome from his ladylove."

At that he laughed, kissed Bess on the cheek, and went downstairs.

FORTY-THREE

Sunday 5 September 1886

On the Playing Field in Broadway

Everyone at Russell House, even the housemaid, departed after a quick luncheon to assemble on the playing field at the southern end of the village. We were reunited with the Barnard family on the way, and made a fine and lively group, not excluding Henry James, who had ambled down from Abbots Grange after a morning of writing to join us for lunch. Kitty was of the party as well, but David Cowan had left earlier, as he was to be on the exhibition team with Thomas McCarthy. I was frustrated that I had had no chance at all to talk to David Cowan, especially after the remarks he made at dinner last night—it seemed to me that he, Michael and McCarthy were very likely involved in some political action on behalf of the Irish cause. Perhaps an enemy had uncovered their plot, and Michael's death was part of that?

I hoped that being among all these Irish folk at the rugby exhibition would somehow reveal some truths to me. I had never been involved in a case that was so ephemeral! It was quite annoying.

As we approached the field, I responded to a question from Ned that I knew nothing of the sport of rugby (I know even less about cricket, I have to say), so was treated to an amusing summary of the game by him.

"It's nothing in the world but a chap running with a ball in hand and passing it backwards to his mates, all whilst heading forward to plunk said ball over the goal-line," he said.

"That sounds exceedingly simple," I said. "I expect I can follow that."

Frank Millet intervened, a note of humorous scorn in his voice. "It does indeed sound simple, the way Ned puts it," he said. "But the doing of it is tremendously complex, you see, and depends upon superior coordination of teamwork—this is not a single star player's game," he wound up. Ned smiled broadly and winked at me, so I knew he had been baiting Mr. Millet.

"The original of the game allowed for *hacking*," Frank continued, in rather a professorial tone. "This gave players the go-ahead to kick each other's shins and bring them down, but that was ruled out some years ago as too injurious."

"Sounds positively medieval to me," I said, and was pleased to hear Ned's outright laugh at that.

We gained the field—actually a large meadow recently mowed to flatness, with trees all around it—along with what looked like the residents of the whole village, and the surrounding farms and hamlets. Lucia and Lily had provided picnic hampers of fruit and bread, bottles of cold lemonade and ginger beer, and sweets for the children. There were of course no formal chairs or stands such as are erected at official playing or racing fields, so we all just made ourselves comfortable on blankets and cushions on the short grass around the edges. Our party was fortunate in having a good spot near the field but under some trees, against which we could lean our backs as we sat, and also be shaded from the sun that peeped from the clouds more and more as the afternoon wore on.

A number of speeches preceded the actual game, which I found exceedingly tiresome—they were all about *sportsmanship* and *Ireland taking the prize* and such like competitive boasting—and soon I was up and about from my seat on the grass, to make my way slowly through the gathered crowd and keep my eyes open for—well, for anything or anyone suspicious. John and Ned were doing the same, while Lucia was too engaged with minding the children and keeping an eye on the state of the picnic baskets to help us as she might want.

McCarthy made a splendid figure as he ran up and down the field, and even to my ignorant eyes, David Cowan looked to be holding up his end competently. I observed the various groups of people in the audience— families, mainly, and groups of young boys and men who were rapt in awe of the spectacle, breaking into cheers at intervals when something happened on the field to excite them. Everyone looked ordinary, and everyone looked like they belonged.

And then suddenly there were three people who didn't.

The first oddity I saw was Mr. Poole, the village constable, who stood alone, off on the sidelines at the center of the field, but in the dark shade of a large tree, hands in pockets though standing stiffly. His head turned slowly as he watched one figure go up and down the field—as far as I could tell, he was tracking Thomas McCarthy as he ran back and forth. I recalled Mr. Hesford's obvious reluctance to have the constable informed of the activities of the Irish men the night Michael was killed, and felt unsettled watching the officer now.

The second suspicious circumstance occurred when two men, dressed in dark suits and what I could only call "City" hats, approached Mr. Poole and began to talk with him. They clearly were not villagers, based on what everyone else in the crowd looked like.

If I had to guess, I would say that they were from the ministry in Her Majesty's government known as the Home Office.

I continued watching them, drawing as near as I dared, but too far to overhear any of their conversation. Some triumph or other from the field brought most of the crowd to their feet, cheering and yelling, and my view was obscured for some minutes. When I could once again see in the right direction, none of the three men were any longer under that large tree. I hastened back to find John and Ned at our rendezvous point near the main pathway into the meadow, and having gained the path, waited impatiently some time until they both showed up. I told them my observations.

"It certainly is interesting what you observed about Mr. Poole," Ned conceded. "But how are you so sure that the two men who approached him are from the Home Office?"

John and I exchanged knowing looks at this, and he offered an explanation. "Violet and I have had some rather close acquaintance with that type of person," he said, while I couldn't help but smile, thinking of our various exploits and the sometimes rather fraught "acquaintance" with police, international detectives, and government agents. John continued, "All things considered, I'd trust Vi's judgement in this matter."

Ned looked perplexed, but gave way to our expertise. "What is it you conjecture they might be doing here?" he asked.

I frowned. "I feel sure it has to do with the Irish troubles that have beset the kingdom in the last two months, ever since the Home Rule legislation failed." I tapped my fingers to my lips, thinking. "Whatever it is, we must keep close to McCarthy, and along with him, David Cowan and Kitty as well."

"Kitty!" exclaimed Ned. "What has she to do with any-thing?

"Oh, I expect there's more to your pretty Irish model than appears to be the case," I said. We turned to look at the game field as applause from the crowd indicated the match was at an end, and the sight of McCarthy and David Cowan lifted onto the shoulders of several men made the winning team clear.

"We must hurry now," I said. "Go to McCarthy, and stick to him—go with him back to the Lygon Arms," I told them. "I'll find Kitty and walk with her back to Russell House. And," I added with sudden inspiration, "see if you can get Frank to invite Thomas McCarthy over to dinner again tonight—he'll come on Kitty's account, I feel sure— and then we'll be able to keep him under our eyes."

In the event, our whole group of Russell House denizens accompanied the famous athlete to the Lygon Arms, and while we dawdled in the front yard before moving on—John and Ned said they would wait for McCarthy to bathe and dress before escorting him to the house—I had a moment's word with Mr. Hesford, ever steady at his post at the hotel door.

"Mr. Hesford, pray," I said. "Have you picked up any more information about any unusual visitors to the village in the last day or so?" I didn't want to put ideas in his head, so said nothing of my own suspicions.

The good man cast down his eyes, and taking my elbow gently, led us a step or two out of the main entrance. "I have heard it said that two gentlemen employed by Her gracious Majesty's government have made an appearance, likely in relation to the Irish question, as we have discussed previously," he said in a soft whisper, all the while looking about him as if merely giving me directions and staying at his post.

I smiled in satisfaction, and again marvelled at the unquestionable authority of village gossips.

A large party was just alighting from a coach that pulled up before the hotel, and Mr. Hesford was required to be off, and I wasn't sure I had heard his parting words. It sounded like *'another such to keep an eye on'* but if he said a name, I did not hear it.

* * *

FORTY-FOUR

15 OCTOBER 1726

At the Olde Swan Inn

TIM STRUGGLED TO FREE HIS HANDS AS HE LAY, bound and
gagged, in a pile of straw at one end of the stables. The
two soldiers who had brought him there, and bound him,
sat at some distance, looking out the open half-door to the
barn. It was a clear and lovely day, with soft clouds above
and a light wind. The thought made Tim wretched, as he
pictured the highwayman Tremayne being shot down in
the courtyard, in the full warm light of the sun, and Bess
there to see it all happen.

He was miserable, and sorry he had ever written that
letter to Mr. Wells in Oxford. Sure, he loved Bess, but he
never would want her to come to grief, or her father, or
Germaine. Now they all knew of his treachery. He felt a
full Judas, he did, and vowed to himself he would not
accept any reward for his part in the capture of the
Highwayman.

He wished he'd never been born.

Suddenly he heard rough voices outside the barn, and
the two soldiers at the door came to attention. Potter, the
surly soldier that had talked to him and beat him, gave
them some orders and then walked away. Tim's guards

came back to where they'd put him, bent down and made sure his ropes were secure, and stood there looking down at him for a minute. One of them, younger and less hardened than the others, said to his fellow, "Should we take out his gag, he's prolly thirsty, eh?"

The other one shrugged. "Do wot ye will, then," and turning away, walked toward the door.

The kindly soldier took off the rag they'd wound around Tim's head, covering his mouth, and offered him some water from his flask. Tim drank greedily, sputtered a bit, then thanked the man, who appeared not a bit older than himself.

"I'm sorry to leave ye like this," the soldier said as he tied the rag around Tim's mouth again. "But we canna let ye go, eh? We expect the Highwayman in daylight, yes? As you said? So it'll all be over soon. Then ye'll be free agin." He capped up his flask and made for the door, closing it fully behind him, and shutting out the sunlight that had been pouring in.

Tim lay back, exhausted from the whole ordeal, and tried to force his weary mind to think of what he should do. Hours passed as he drifted in and out of sleep, and when he finally woke to full attention, the utter darkness of the stables told him the night had come. He was puzzled, and then hopeful. Surely he would have wakened if Tremayne had come, and been either shot or taken by the soldiers. Maybe he had been warned away! Maybe nothing bad was going to happen.

Just then he heard the door to his own little room in the stables open—it creaked when it did. A moment later, he heard Sam's soft voice calling to him.

"Tim! Tim! Are ye there?"

Tim made himself sit up, and felt the urgency of his need to pee weigh on him. He stifled a groan, and instantly Sam was with him—he pulled out a pocketknife and began sawing away at the ropes that bound his friend. In moments, Tim was free, and tore away the gag from his mouth.

"Wot's goin' on then, Tim?" Sam asked, his eyes wide and frightened. "We was that worret when we didnae see ye at noon." Tim remembered then that he was supposed to meet Sam at his parents' home to collect some items they were planning to cart down to market to sell.

"No time, Sam, to tell thee, but say, are the soldiers still at the inn?" Tim said, feeling like he wanted to hug the boy, he was so glad to see him. He slowly rose to his feet, testing his sore ankles and hips, and feeling the bruises from the kicking he'd received. After a few minutes, the strength flowed back into him.

Sam nodded nervously. "Yes, I seen them through the window, so I came here to find ye."

He knew what he had to do. "What o'clock is it, boy?"

Sam stuttered out a reply. "Near midnight, I'm guessin'," he said. "I heard the bells for the three quarters as I was almost here."

"Now, Sam, lissen to me, and lissen hard," Tim said, taking the boy firmly by the shoulders. "These soldiers here, they're King's Men, and they are not to be messed with, yes?"

Sam nodded, his eyes huge.

• • •

"Get thee home, out of sight, and say nothin to nobody, y'hear? Not thy mum, nor thy dad, *no one*." Tim feared for all of their lives if the soldiers were crossed. He shook the boy lightly. "Understand? Nothin' to nobody— or them soldiers'll run thee through like a stuck pig!"

Sam nodded again, and crossed his heart for good measure.

"Good lad, off thou go, and tomorrow we'll laugh at all this, yes?" Tim prayed he was right to promise such a thing, and heaved a sigh of relief as he watched Sam slip out as quietly as he had come, and no shouts or noise outside to indicate he'd been seen. He felt confident that the soldiers would not be back to check on him this night. They might still be expecting Tremayne to show up—but if he didn't, then they would go away.

But now he would be off to Squire Robert's to get help—surely the man would help Bess in her hour of need? The Squire could make the soldiers go away, if he would. Tim feared he could not get to the Squire in time, should anything happen while he was trying to get there. He collected a warm coat, took a flask of water, and was gone into the dark before five minutes had passed.

* * *

Richard and Germaine sat together in the back of the tavern, watched over by Potter and the soldiers there. When Germaine was ordered to get some food, two of them went with her to the kitchen, and watched her sullenly as she gathered bread and cheese to bring back. A few times she asked to go look after their captain, and was escorted to the snug as well, where she gave him more willow bark tea and tried to feed him a little broth. This was a strong, hectic fever, though, and had seized his lungs, and even her considerable skills weren't making much of an inroad on the captain's suffering; he was mostly unconscious, occasionally murmuring in his troubled sleep, and coughing roughly. His men, all but Potter, looked worried.

It was now dark outside, and the moon was rising. Richard felt consumed by desperation and fear. He had no idea what was happening with Bess in the room above, although all was deathly quiet. He thought of Tim, beaten and dragged to the stables, and he felt a moment's pity, but his heart was hardened against the man who'd brought this upon them—not Tim, whose actions had certainly brought the soldiers here, but Tremayne, the Highwayman of the Hill! And his Bess was the beloved of such a man, and loved him as well. Germaine had confessed to him that she knew Bess had sent a message to Tremayne, but she swore she knew nothing of his being the Highwayman, or how Tim could have found that out. Richard could hardly make sense of it, and was reduced to simply praying, over and over in his head, *God of mercy, save us all.*

* * *

Night came on. Once, just after sunset, Bess heard voices outside the courtyard gate, which was closed and locked— the soldiers had made a sign, badly lettered, that said the inn was shut due to sickness—she heard someone rattle the gate, but after a few minutes, they faded away. She had heard the soldier say that Tim told them Tremayne would come in the daylight—so he must have overheard her and Tremayne talking that night, when Tim had gone to Oxford. But he didn't know that they had changed their plan, and that Tremayne was to appear tonight, at midnight, under the full moon. But the soldiers hadn't left—apparently they had decided to just wait through the night.

The soldiers assigned to the watch in her chamber knelt at the windows; earlier they had taken turns sleeping, but ever since moonrise, they were both alert, their muskets set on the windowsill, trained on the courtyard below. Potter came to the door one time, checked with them about their positions, and with a leer and another kiss on the cheek, he left her, still tied to the post, the musket poised beneath her breast. She could see through the window that someone had gone down and opened the courtyard gate, for Tremayne to ride in freely.

In the darkened room, Bess stealthily pulled and stretched her hands to loosen the ropes, and though it hurt til she was sure it drew blood, she managed to get her right hand down far enough for a single finger to touch the trigger of the musket that was bound at her side. It had taken hours, but she had gained her objective.

She strained her eyes to see through the open windows to the road, bright as a ribbon threaded through the hills in the astonishing light of the moon, and her ears were alert to the sound of his horse.

Soon after the old clock in the hallway struck the three quarters after eleven, she heard a faint sound. *Tlot tlot tlot tlot*—his horse, riding confidently through the night, sure

* * *

in the bright moonlight—*tlot tlot tlot*—he drew near, soon he would ride into the courtyard, and call her name to the window. She drew a deep, quavering breath.

Her finger tightened on the trigger.

And pulled.

FORTY-FIVE

SUNDAY 5 SEPTEMBER 1886

Night Falls at Russell House

THE GENTLE AUTUMN NIGHT CREPT IN whilst the revels at Russell House continued in full force. John was begged to play mazurkas on the piano after dinner so that all who were so inclined might dance in the large drawing room. The tables and sofas had been moved back, the rug rolled up, and several couples, including the children, were merrily swinging each other round the room.

I admit I was one of the party, although I have never been as adept at dancing as I have been at conversing, thinking or writing. But I jounced along with Ned leading the way, for two full dances, then begged off further, as I was quite out of breath. I was amused to see Lucia coax Henry James onto the floor, where he cut a very creditable figure; I expect the dinner wine, which flowed freely, had something to do with his amenability to joining such activity. Kitty and McCarthy danced several times together

* * *

and, watching them, I could see there was a great deal of mutual attraction and understanding between them.

But I was too nervous and watchful, as the evening drew to a close, to spare many thoughts for frivolity. The Barnards had soon departed with their active brood, and Lily had taken Kate up to bed shortly after; John was playing something a little more melancholy than dance tunes, and everyone seemed content—after replacing the rug and chairs—to find a seat and relax with a final sip or two of cognac or port.

"Violet, my dear," said Frank Millet, casting an amiable glance my way, "can I tempt you with another cigar this evening?" He didn't try to hide his amused smile as he said this, and grinned even more broadly when I shook my head and answered, "Even so dissolute a character as I, Frank," I said, smiling, "even I have my limits."

His attention being claimed by Thomas McCarthy at that moment, I took the opportunity to rise and wander over to the hallway a little way down from the drawing room, whose windows gave on the courtyard that led to the front gate, but also part of the gardens near the back of the house. I slipped behind a partially drawn, heavy curtain, which gave me the darkness I required to survey the lawn and courtyard outside. The moon was rising, and being more than halfway to full, shed a white light that illuminated the outside world in exquisite detail. As I watched, I saw movement in the shadows under the trees nearest to the courtyard. I trained my eyes to the spot and held very still, and after a moment, I saw them: the two Home Office agents, lying in wait outside the house!

• • •

I caught my breath, my hand at my throat, for I sensed the danger they posed—they were undoubtedly here for McCarthy, perhaps for David Cowan as well, as he seemed to be closely allied with the rugby player. Would they arrest him as he left the house? Would they dare even shoot at him—using more direct means to eliminate him than they had, perhaps, used on poor Michael?

As these possibilities ran through my head, the two men merged with the shadows, and I could not see exactly where they had hid themselves. I turned swiftly away and went back to the drawing room to fetch John and Ned, but even as I returned, I could hear the sounds of people saying good night and taking their leave. When I opened the door to the drawing room, the first thing I noted was that neither Kitty nor McCarthy were any longer there.

Quelling a growing sense of panic, I nearly ran over to John, still seated at the piano.

"Where is Kitty?" I whispered to him. "Where is McCarthy?"

John looked around in surprise, then consternation. "There were here just moments ago," he said. He looked closely at me. "Why? What's going on, Vi?"

"The two Home Office agents, I saw them, they're hiding in the shadows of the trees alongside the lawn." I made an impatient gesture. "We must go outside, quickly, and warn McCarthy."

At that, John leaped up from the piano, called to Ned who responded instantly, and the three of us ran to the door that led to the courtyard. There a scene awaited us that I had feared in my heart, and wished would never become real.

* * *

McCarthy and Kitty stood in the courtyard, illumined by the kitchen lights that poured out of the back windows, casting shadows all around them. In front of them stood the two agents, one of whom appeared to be addressing the rugby player; he had his hand out, palm down, as if calming the pair they were confronting.

John, in his great height, walked up coolly toward the Home Office agents.

"What is going on here, may I ask?" he said, sounding civil enough.

"This is Her Majesty's business, and none of yours," the agent, the younger of the two it seemed, replied evenly.

"I say," interposed Ned, "this is my house, and I demand an explanation for this—" he wasn't sure what to call it, but waved his hand in McCarthy's direction.

The other agent put his hand in his coat pocket, and appeared to be drawing something out of it—I feared the worst—and when a flash of metal made it seem to be a gun, Kitty gave a sharp cry, and placed herself directly in front of McCarthy, holding her arms wide so as to cover him.

"There's no need for that, Miss," the agent said, holding up what he had in his hands—not a gun after all, but a pair of handcuffs, the metal glinting in the moonlight.

"And there's no need for those!" John said angrily. "Under what pretense are you taking this man into custody?"

Ned seconded John's indignation, and demanded to see a warrant, if they were here to arrest McCarthy.

I had been slowly creeping closer to where Kitty and McCarthy stood, she still attempting to shield him from whatever injustice was about to be done. I'm not sure what I thought I was going to do, or when, but something impelled me to get ever closer. Soon I could have touched her arm if I reached out. McCarthy had put his hands on her shoulders, and looked as if he would pull her aside and place himself in front of her.

At that moment I saw a movement in the hedge directly across from where we stood—and the next moment saw Mr. Poole, the constable, step forward, his arm raised, pointing a pistol at Kitty and McCarthy, his finger on the trigger.

"No!" I cried out, and the gun he held swung toward me, then back to Kitty again.

"Hey there, you, put that pistol down!" yelled the older agent.

Mr. Poole sneered, his eyes alight with a crazed look. He actually turned the gun in the direction of the agent, and laughed. "I made a little mistake the other night, but I'll get this traitorous Irishman this time, and why not an Irish woman as well!" And he turned to fire at Kitty and McCarthy, but at that instant I rushed forward —indeed, I felt as if I had been pushed from behind by unseen hands—directly at Kitty. Grabbing her outstretched arm, I fell forward with all my weight and force, and knocked all three of us to the ground—myself, Kitty and McCarthy. I felt a searing sting on my left arm as I went down.

Pandemonium ensued, and I believe I fainted.

When I came to, which was really only moments later, Lucia and Kitty were bending over me, my head in Lucia's lap as I lay on the ground, with John and Ned holding lanterns aloft so they might tend to my wound.

Wounded! I had actually been shot by Mr. Poole! Well, *mildly grazed* is a more correct way to put it, the gabardine of my sleeve having been but slightly torn, and a shallow slash—like a bad encounter with a thorn bush— stretched some few inches across my upper arm. Nonetheless, I was fully prepared to be treated as a heroine, and made a fuss over, as Lucia and Kitty were happy to do.

They helped me stand up, and get into the house, where the two Home Office agents had commandeered the sitting room next to the kitchen, and were interrogating Mr. Poole for all they were worth. I motioned to Lucia that I wanted to be there and listen in, to which she acceded readily, so we stood in the doorway and observed all we could.

The first thing that astonished me was seeing Mr. Andrew Hesford, the doorman of the Lygon Arms, standing guard over the downcast Constable Poole, looming over the man with a very menacing mien. I was gratified to hear that the older government agent was asking him the very question I had formed in my mind.

"Whatever led you to be so near to Mr. Poole, sir, that you were so readily able to subdue him?"

Mr. Hesford looked down modestly, and said, "I had my suspicions, sir, about Mr. Poole and the recent incident here at Russell House—" here he nodded to Ned and John, who were standing nearby. "The constable is well-known for taking against the Irish, here in Broadway, and there's others that saw him in places he shouldn't have been, that's all I'm saying. So," he wound up succinctly, "I followed him from the Lygon Arms, as he himself was following Mr. McCarthy here, and I laid in wait behind Mr. Poole, watching to see what he might do."

The two agents exchanged glances at this, but their looks were inscrutable. "Your assistance is greatly appreciated, Mr. Hesford," said the older one. "You shall be commended for your observation and your quick thinking."

Mr. Hesford nodded his head with great dignity, then looking over at me, trouble returned to his face. "I shall never forgive myself for being too late, and causing harm to Miss Vernon Lee, a most courageous young lady, if I may be so bold as to say." And he bowed in my direction.

Kitty, who was now wrapped in McCarthy's arms, spoke up, directing her anger to Constable Poole. "And so you killed poor Michael, you horrible man! You should be hanged!"

The two agents looked grim at this, and decided there was no doubt a better place for them to pursue this new wrinkle in the situation. They pulled Mr. Poole up from the sofa, and in consultation with Mr. Hesford, determined that one of the locked storerooms at the Lygon Arms would serve as a jail for the time being. The four men left quickly, along with Thomas McCarthy and David Cowan, with whom they said they would like to consult—but not take into custody.

The rest of us—John, Ned, Lucia and Kitty—stared at each other for some moments in wonder and amazement, then sat down with tired relief on various chairs and sofas while John reached over to a cabinet and brought out a bottle of wine.

"To Violet," he said. They all drank my health, and then I, stealing a glance at Lucia, raised my glass again.

"To Bess, the landlord's daughter," I said.

EPILOGUE

Il Palmerino, Florence, 1928

I WAS OBLIGED TO LEAVE BROADWAY within two days after the events I have described above. I was content to go, especially as I was bound for the warmer winter in Florence, which is a happy alternative to anything London has to offer during the wretched weather that reigns during those months. Before I left the village, however, two or three interesting things occurred of which I feel I owe to you, dear Reader, to inform you.

First, on the Monday after that electrifying Sunday, Mr. Alfred Parsons returned from his fishing trip, and Mr. Henry James departed. Lucia had insisted on walking to the Lygon Arms to see him off in his carriage, but I was able to hang back, claiming a little indisposition due to my wounded arm.

Mr. Parsons, sturdy man that he is, showed up at Russell House on his own, and was amazed and astounded to hear of the events of the past three days. At my urging, John and I had a private word with Mr. Parsons, who was greatly perturbed at hearing about the pitchfork holes in the Garden Painting canvas, and admitted that his pitchfork was probably the cause of the holes, though unknown to him at the time. He apologized profusely to John, and was only somewhat mollified when John assured him that the painting was now much more interesting—*felix culpa!*—as a square than a rectangle, and thanked him for his help!

The more serious charge of the death of the blue bird, which I had become convinced was due to Mr. Parsons' unmanageable irritation at the creature and its insalubrious activities in his pristine garden, was denied by him with persistent indignation. He would never harm a living creature, even one so annoying as that blue bird, he protested, and in the end, we were obliged to accept our failure in solving that particular mystery. We told him our suspicions regarding his fall down the ice house steps, but he waved the incident away as not worth bothering about, as he was perfectly all right.

Monday afternoon brought round a visitor to Russell House—Thomas McCarthy, who came to thank me again, on his own account and Kitty's, and to take leave as he was continuing on to London in the furtherance of his Irish Athletic Association promotional tour. Kitty had already confessed to us that McCarthy was the one who had left the note in the birdhouse (I didn't ask her about the other one I saw in her room!)—and when I asked if she thought he had also pushed Alfred Parsons down the icehouse steps, she looked ashamed and guilty, but said she really couldn't speak to that—which was enough for me. It was what I had assumed, especially given the evidence of the Irish lapel pin, which I believe Ned managed to quietly return to the rugby player. Kitty and McCarthy clearly were in love with each other, and I'm sure she hadn't wanted to implicate her beloved any more than necessary, so I let it pass.

• • •

Ned and John and I discussed at some length, after McCarthy had gone, the possibilities of that "Association" being a bit more political than athletic, which in time, I learned that it was—so the Home Office agents were actually on the right trail, albeit somewhat incompetently. Michael was a new recruit, and an enthusiastic one, to the Cause, and he and McCarthy had met secretly down at the brook to discuss certain plans for action in London (we hoped they were not violent plans). Sadly, Home Rule for the Irish was destined to wait nearly three more decades until December 1922, when the Irish Free State was established under the Anglo-Irish Treaty. The treaty ended the three-year Irish War of Independence between the forces of the Irish Republic—the Irish Republican Army—and British Crown forces.

It was a day of visitors! Mr. Andrew Hesford appeared to inquire as to my continued good health, and also to inform us that Constable Poole—merely Mr. Poole now—had been taken into custody by the Sheriff of Evesham, and would be charged with the murder of Michael Kelly, to which he had confessed fully—having decided to take the law into his own hands by assaulting the man he thought was Thomas McCarthy, to punish him for starting the Irish Athletic Association.

After Mr. Hesford departed, John wanted to be painting again, as there had been no gathering in the garden on Sunday—and I watched from a comfortable seat as the luminous painting of the Barnard girls continued to take shape. I'll just say here, *obiter dictum,* that when "Carnation, Lily, Lily, Rose" made its official debut in the Royal Academy's Summer Exhibition of 1887, it was greeted by a fiercely divided audience. *The Art Journal* noted that "Mr. Sargent is certainly the most discussed artist of the year… as artists almost come to blows over this picture." John's reputation was fully restored—there is nothing like controversy to whet the public's appetite. Most amusingly, some twenty years later, John's previously despised "Madame X" was purchased by the Metropolitan Museum of New York for an enormous sum! John referred to it as "probably the best thing I've done." Such are the revolutions of time and taste.

I wish I could say the same for my "controversial" *Miss Brown*—but its day of infamy soon passed, I rallied my forces and achieved other literary triumphs—including several ghost stories, which my experiences of the supernatural at Russell House taught me to take the genre more seriously.

I was to leave on the Wednesday morning, taking the coach to Evesham and then the train to London, so on Tuesday afternoon, I asked Lucia if she would accompany me to make another visit to Miss Marshall. I desperately wanted to hear the end of the story of Bess and the Highwayman.

This is a faithful account of what she told us, and I will say now that I am grateful to have been acquainted with—and literally pushed into the role of heroine by—the tragic and beautiful ghost of Russell House.

* * *

"Let me see, where did I leave off last time? You must forgive an old woman, Miss Lee and Miss Millet, whose body is less governable than her mind." Miss Marshall, dressed in her quaint clothes, and offering us tea and cake, was as obliging as before—in addition to having shown Lucia all the antique clothing in her wardrobes.

"I believe you were at the part, ma'am," I prompted, "where there was some betrayal by a stableman at the Olde Swan Inn, and soldiers had been called in to capture the Highwayman?"

"Ah, yes, how good of you to remember," said the old lady. "Yes. Well, the stableman was promised a reward if the soldiers captured the Highwayman, but I recall there was something about him deciding not to accept it in the end, given how tragic it all was." She sighed, almost as if she had been present at the time herself, and sorrowed at the memory. She gazed out the window for a moment, and said, "For many years, there was a gravestone at St. Eadburgha's, where the Squire had them buried together, but it's long since fallen to the wind and the rain."

Lucia and I exchanged glances, but stayed silent, waiting for Miss Marshall to continue. She had closed her eyes again, like the time before, and spoke in a soft voice, almost singing:

> *He did not come in the dawning. He did*
> *   not come at noon;*
> *And out of the tawny sunset, before the*
> *   rise of the moon,*
> *When the road was a gypsy's ribbon,*
> *   looping the purple moor,*
> *A red-coat troop came marching—*
> *   Marching—marching—*

*King George's men came marching, up
to the old inn-door.*

*They said no word to the landlord. They
drank his ale instead.*
*But they gagged his daughter, and
bound her, to the foot of her narrow
bed.*
*Two of them knelt at her casement, with
muskets at their side!*
There was death at every window;
And hell at one dark window;
*For Bess could see, through her
casement, the road that he would ride.*

*They had tied her up to attention, with
many a sniggering jest.*
*They had bound a musket beside her,
with the muzzle beneath her breast!*
*"Now, keep good watch!" and they
kissed her. She heard the doomed man
say—*
Look for me by moonlight;
Watch for me by moonlight;
*I'll come to thee by moonlight, though
hell should bar the way!*

*She twisted her hands behind her; but all
the knots held good!*
*She writhed her hands till her fingers
were wet with sweat or blood!*

• • •

They stretched and strained in the
  darkness, and the hours crawled by
  like years
Till, now, on the stroke of midnight,
    Cold, on the stroke of midnight,
The tip of one finger touched it! The
  trigger at least was hers!

The tip of one finger touched it. She
  strove no more for the rest.
Up, she stood up to attention, with the
  muzzle beneath her breast.
She would not risk their hearing; she
  would not strive again;
For the road lay bare in the moonlight;
    Blank and bare in the moonlight;
And the blood of her veins, in the
  moonlight, throbbed to her love's
  refrain.

Tlot-tlot; tlot-tlot! Had they heard it?
  The horsehoofs ringing clear;
Tlot-tlot; tlot-tlot, in the distance? Were
  they deaf that they did not hear?
Down the ribbon of moonlight, over the
  brow of the hill,
The highwayman came riding—
    Riding—riding—
The red coats looked to their priming!
  She stood up, straight and still.

Tlot-tlot, in the frosty silence! Tlot-tlot,
  in the echoing night!

Nearer he came and nearer. Her face
was like a light.
Her eyes grew wide for a moment; she
drew one last deep breath,
Then her finger moved in the moonlight,
Her musket shattered the
moonlight,
Shattered her breast in the moonlight
and warned him—with her death.

He turned. He spurred to the west; he
did not know who stood
Bowed, with her head o'er the musket,
drenched with her own blood!
Not till the dawn he heard it, and his
face grew grey to hear
How Bess, the landlord's daughter,
The landlord's black-eyed
daughter,
Had watched for her love in the
moonlight, and died in the darkness
there.

Back, he spurred like a madman,
shrieking a curse to the sky,
With the white road smoking behind him
and his rapier brandished high.
Blood red were his spurs in the golden
noon; wine-red was his velvet coat;
When they shot him down on the
highway,
Down like a dog on the highway,

• • •

And he lay in his blood on the highway,
  with a bunch of lace at his throat.

And still of a winter's night, they say,
  when the wind is in the trees,
When the moon is a ghostly galleon
  tossed upon cloudy seas,
When the road is a ribbon of moonlight
  over the purple moor,
A highwayman comes riding—
      Riding—riding—
A highwayman comes riding, up to the
  old inn-door.

Over the cobbles he clatters and clangs
  in the dark inn-yard.
He taps with his whip on the shutters,
  but all is locked and barred.
He whistles a tune to the window, and
  who should be waiting there
But the landlord's black-eyed daughter,
      Bess, the landlord's daughter,
Plaiting a dark red love-knot into her
  long black hair.

SPECIAL LINKS AND FURTHER INFORMATION

"The Highwayman" by Alfred Noyes, was first published in the August 1906 issue of *Blackwood's Magazine*, based in Edinburgh, Scotland. In the *Epilogue*, Miss Marshall presents "Part Two" of the original *Highwayman* poem by Alfred Noyes. To complete the story, here is Part One.

PART ONE

The wind was a torrent of darkness
    among the gusty trees.
The moon was a ghostly galleon tossed
    upon cloudy seas.
The road was a ribbon of moonlight over
    the purple moor,
And the highwayman came riding—
      Riding—riding—
The highwayman came riding, up to the
    old inn-door.

He'd a French cocked-hat on his
    forehead, a bunch of lace at his chin,
A coat of the claret velvet, and breeches
    of brown doe-skin.
They fitted with never a wrinkle. His
    boots were up to the thigh.
And he rode with a jewelled twinkle,
      His pistol butts a-twinkle,
His rapier hilt a-twinkle, under the
    jewelled sky.

Over the cobbles he clattered and
  clashed in the dark inn-yard.
He tapped with his whip on the shutters,
  but all was locked and barred.
He whistled a tune to the window, and
  who should be waiting there
But the landlord's black-eyed daughter,
    Bess, the landlord's daughter,
Plaiting a dark red love-knot into her
  long black hair.

And dark in the dark old inn-yard a
  stable-wicket creaked
Where Tim the ostler listened. His face
  was white and peaked.
His eyes were hollows of madness, his
  hair like mouldy hay,
But he loved the landlord's daughter,
    The landlord's red-lipped daughter.
Dumb as a dog he listened, and he heard
  the robber say—

"One kiss, my bonny sweetheart, I'm
  after a prize to-night,
But I shall be back with the yellow gold
  before the morning light;
Yet, if they press me sharply, and harry
  me through the day,
Then look for me by moonlight,
    Watch for me by moonlight,
I'll come to thee by moonlight, though
  hell should bar the way."

He rose upright in the stirrups. He scarce
  could reach her hand,
But she loosened her hair in the
  casement. His face burnt like a brand
As the black cascade of perfume came
  tumbling over his breast;
And he kissed its waves in the
  moonlight,
      (O, sweet black waves in the
  moonlight!)
Then he tugged at his rein in the
  moonlight, and galloped away to the
  west.

* * *

Here is a link for a very emotional and beautiful version by
Loreena McKennit of "The Highwayman":
https://www.youtube.com/watch?v=DhT3HzCDX5k

* * *

THE ORIGIN OF THE TITLE:
"CARNATION, LILY, LILY, ROSE"

Here is a link for a sung version of "Ye, Shepherds, Tell
Me, Tell Me", which is the song that the "Carnation, Lily,
Lily, Rose" title comes from; it was a popular music hall
song at the time:
https://www.youtube.com/watch?v=IlzcmCr-UPE

AUTHOR'S NOTES

There is abundant information about Broadway Village online, and several books published on the subject of the American Artists there, both separately and as a group, and any number of essays and books about Sargent and his famous painting that he created there. There is scant evidence that Vernon Lee (Violet Paget) visited her friend in Broadway—only one sentence in Veneta Colby's biography of Vernon Lee, which says "Lee visited her friend John Sargent in Broadway." So I'm going with that!

I was blessed to be a temporary inhabitant of Broadway in the fall of 2022, where I stayed at The Manor Cottages, run by Debbie Tanser-Williamson and her husband on an estate that harks back several centuries. Through her good offices, I was introduced to the current owners of Russell House, who generously invited me in and showed me around the grounds, telling me little details of what it might have been like in the 1880s, including the story of the "ghost" of Russell House, which sparked the idea for my novel.

Walking across the fields from the Manor into the village of Broadway, or in the other direction to St. Eadburgha's ancient church, was deeply evocative of what it must have been like more than a hundred years previously. Sheep grazed in the meadows, magpies cawed and flew in circles above, and the clouds formed ever-changing paintings of shadow and light in the sky and on the land.

My readers always want to know who's real and who's not, so here's a list (other than Violet and John, of course):

REAL CHARACTERS: Frank and Lily Millet and their children; Lucia Millet, Frank's sister; Fred and Alice Barnard and their children; Ned (Edwin Austin) Abbey; Alfred Parsons; Henry James; Thomas McCarthy (a real rugby player who started the Irish Athletic Association in 1886); Miss Marshall (who is mentioned in a letter from Lucia Millet to her family). Sadly, Laurence Millet died in 1891, aged 19, of a congenital heart disease, and his father Frank was one of the unfortunate passengers on the doomed Titanic in April 1912; his body was recovered and he was buried in Bridgewater, Massachusetts.

FICTIONAL CHARACTERS: Kitty O'Byrne (al-though her character was based on a real "red-haired model" in a painting by Frank Millet, her name is fictional), David Cowan, Michael Flynn, Constable Poole, Dr. White, any other minor characters.

SPECIAL CHARACTER: Mr. Andrew Hesford happens to be the name of the actual, present-day doorman at the Lygon Arms. When I visited Broadway, I stopped in and he was very hospitable, informative and entertaining. I asked him if he would mind if I used his name for a character in the novel I was writing, and he was delighted to say yes. He turned out to be more of a major character (in the novel!) than I had imagined, so, Andrew, I hope you like your esteemed "ancestor"!

A Word about *Thee* and *Thou* ....

In the chapters taking place in 1726, the characters use the older style of address: you/ye were used when talking to multiple persons or to a person of a higher status, to show respect. Thee/thou were used among familiars, intimates and to children or "inferiors" (as when Squire Robert addresses Bess and her father). The verb forms ending in -est or -eth were still in use at that time (giveth, hast, etc.) but such usage varied throughout the kingdom, and would die out as the century progressed.

ACKNOWLEDGEMENTS

My most heartfelt gratitude goes to Marc Simpson, author and an expert on 19th-century American art. Marc generously shared with me his PhD dissertation, "Reconstructing the Golden Age: American Artists in Broadway, Worcestershire, 1885 to 1889" (Yale University, May 1993), which helped me establish an almost hour-by-hour account of the specific days I chose to use in my novel (September 3-8, 1886), particularly through gleaning facts and delightful anecdotes from the voluminous letters of Lucia Millet to her family. Marc was one of the first beta readers for my initial book on Singer Sargent (*Portraits of an Artist*), and he also read over this fifth mystery to help me accurately portray the persons and places depicted (within fictional license of course). When I initially relayed my intention to him of writing about Sargent's time in Broadway, I remarked that "all I need is a murder"—and he promptly told me about the Blue Bird—an actual event chronicled in one of the charming, chatty letters of Lucia Millet to her family—and that gave me the starting point for the mystery in *The Light in the Garden*.

I am also indebted to the current owners of Russell House, Andrew Dakin and Malcolm Rogers, who welcomed me to their home during my research visit to Broadway, told me about the ghost, and showed me around the house and gardens, with many stories of interest about those American inhabitants almost 150 years ago. Debbie Tanser-Williamson, head of the Broadway Historical Society and former Arts Festival director, was also very helpful during my visit, providing important local information about the era, while I stayed at The Manor Cottages owned by her and her husband.

Finally, thanks to my faithful beta readers Robert Densmore and Jay Miller, who always love spending time with John and Violet, and who always let me know if there's too much or too little of anything in the book.

Any and all mistakes or errors of judgement in this novel are completely my own.

OTHER BOOKS BY MARY F. BURNS

Portraits of an Artist:
A Novel about John Singer Sargent

The Sargent/Paget Mysteries

The Spoils of Avalon – Book One
The Love for Three Oranges – Book Two
The Unicorn in the Mirror – Book Three
The Eleventh Commandment – Book Four

Other Historical Fiction

Isaac and Ishmael: A Novel of Genesis
J-The Woman Who Wrote the Bible
Ember Days
Of Ripeness & The River

Short Fiction Series: A Classic & A Sequel

In the Cage by Henry James + *At Chalk Farm*
Crapy Cornelia by Henry James + *The Grace of Uncertainty*

Non-Fiction

Reading Mrs. Dalloway

To see book trailers, contact the author, and order these
books, please visit the author's website at
www.maryfburns.com

Printed in Great Britain
by Amazon

23079078R00188